GHOST
STORIES

Selected by
Giles Gordon

BLOOMSBURY
CLASSICS

First published 1996
This compilation by Giles Gordon © 1996
by Bloomsbury Publishing Plc
The copyright of the individual contributors
remains with the respective authors
The moral right of the authors has been asserted

Bloomsbury Publishing Plc, 2 Soho Square,
London W1V 6HB
A CIP catalogue record for this book is available
from the British Library

ISBN 07475 2914 0

10 9 8 7 6 5 4 3 2 1

Typeset in Great Britain by
Hewer Text Composition Services, Edinburgh
Printed in Great Britain by St Edmundsbury Press, Suffolk
Jacket design by Jeff Fisher

Acknowledgements

Elizabeth Bowen: 'The Apple Tree', © Elizabeth Bowen 1934,
reprinted by permission of Curtis Brown, London.
Montague Rhodes James: 'The Stalls of Barchester Cathedral',
reprinted by permission of N.J.R. James.
Rudyard Kipling: 'The Phantom 'Rickshaw', reprinted by
permission of A.P. Watt on behalf of The National Trust for Places
of Historic Interest or Natural Beauty.
Walter de la Mare: 'The Quincunx', reprinted by permission of
The Literary Trustees of Walter de la Mare and the Society of
Authors as their representative.
Muriel Spark: 'The Leaf-Sweeper', reprinted by permission of
David Higham Associates.

CONTENTS

1 A true relation of the apparition of
  one Mrs. Veal the next day after her
  death to one Mrs. Bargrave at
  Canterbury the 8th of September, 1705
  DANIEL DEFOE   1

2 The Tapestried Chamber
  SIR WALTER SCOTT   13

3 The Lady with the Velvet Collar
  WASHINGTON IRVING   33

4 The Gray Champion
  NATHANIEL HAWTHORNE   40

5 No. 1 Branch Line: The Signalman
  CHARLES DICKENS   50

6 The Dream Woman
  WILKIE COLLINS   67

7 A Horseman in the Sky
  AMBROSE BIERCE   93

8 The Jolly Corner
  HENRY JAMES   101

9 The Stalls of Barchester Cathedral
  MONTAGUE RHODES JAMES   146

10 The Phantom 'Rickshaw
  RUDYARD KIPLING   166

11 The Quincunx
   WALTER DE LA MARE   195
12 The Apple Tree
   ELIZABETH BOWEN   209
13 The Leaf-Sweeper
   MURIEL SPARK   225

A true relation of the apparition of one Mrs. Veal the next day after her death to one Mrs. Bargrave at Canterbury the 8th of September, 1705

Daniel Defoe

This thing is so rare in all its circumstances, and on so good authority, that my reading and conversation has not given me anything like it. It is fit to gratify the most ingenious and serious inquirer. Mrs. Bargrave is the person to whom Mrs. Veal appeared after her death; she is my intimate friend, and I can avouch for her reputation for these last fifteen or sixteen years, on my own knowledge; and I can confirm the good character she had from her youth to the time of my acquaintance. Though, since this relation, she is calumniated by some people that are friends to the brother of Mrs. Veal who appeared, who think the relation of this appearance to be a reflection, and endeavor what they can to blast Mrs. Bargrave's reputation and to laugh the story out of countenance. But the circumstances thereof, and the cheerful disposition of Mrs. Bargrave, notwithstanding the unheard-of ill usage of a very wicked husband, there is not the least sign of dejection in her face; nor did I ever hear her let fall a desponding or murmuring expression; nay, not when actually under her husband's barbarity, which I have been witness to, and several other persons of undoubted reputation.

Now you must know that Mrs. Veal was a maiden gentlewoman of about thirty years of age, and for some years last past had been troubled with fits, which were perceived coming on her by her going off from her discourse very abruptly to some impertinence. She was maintained by an only brother, and kept his house in Dover. She was a very pious woman, and her brother a very sober man to all appearance; but now he does all he can to null and quash the story. Mrs. Veal was intimately acquainted with Mrs. Bargrave from her childhood. Mrs. Veal's circumstances were then mean; her father did not take care of his children as he ought, so that they were exposed to hardships. And Mrs. Bargrave in those days had as unkind a father, though she wanted for neither food nor clothing; whilst Mrs. Veal wanted for both. So that it was in the power of Mrs. Bargrave to be very much her friend in several instances, which mightily endeared Mrs. Veal, insomuch that she would often say, 'Mrs. Bargrave, you are not only the best, but the only friend I have in the world; and no circumstances of life shall ever dissolve my friendship.' They would often condole each other's adverse fortune, and read together 'Drelincourt upon Death', and other good books; and so, like two Christian friends, they comforted each other under their sorrow.

Some time after, Mr. Veal's friends got him a place in the custom-house at Dover, which occasioned Mrs. Veal, by little and little, to fall off from her intimacy with Mrs. Bargrave, though there was never any such thing as a quarrel; but an indifferency came on by degrees, till at last Mrs. Bargrave had not seen her in two years and a half, though above a twelvemonth of the time Mrs. Bargrave had been absent from Dover, and this last half-year has been in Canterbury about two months of the time, dwelling in a house of her own.

In this house, on the eighth of September last, viz., 1705, she was sitting alone in the forenoon, thinking over her unfortunate life, and arguing herself into a due resignation to Providence, though her condition seemed hard: 'And,' said she, 'I have been provided for hitherto, and doubt not but I shall be still, and am well satisfied that my afflictions shall end when it is most fit for me.' And then took up her sewing work, which she had no sooner done but she hears a knocking at the door; she went to see who it was there, and this proved to be Mrs. Veal, her old friend, who was in a riding habit. At that moment of time the clock struck twelve at noon.

'Madam,' says Mrs. Bargrave, 'I am surprised to see you, you have been so long a stranger'; but told her she was glad to see her, and offered to salute her, which Mrs. Veal complied with, till their lips almost touched, and then Mrs. Veal drew her hand across her own eyes, and said, 'I am not very well,' and so waived it. She told Mrs. Bargrave she was going on a journey, and had a great mind to see her first. 'But,' says Mrs. Bargrave, 'how came you to take a journey alone? I am amazed at it, because I know you have so fond a brother.' 'Oh,' says Mrs. Veal, 'I gave my brother the slip, and came away, because I had so great a mind to see you before I took my journey.' So Mrs. Bargrave went in with her into another room within the first, and Mrs. Veal sat herself down in an elbow chair, in which Mrs. Bargrave was sitting when she heard Mrs. Veal knock. 'Then,' says Mrs. Veal, 'my dear friend, I am come to renew our old friendship again, and to beg your pardon for my breach of it; and if you can forgive me, you are one of the best of women.' 'Oh,' says Mrs. Bargrave, 'don't mention such a thing; I have not had an uneasy thought about it. I can easily forgive it.' 'What did you think of me?' says

Mrs. Veal. Says Mrs. Bargrave, 'I thought you were like
the rest of the world, and that prosperity had made you
forget yourself and me.' Then Mrs. Veal reminded
Mrs. Bargrave of the many friendly offices she did her
in former days, and much of the conversation they had
with each other in the time of their adversity; what
books they read, and what comfort in particular they
received from Drelincourt's 'Book of Death', which was
the best, she said, on that subject was ever wrote. She also
mentioned Doctor Sherlock, and two Dutch books,
which were translated, wrote upon death, and several
others. But Drelincourt, she said, had the clearest notions
of death and of the future state of any who have handled
that subject. Then she asked Mrs. Bargrave whether she
had Drelincourt. She said, 'Yes.' Says Mrs. Veal, 'Fetch
it.' And so Mrs. Bargrave goes upstairs and brings it
down. Says Mrs. Veal, 'Dear Mrs. Bargrave, if the eyes of
our faith were as open as the eyes of our body, we should
see numbers of angels about us for our guard. The
notions we have of Heaven now are nothing like what
it is, as Drelincourt says; therefore be comforted under
your afflictions, and believe that the Almighty has a
particular regard to you, and that your afflictions are
marks of God's favor; and when they have done the
business they were sent for, they shall be removed from
you. And believe me, my dear friend, believe what I say
to you, one minute of future happiness will infinitely
reward you for all your sufferings. For I can never
believe' (and claps her hand upon her knee with a great
deal of earnestness, which, indeed, ran through all her
discourse) 'that ever God will suffer you to spend all your
days in this afflicted state. But be assured that your
afflictions shall leave you, or you them, in a short
time.' She spake in that pathetical and heavenly manner

that Mrs. Bargrave wept several times, she was so deeply affected with it.

Then Mrs. Veal mentioned Doctor Horneck's 'Ascetic', at the end of which he gives an account of the lives of the primitive Christians. Their pattern she recommended to our imitation, and said, 'Their conversation was not like this of our age. For now,' says she, 'there is nothing but frothy vain discourse, which is far different from theirs. Theirs was to edification, and to build one another up in the faith, so that they were not as we are, nor are we as they are. But,' said she, 'we might do as they did; there was a hearty friendship among them; but where is it now to be found?' Says Mrs. Bargrave, 'It is hard indeed to find a true friend in these days.' Says Mrs. Veal, 'Mr. Norris has a fine copy of verses, called *Friendship in Perfection*, which I wonderfully admire. Have you seen the book?' says Mrs. Veal. 'No,' says Mrs. Bargrave, 'but I have the verses of my own writing out.' 'Have you?' says Mrs. Veal; 'then fetch them'; which she did from above stairs, and offered them to Mrs. Veal to read, who refused, and waived the thing, saying, 'holding down her head would make it ache'; and then desired Mrs. Bargrave to read them to her, which she did. As they were admiring *Friendship*, Mrs. Veal said, 'Dear Mrs. Bargrave, I shall love you forever.' In the verses there is twice used the word 'Elysium'. 'Ah!' says Mrs. Veal, 'these poets have such names for Heaven.' She would often draw her hand cross her own eyes, and say, 'Mrs. Bargrave, don't you think I am mightily impaired by my fits?' 'No,' says Mrs. Bargrave; 'I think you look as well as ever I knew you.'

After all this discourse, which the apparition put in words much finer than Mrs. Bargrave said she could pretend to, and was much more than she can remember

– for it cannot be thought that an hour and three-quarters conversation could all be retained, though the main of it she thinks she does – she said to Mrs. Bargrave she would have her write a letter to her brother, and tell him she would have him give rings to such and such; and that there was a purse of gold in her cabinet, and that she would have two broad pieces given to her cousin Watson.

Talking at this rate, Mrs. Bargrave thought that a fit was coming upon her, and so placed herself in a chair just before her knees, to keep her from falling to the ground, if her fits should occasion it; for the elbow chair, she thought, would keep her from falling on either side. And to divert Mrs. Veal, as she thought, she took hold of her gown-sleeve several times, and commended it. Mrs. Veal told her it was a scoured silk, and newly made up. But, for all this, Mrs. Veal persisted in her request, and told Mrs. Bargrave she must not deny her. And she would have her tell her brother all their conversation when she had an opportunity. 'Dear Mrs. Veal,' says Mrs. Bargrave, 'this seems so impertinent that I cannot tell how to comply with it; and what a mortifying story will our conversation be to a young gentleman.' 'Well,' says Mrs. Veal, 'I must not be denied.' 'Why,' says Mrs. Bargrave, 'it is much better, methinks, to do it yourself.' 'No,' says Mrs. Veal; 'though it seems impertinent to you now, you will see more reason for it hereafter.' Mrs. Bargrave, then, to satisfy her importunity, was going to fetch a pen and ink, but Mrs. Veal said, 'Let it alone now and do it when I am gone; but you must be sure to do it'; which was one of the last things she enjoined her at parting, and so she promised her.

Then Mrs. Veal asked for Mrs. Bargrave's daughter. She said she was not at home. 'But if you have a mind to see her,' says Mrs. Bargrave, 'I'll send for her.' 'Do,' says Mrs. Veal; on which she left her, and went to a neighbor's to send for her; and by the time Mrs. Bargrave was returning, Mrs. Veal was got without the door in the street, in the face of the beast-market, on a Saturday (which is market-day), and stood ready to part as soon as Mrs. Bargrave came to her. She asked her why she was in such haste. She said she must be going, though perhaps she might not go her journey till Monday; and told Mrs. Bargrave she hoped she should see her again at her cousin Watson's before she went whither she was agoing. Then she said she would not take her leave of her, and walked from Mrs. Bargrave, in her view, till a turning interrupted the sight of her, which was three-quarters after one in the afternoon.

Mrs. Veal died the seventh of September, at twelve o'clock at noon, of her fits, and had not above four hours' senses before her death, in which time she received the sacrament. The next day after Mrs. Veal's appearing, being Sunday, Mrs. Bargrave was mightily indisposed with a cold and a sore throat, that she could not go out that day; but on Monday morning she sends a person to Captain Watson's to know if Mrs. Veal were there. They wondered at Mrs. Bargrave's inquiry, and sent her word she was not there, nor was expected. At this answer, Mrs. Bargrave told the maid she had certainly mistook the name or made some blunder. And though she was ill, she put on her hood and went herself to Captain Watson's, though she knew none of the family, to see if Mrs. Veal was there or not. They said they wondered at her asking, for that she had not been in town; they were sure, if she had, she would have been there. Says Mrs. Bargrave, 'I am sure she was with me on Saturday almost two hours.' They said it was impossible, for they must have seen her if she had. In comes Captain Watson, while they were in dispute, and said that Mrs. Veal was certainly dead, and her escutcheons were making. This strangely surprised Mrs. Bargrave, who went to the person immediately who had the care of them, and found it true. Then she related the whole story to Captain Watson's family; and what gown she had on, and how striped; and that Mrs. Veal told her it was scoured. Then Mrs. Watson cried out, 'You have seen her indeed, for none knew but Mrs. Veal and myself that the gown was scoured.' And Mrs. Watson owned that she described the gown exactly; 'for,' said she, 'I helped her to make it up.' This Mrs. Watson blazed all about the town, and avouched the demonstration of truth of Mrs. Bargrave's seeing Mrs. Veal's apparition. And Captain Watson carried two gentlemen immediately to Mrs. Bargrave's house to hear the relation from her own mouth. And then it spread so fast that gentlemen and persons of quality, the judicious and sceptical part of the world, flocked in upon her, which at last became such a task that she was forced to go out of the way; for they were in general extremely satisfied of the truth of the thing, and plainly saw that Mrs. Bargrave was no hypochondriac, for she always appears with such a cheerful air and pleasing mien that she has gained the favor and esteem of all the gentry, and it is thought a great favor if they can but get the relation from her own mouth. I should have told you before that Mrs. Veal told Mrs. Bargrave that her sister and brother-in-law were just come down from London to see her. Says Mrs. Bargrave, 'How came you to order matters so strangely?' 'It could not be helped,' said Mrs. Veal. And her brother and sister did come to see her, and entered the town of Dover just as Mrs. Veal was expiring. Mrs. Bargrave asked her whether she would not drink some tea. Says Mrs. Veal, 'I do not care if I do; but I'll warrant this mad fellow' – meaning Mrs. Bargrave's husband – 'has broke all your trinkets.' 'But,' says Mrs. Bargrave, 'I'll get something to drink in for all that'; but Mrs. Veal waived it, and said, 'It is no matter; let it alone'; and so it passed.

All the time I sat with Mrs. Bargrave, which was some hours, she recollected fresh sayings of Mrs. Veal. And one material thing more she told Mrs. Bargrave, that old Mr. Breton allowed Mrs. Veal ten pounds a year, which was a secret, and unknown to Mrs. Bargrave till Mrs. Veal told it her.

Mrs. Bargrave never varies in her story, which puzzles those who doubt of the truth, or are unwilling to believe it. A servant in a neighbor's yard adjoining to Mrs. Bargrave's house heard her talking to somebody an hour of the time Mrs. Veal was with her. Mrs. Bargrave went out to her next neighbor's the very moment she parted with Mrs. Veal, and told what ravishing conversation she had with an old friend, and told the whole of it. Drelincourt's 'Book of Death' is, since this happened, bought up strangely. And it is to be observed that, notwithstanding all this trouble and fatigue Mrs. Bargrave has undergone upon this account, she never took the value of a farthing, nor suffered her daughter to take anything of anybody, and therefore can have no interest in telling the story.

But Mr. Veal does what he can to stifle the matter, and said he would see Mrs. Bargrave; but yet it is certain matter of fact that he has been at Captain Watson's since the death of his sister, and yet never went near Mrs. Bargrave; and some of his friends report her to be a great liar, and that she knew of Mr. Breton's ten pounds a year.

But the person who pretends to say so has the reputation of a notorious liar among persons which I know to be of undoubted repute. Now, Mr. Veal is more a gentleman than to say she lies, but says a bad husband has crazed her; but she needs only present herself and it will effectually confute that pretence. Mr. Veal says he asked his sister on her death-bed whether she had a mind to dispose of anything. And she said no. Now what the things which Mrs. Veal's apparition would have disposed of were so trifling, and nothing of justice aimed at in their disposal, that the design of it appears to me to be only in order to make Mrs. Bargrave so to demonstrate the truth of her appearance as to satisfy the world of the reality thereof as to what she had seen and heard, and to secure her reputation among the reasonable and understanding part of mankind. And then, again, Mr. Veal owns that there was a purse of gold; but it was not found in her cabinet, but in a comb-box. This looks improbable; for that Mrs. Watson owned that Mrs. Veal was so very careful of the key of her cabinet that she would trust nobody with it; and if so, no doubt she would not trust her gold out of it. And Mrs. Veal's often drawing her hands over her eyes, and asking Mrs. Bargrave whether her fits had not impaired her, looks to me as if she did it on purpose to remind Mrs. Bargrave of her fits, to prepare her not to think it strange that she should put her upon writing to her brother, to dispose of rings and gold, which looked so much like a dying person's bequest; and it took accordingly with Mrs. Bargrave as the effect of her fits coming upon her, and was one of the many instances of her wonderful love to her and care of her, that she should not be affrighted, which, indeed, appears in her whole management, particularly in her coming to her in the daytime, waiving the salutation, and when she was alone; and then the manner of her parting, to prevent a second attempt to salute her.

Now, why Mr. Veal should think this relation a reflection − as it is plain he does, by his endeavoring to stifle it − I cannot imagine; because the generality believe her to be a good spirit, her discourse was so heavenly. Her two great errands were, to comfort Mrs. Hargrave in her affliction, and to ask her forgiveness for her breach of friendship, and with a pious discourse to encourage her. So that, after all, to suppose that Mrs. Bargrave could hatch such an invention as this, from Friday noon to Saturday noon − supposing that she knew of Mrs. Veal's death the very first moment − without jumbling circumstances, and without any interest, too, she must be more witty, fortunate, and wicked, too, than any indifferent person, I dare say, will allow. I asked Mrs. Bargrave several times if she was sure she felt the gown. She answered, modestly, 'If my senses be to be relied on, I am sure of it.' I asked her if she heard a sound when she clapped her hand upon her knee. She said she did not remember she did, and she said she appeared to be as much a substance as I did who talked with her. 'And I may,' said she, 'be as soon persuaded that your apparition is talking to me now as that I did not really see her; for I was under no manner of fear, I received her as a friend, and parted with her as such. I would not,' says she, 'give one farthing to make any one believe it; I have no interest in it; nothing but trouble is entailed upon me for a long time, for aught that I know; and, had it not come to light by accident, it would never have been made public.' But now she says she will make her own private use of it, and keep herself out of the way as much as she can; and so she has done since. She says she had a gentleman who came thirty miles to her to hear the relation; and that she had told it to a roomful of people at a time. Several particular gentlemen have had the story from Mrs. Bargrave's own mouth.

This thing has very much affected me, and I am as well satisfied as I am of the best-grounded matter of fact. And why we should dispute matter of fact, because we cannot solve things of which we can have no certain or demonstrative notions, seems strange to me; Mrs. Bargrave's authority and sincerity alone would have been undoubted in any other case.

The Tapestried Chamber

Sir Walter Scott

The following narrative is given from the pen, so far as
memory permits, in the same character in which it was
presented to the Author's ear; nor has he claim to further
praise, or to be more deeply censured, than in proportion
to the good or bad judgment which he has employed in
selecting his materials, as he has studiously avoided any
attempt at ornament which might interfere with the
simplicity of the tale.

At the same time it must be admitted, that the
particular class of stories which turns on the marvellous
possesses a stronger influence when told than when
committed to print. The volume taken up at noonday,
though rehearsing the same incidents, conveys a much
more feeble impression than is achieved by the voice of
the speaker on a circle of fireside auditors, who hang
upon the narrative as the narrator details the minute
incidents which serve to give it authenticity, and lowers
his voice with an affectation of mystery while he
approaches the fearful and wonderful part. It was with
such advantages that the present writer heard the
following events related, more than twenty years since,
by the celebrated Miss Seward of Litchfield, who to her
numerous accomplishments added, in a remarkable
degree, the power of narrative in private conversation.
In its present form the tale must necessarily lose all the
interest which was attached to it by the flexible voice and

intelligent features of the gifted narrator. Yet still, read aloud, to an undoubting audience by the doubtful light of the closing evening, or, in silence, by a decaying taper, and amidst the solitude of a half-lighted apartment, it may redeem its character as a good ghost-story. Miss Seward always affirmed that she had derived her information from an authentic source, although she suppressed the names of the two persons chiefly concerned. I will not avail myself of any particulars I may have since received concerning the localities of the detail, but suffer them to rest under the same general description in which they were first related to me; and, for the same reason, I will not add to, or diminish, the narrative by any circumstance, whether more or less material, but simply rehearse, as I heard it, a story of supernatural terror.

About the end of the American war, when the officers of Lord Cornwallis's army, which surrendered at York-town, and others, who had been made prisoners during the impolitic and ill-fated controversy, were returning to their own country, to relate their adventures and repose themselves after their fatigues, there was amongst them a general officer, to whom Miss S. gave the name of Browne, but merely, as I understood, to save the inconvenience of introducing a nameless agent in the narrative. He was an officer of merit, as well as a gentleman of high consideration for family and attainments.

Some business had carried General Browne upon a tour through the western counties, when, in the conclusion of a morning stage, he found himself in the vicinity of a small country town, which presented a scene of uncommon beauty, and of a character peculiarly English.

The little town, with its stately old church, whose tower bore testimony to the devotion of ages long past, lay amidst pastures and cornfields of small extent, but bounded and divided with hedgerow timber of great age and size. There were few marks of modern improvement. The environs of the place intimated neither the solitude of decay nor the bustle of novelty; the houses were old, but in good repair; and the beautiful little river murmured freely on its way to the left of the town, neither restrained by a dam nor bordered by a towing-path.

Upon a gentle eminence, nearly a mile to the southward of the town, were seen, amongst many venerable oaks and tangled thickets, the turrets of a castle, as old as the wars of York and Lancaster, but which seemed to have received important alterations during the age of Elizabeth and her successor. It had not been a place of great size; but whatever accommodation it formerly afforded was, it must be supposed, still to be obtained within its walls; at least, such was the inference which General Browne drew from observing the smoke arise merrily from several of the ancient wreathed and carved chimney-stalks. The wall of the park ran alongside of the highway for two or three hundred yards; and through the different points by which the eye found glimpses into the woodland scenery it seemed to be well stocked. Other points of view opened in succession – now a full one of the front of the old castle, and now a side glimpse at its particular towers, the former rich in all the bizarrerie of the Elizabethan school, while the simple and solid strength of other parts of the building seemed to show that they had been raised more for defence than ostentation.

Delighted with the partial glimpses which he obtained
of the castle through the woods and glades by which this
ancient feudal fortress was surrounded, our military
traveller was determined to inquire whether it might
not deserve a nearer view, and whether it contained
family pictures or other objects of curiosity worthy of a
stranger's visit, when, leaving the vicinity of the park, he
rolled through a clean and well-paved street, and stopped
at the door of a well-frequented inn.

Before ordering horses to proceed on his journey,
General Browne made inquiries concerning the pro-
prietor of the château which had so attracted his
admiration; and was equally surprised and pleased at
hearing in reply a nobleman named whom we shall call
Lord Woodville. How fortunate! Much of Browne's
early recollections, both at school and at college, had
been connected with young Woodville, whom, by a
few questions, he now ascertained to be the same with
the owner of this fair domain. He had been raised to
the peerage by the decease of his father a few months
before, and, as the General learned from the landlord,
the term of mourning being ended, was now taking
possession of his paternal estate, in the jovial season of
merry autumn, accompanied by a select party of
friends, to enjoy the sports of a country famous for
game.

This was delightful news to our traveller. Frank
Woodville had been Richard Browne's fag at Eton, and
his chosen intimate at Christ Church; their pleasures and
their tasks had been the same; and the honest soldier's
heart warmed to find his early friend in possession of so
delightful a residence, and of an estate, as the landlord
assured him with a nod and a wink, fully adequate to
maintain and add to his dignity. Nothing was more natural

than that the traveller should suspend a journey which there was nothing to render hurried to pay a visit to an old friend under such agreeable circumstances.

The fresh horses, therefore, had only the brief task of conveying the General's travelling-carriage to Woodville Castle. A porter admitted them at a modern Gothic lodge, built in that style to correspond with the castle itself, and at the same time rang a bell to give warning of the approach of visitors. Apparently the sound of the bell had suspended the separation of the company, bent on the various amusements of the morning; for, on entering the court of the château, several young men were lounging about in their sporting-dresses, looking at and criticising the dogs, which the keepers held in readiness to attend their pastime. As General Browne alighted, the young lord came to the gate of the hall, and for an instant gazed, as at a stranger, upon the countenance of his friend, on which war, with its fatigues and its wounds, had made a great alteration. But the uncertainty lasted no longer than till the visitor had spoken, and the hearty greeting which followed was such as can only be exchanged betwixt those who have passed together the merry days of careless boyhood or early youth.

'If I could have formed a wish, my dear Browne,' said Lord Woodville, 'it would have been to have you here, of all men, upon this occasion, which my friends are good enough to hold as a sort of holiday. Do not think you have been unwatched during the years you have been absent from us. I have traced you through your dangers, your triumphs, your misfortunes, and was delighted to see that, whether in victory or defeat, the name of my old friend was always distinguished with applause.'

The General made a suitable reply, and congratulated his friend on his new dignities, and the possession of a place and domain so beautiful.

'Nay, you have seen nothing of it as yet,' said Lord Woodville, 'and I trust you do not mean to leave us till you are better acquainted with it. It is true, I confess, that my present party is pretty large, and the old house, like other places of the kind, does not possess so much accommodation as the extent of the outward walls appears to promise. But we can give you a comfortable old-fashioned room, and I venture to suppose that your campaigns have taught you to be glad of worse quarters.'

The General shrugged his shoulders and laughed. 'I presume,' he said, 'the worst apartment in your château is considerably superior to the old tobacco-cask in which I was fain to take up my night's lodging when I was in the bush, as the Virginians call it, with the light corps. There I lay, like Diogenes himself, so delighted with my covering from the elements, that I made a vain attempt to have it rolled on to my next quarters; but my commander for the time would give way to no such luxurious provision, and I took farewell of my beloved cask with tears in my eyes.'

'Well, then, since you do not fear your quarters,' said Lord Woodville, 'you will stay with me a week at least. Of guns, dogs, fishing-rods, flies, and means of sport by sea and land, we have enough and to spare; you cannot pitch on an amusement but we will find the means of pursuing it. But if you prefer the gun and pointers, I will go with you myself, and see whether you have mended your shooting since you have been amongst the Indians of the back settlements.'

The General gladly accepted his friendly host's proposal in all its points. After a morning of manly exercise, the company met at dinner, where it was the delight of Lord Woodville to conduce to the display of the high properties of his recovered friend, so as to recommend him to his guests, most of whom were persons of distinction. He led General Browne to speak of the scenes he had witnessed; and as every word marked alike the brave officer and the sensible man, who retained possession of his cool judgment under the most imminent dangers, the company looked upon the soldier with general respect, as on one who had proved himself possessed of an uncommon portion of personal courage – that attribute, of all others, of which everybody desires to be thought possessed.

The day at Woodville Castle ended as usual in such mansions. The hospitality stopped within the limits of good order; music, in which the young lord was a proficient, succeeded to the circulation of the bottle; cards and billiards, for those who preferred such amusements, were in readiness; but the exercise of the morning required early hours, and not long after eleven o'clock the guests began to retire to their several apartments.

The young lord himself conducted his friend, General Browne, to the chamber destined for him, which answered the description he had given of it, being comfortable, but old-fashioned. The bed was of the massive form used in the end of the 17th century, and the curtains of faded silk, heavily trimmed with tarnished gold. But then the sheets, pillows, and blankets looked delightful to the campaigner, when he thought of his 'mansion, the cask'. There was an air of gloom in the tapestry hangings which, with their worn-out graces, curtained the walls of the little chamber, and gently undulated as the autumnal breeze found its way through the ancient lattice-window, which pattered and whistled as the air gained entrance. The toilet, too, with its mirror, turbaned, after the manner of the beginning of the century, with a coiffure of murrey-colored silk, and its hundred strange-shaped boxes, providing for arrangements which had been obsolete for more than fifty years, had an antique, and in so far a melancholy, aspect. But nothing could blaze more brightly and cheerfully than the two large wax candles; or if aught could rival them, it was the flaming, bickering fagots in the chimney, that sent at once their gleam and their warmth through the snug apartment, which, notwithstanding the general antiquity of its appearance, was not wanting in the least convenience that modern habits rendered either necessary or desirable.

'This is an old-fashioned sleeping-apartment, General,' said the young lord; 'but I hope you find nothing that makes you envy your old tobacco-cask.'

'I am not particular respecting my lodgings,' replied the General; 'yet were I to make any choice, I would prefer this chamber by many degrees to the gayer and more modern rooms of your family mansion. Believe me, that when I unite its modern air of comfort with its venerable antiquity, and recollect that it is your lordship's property, I shall feel in better quarters here than if I were in the best hotel London could afford.'

'I trust – I have no doubt – that you will find yourself as comfortable as I wish you, my dear General,' said the young nobleman; and once more bidding his guest good-night, he shook him by the hand and withdrew.

The General once more looked around him, and internally congratulating himself on his return to peace-

ful life, the comforts of which were endeared by the
recollection of the hardships and dangers he had lately
sustained, undressed himself, and prepared for a luxurious night's rest.

Here, contrary to the custom of this species of tale, we
leave the General in possession of his apartment until the
next morning.

The company assembled for breakfast at an early hour,
but without the appearance of General Browne, who
seemed the guest that Lord Woodville was desirous of
honoring above all whom his hospitality had assembled
around him. He more than once expressed surprise at the
General's absence, and at length sent a servant to make
inquiry after him. The man brought back information
that General Browne had been walking abroad since an
early hour of the morning, in defiance of the weather,
which was misty and ungenial.

'The custom of a soldier,' said the young nobleman to
his friends; 'many of them acquire habitual vigilance, and
cannot sleep after the early hour at which their duty
usually commands them to be alert.'

Yet the explanation which Lord Woodville thus
offered to the company seemed hardly satisfactory to
his own mind, and it was in a fit of silence and
abstraction that he awaited the return of the General.
It took place near an hour after the breakfast-bell had
rung. He looked fatigued and feverish. His hair, the
powdering and arrangement of which was at this time
one of the most important occupations of a man's
whole day, and marked his fashion as much as, in the
present time, the tying of a cravat, or the want of one,
was dishevelled, uncurled, void of powder, and dank
with dew. His clothes were huddled on with a careless
negligence remarkable in a military man, whose real or

supposed duties are usually held to include some attention to the toilet; and his looks were haggard and ghastly in a peculiar degree.

'So you have stolen a march upon us this morning, my dear General,' said Lord Woodville; 'or you have not found your bed so much to your mind as I had hoped and you seemed to expect. How did you rest last night?'

'Oh, excellently well – remarkably well – never better in my life!' said General Browne rapidly, and yet with an air of embarrassment which was obvious to his friend. He then hastily swallowed a cup of tea, and, neglecting or refusing whatever else was offered, seemed to fall into a fit of abstraction.

'You will take the gun to-day, General?' said his friend and host, but had to repeat the question twice ere he received the abrupt answer, 'No, my lord; I am sorry I cannot have the honor of spending another day with your lordship: my post-horses are ordered, and will be here directly.'

All who were present showed surprise, and Lord Woodville immediately replied, 'Post-horses, my good friend! what can you possibly want with them, when you promised to stay with me quietly for at least a week?'

'I believe,' said the General, obviously much embarrassed, 'that I might, in the pleasure of my first meeting with your lordship, have said something about stopping here a few days; but I have since found it altogether impossible.'

'That is very extraordinary,' answered the young nobleman. 'You seemed quite disengaged yesterday, and you cannot have had a summons to-day; for our post has not come up from the town, and therefore you cannot have received any letters.'

General Browne, without giving any further explanation, muttered something of indispensable business, and
insisted on the absolute necessity of his departure in a
manner which silenced all opposition on the part of his
host, who saw that his resolution was taken, and forbore
all further importunity.

'At least, however,' he said, 'permit me, my dear
Browne, since go you will or must, to show you the
view from the terrace, which the mist, that is now rising,
will soon display.'

He threw open a sash-window and stepped down
upon the terrace as he spoke. The General followed him
mechanically, but seemed little to attend to what his host
was saying, as, looking across an extended and rich
prospect, he pointed out the different objects worthy
of observation. Thus they moved on till Lord Woodville
had attained his purpose of drawing his guest entirely
apart from the rest of the company, when, turning round
upon him with an air of great solemnity, he addressed
him thus:

'Richard Browne, my old and very dear friend, we are
now alone. Let me conjure you to answer me upon the
word of a friend and the honor of a soldier. How did you
in reality rest during last night?'

'Most wretchedly indeed, my lord,' answered the
General, in the same tone of solemnity; 'so miserably,
that I would not run the risk of such a second night, not
only for all the lands belonging to this castle, but for all
the country which I see from this elevated point of
view.'

'This is most extraordinary,' said the young lord, as if
speaking to himself; 'then there must be something in the
reports concerning that apartment.' Again turning to the
General, he said: 'For God's sake, my dear friend, be

candid with me, and let me know the disagreeable particulars which have befallen you under a roof where, with consent of the owner, you should have met nothing save comfort.'

The General seemed distressed by this appeal, and paused a moment before he replied. 'My dear lord,' he at length said, 'what happened to me last night is of a nature so peculiar and so unpleasant, that I could hardly bring myself to detail it even to your lordship, were it not that, independent of my wish to gratify any request of yours, I think that sincerity on my part may lead to some explanation about a circumstance equally painful and mysterious. To others, the communication I am about to make might place me in the light of a weak-minded, superstitious fool, who suffered his own imagination to delude and bewilder him; but you have known me in childhood and youth, and will not suspect me of having adopted in manhood the feelings and frailties from which my early years were free.' Here he paused, and his friend replied.

'Do not doubt my perfect confidence in the truth of your communication, however strange it may be,' replied Lord Woodville; 'I know your firmness of disposition too well to suspect you could be made the object of imposition, and am aware that your honor and your friendship will equally deter you from exaggerating whatever you may have witnessed.'

'Well, then,' said the General, 'I will proceed with my story as well as I can, relying upon your candor, and yet distinctly feeling that I would rather face a battery than recall to my mind the odious recollections of last night.'

He paused a second time, and then perceiving that Lord Woodville remained silent and in an attitude of attention, he commenced, though not without obvious reluctance, the history of his night adventures in the Tapestried Chamber.

'I undressed and went to bed, so soon as your lordship left me yesterday evening; but the wood in the chimney, which nearly fronted my bed, blazed brightly and cheerfully, and, aided by a hundred exciting recollections of my childhood and youth, which had been recalled by the unexpected pleasure of meeting your lordship, prevented me from falling immediately asleep. I ought, however, to say, that these reflections were all of a pleasant and agreeable kind, grounded on a sense of having for a time exchanged the labor, fatigues, and dangers of my profession for the enjoyments of a peaceful life, and the reunion of those friendly and affectionate ties which I had torn asunder at the rude summons of war.

'While such pleasing reflections were stealing over my mind, and gradually lulling me to slumber, I was suddenly aroused by a sound like that of the rustling of a silken gown, and the tapping of a pair of high-heeled shoes, as if a woman were walking in the apartment. Ere I could draw the curtain to see what the matter was, the figure of a little woman passed between the bed and the fire. The back of this form was turned to me, and I could observe, from the shoulders and neck, it was that of an old woman, whose dress was an old-fashioned gown, which, I think, ladies call a sacque – that is, a sort of robe completely loose in the body, but gathered into broad plaits upon the neck and shoulders, which fall down to the ground, and terminate in a species of train.

'I thought the intrusion singular enough, but never harbored for a moment the idea that what I saw was anything more than the mortal form of some old woman about the establishment, who had a fancy to dress like her grandmother, and who, having perhaps, as your lordship mentioned that you were rather straitened for room, been dislodged from her chamber for my accommodation, had forgotten the circumstance, and returned by twelve to her old haunt. Under this persuasion I moved myself in bed and coughed a little, to make the intruder sensible of my being in possession of the premises. She turned slowly round, but, gracious Heaven! my lord, what a countenance did she display to me! There was no longer any question what she was, or any thought of her being a living being. Upon a face which wore the fixed features of a corpse were imprinted the traces of the vilest and most hideous passions which had animated her while she lived. The body of some atrocious criminal seemed to have been given up from the grave, and the soul restored from the penal fire, in order to form, for a space, a union with the ancient accomplice of its guilt. I started up in bed, and sat upright, supporting myself on my palms, as I gazed on this horrible spectre. The hag made, as it seemed, a single and swift stride to the bed, where I lay, and squatted herself down upon it, in precisely the same attitude which I had assumed in the extremity of horror, advancing her diabolical countenance within half a yard of mine, with a grin which seemed to intimate the malice and the derision of an incarnate fiend.'

Here General Browne stopped, and wiped from his brow the cold perspiration with which the recollection of his horrible vision had covered it.

'My lord,' he said, 'I am no coward. I have been in all the mortal dangers incidental to my profession, and I may truly boast that no man ever knew Richard Browne dishonor the sword he wears; but in these horrible circumstances, under the eyes, and, as it seemed, almost in the grasp, of the incarnation of an evil spirit, all firmness forsook me, all manhood melted from me like wax in the furnace, and I felt my hair individually bristle. The current of my life-blood ceased to flow, and I sank back in a swoon, as very a victim to panic terror as ever was a village girl or a child of ten years old. How long I lay in this condition I cannot pretend to guess.

'But I was roused by the castle clock striking one, so loud that it seemed as if it were in the very room. It was some time before I dared open my eyes, lest they should again encounter the horrible spectacle. When, however, I summoned courage to look up, she was no longer visible. My first idea was to pull my bell, wake the servants, and remove to a garret or a hay-loft, to be insured against a second visitation. Nay, I will confess the truth, that my resolution was altered, not by the shame of exposing myself, but by the fear that, as the bell-cord hung by the chimney, I might, in making my way to it, be again crossed by the fiendish hag, who, I figured to myself, might be still lurking about some corner of the apartment.

'I will not pretend to describe what hot and cold fever-fits tormented me for the rest of the night, through broken sleep, weary vigils, and that dubious state which forms the neutral ground between them. A hundred terrible objects appeared to haunt me; but there was the great difference betwixt the vision which I have described and those which followed, that I knew the last to be deceptions of my own fancy and over-excited nerves.

'Day at last appeared, and I rose from my bed ill in health and humiliated in mind. I was ashamed of myself as a man and a soldier, and still more so at feeling my own extreme desire to escape from the haunted apartment, which, however, conquered all other considerations; so that, huddling on my clothes with the most careless haste, I made my escape from your lordship's mansion, to seek in the open air some relief to my nervous system, shaken as it was by this horrible rencounter with a visitant, for such I must believe her, from the other world. Your lordship has now heard the cause of my discomposure, and of my sudden desire to leave your hospitable castle. In other places I trust we may often meet; but God protect me from ever spending a second night under that roof!'

Strange as the General's tale was, he spoke with such a deep air of conviction, that it cut short all the usual commentaries which are made on such stories. Lord Woodville never once asked him if he was sure he did not dream of the apparition, or suggested any of the possibilities by which it is fashionable to explain supernatural appearances, as wild vagaries of the fancy or deceptions of the optic nerves. On the contrary, he seemed deeply impressed with the truth and reality of what he had heard; and, after a considerable pause, regretted, with much appearance of sincerity, that his early friend should in his house have suffered so severely.

'I am the more sorry for your pain, my dear Browne,' he continued, 'that it is the unhappy, though most unexpected, result of an experiment of my own. You must know that, for my father and grandfather's time, at least, the apartment which was assigned to you last night had been shut on account of reports that it was disturbed by supernatural sights and noises. When I came, a few weeks since, into possession of the estate, I

thought the accommodation which the castle afforded
for my friends was not extensive enough to permit the
inhabitants of the invisible world to retain possession of
a comfortable sleeping-apartment. I therefore caused the
Tapestried Chamber, as we call it, to be opened; and,
without destroying its air of antiquity, I had such new
articles of furniture placed in it as became the modern
times. Yet, as the opinion that the room was haunted
very strongly prevailed among the domestics, and was
also known in the neighborhood and to many of my
friends, I feared some prejudice might be entertained by
the first occupant of the Tapestried Chamber, which
might tend to revive the evil report which it had
labored under, and so disappoint my purpose of
rendering it a useful part of the house. I must confess,
my dear Browne, that your arrival yesterday, agreeable
to me for a thousand reasons besides, seemed the most
favorable opportunity of removing the unpleasant
rumors which attached to the room, since your
courage was indubitable, and your mind free of any
preoccupation on the subject, I could not, therefore,
have chosen a more fitting subject for my experiment.'

'Upon my life,' said General Browne, somewhat
hastily, 'I am infinitely obliged to your lordship – very
particularly indebted, indeed. I am likely to remember
for some time the consequences of the experiment, as
your lordship is pleased to call it.'

'Nay, now you are unjust, my dear friend,' said Lord
Woodville. 'You have only to reflect for a single
moment, in order to be convinced that I could not
augur the possibility of the pain to which you have been
so unhappily exposed. I was yesterday morning a
complete sceptic on the subject of supernatural appearances. Nay, I am sure that, had I told you what was said

about that room, those very reports would have induced you, by your own choice, to select it for your accommodation. It was my misfortune, perhaps my error, but really cannot be termed my fault, that you have been afflicted so strangely.'

'Strangely indeed!' said the General, resuming his good temper; 'and I acknowledge that I have no right to be offended with your lordship for treating me like what I used to think myself, a man of some firmness and courage. But I see my post-horses are arrived, and I must not detain your lordship from your amusement.'

'Nay, my old friend,' said Lord Woodville, 'since you cannot stay with us another day, which, indeed, I can no longer urge, give me at least half an hour more. You used to love pictures, and I have a gallery of portraits, some of them by Vandyke, representing ancestry to whom this property and castle formerly belonged. I think that several of them will strike you as possessing merit.'

General Browne accepted the invitation, though somewhat unwillingly. It was evident he was not to breathe freely at ease till he left Woodville Castle far behind him. He could not refuse his friend's invitation, however; and the less so, that he was a little ashamed of the peevishness which he had displayed toward his well-meaning entertainer.

The General, therefore, followed Lord Woodville through several rooms, into a long gallery hung with pictures, which the latter pointed out to his guest, telling the names, and giving some account, of the personages whose portraits presented themselves in progression. General Browne was but little interested in the details which these accounts conveyed to him. They were, indeed, of the kind which are usually found in an old family gallery. Here was a cavalier who had ruined the estate in the royal cause; there a fine lady who had reinstated it by contracting a match with a wealthy Roundhead. There hung a gallant who had been in danger for corresponding with the exiled court at St.-Germain's; here one who had taken arms for William at the Revolution; and there a third that had thrown his weight alternately into the scale of Whig and Tory.

While Lord Woodville was cramming these words into his guest's ear, 'against the stomach of his sense', they gained the middle of the gallery, when he beheld General Browne suddenly start, and assume an attitude of the utmost surprise, not unmixed with fear, as his eyes were caught and suddenly riveted by a portrait of an old lady in a sacque, the fashionable dress of the end of the 17th century.

'There she is!' he exclaimed, 'there she is, in form and features, though inferior in demoniac expression to the accursed hag who visited me last night.'

'If that be the case,' said the young nobleman, 'there can remain no longer any doubt of the horrible reality of your apparition. That is the picture of a wretched ancestress of mine, of whose crimes a black and fearful catalogue is recorded in a family history in my charter-chest. The recital of them would be too horrible; it is enough to say, that in yon fatal apartment incest and unnatural murder were committed. I will restore it to the solitude to which the better judgment of those who preceded me had consigned it; and never shall anyone, so long as I can prevent it, be exposed to a repetition of the supernatural horrors, which could shake such courage as yours.'

Thus the friends, who had met with such glee, parted in a very different mood – Lord Woodville to command the Tapestried Chamber to be unmantled and the door built up; and General Browne to seek in some less beautiful country, and with some less dignified friend, forgetfulness of the painful night which he had passed in Woodville Castle.

The Lady with the Velvet Collar

Washington Irving

On a stormy night, in the tempestuous times of the French revolution, a young German was returning to his lodgings, at a late hour, across the old part of Paris. The lightning gleamed, and the loud claps of thunder rattled through the lofty narrow streets – but I should first tell you something about this young German.

Gottfried Wolfgang was a young man of good family. He had studied for some time at Göttingen, but being of a visionary and enthusiastic character, he had wandered into those wild and speculative doctrines which have so often bewildered German students. His secluded life, his intense application, and the singular nature of his studies, had an effect on both mind and body. His health was impaired; his imagination diseased. He had been indulging in fanciful speculations on spiritual essences, until, like Swedenborg, he had an ideal world of his own around him. He took up a notion, I do not know from what cause, that there was an evil influence hanging over him; an evil genius or spirit seeking to ensnare him and insure his perdition. Such an idea working on his melancholy temperament produced the most gloomy effects. He became haggard and desponding. His friends discovered the mental malady preying upon him, and determined that the best cure was a change of scene; he was sent, therefore, to finish his studies amidst the splendors and gayeties of Paris.

Wolfgang arrived at Paris at the breaking out of the Revolution. The popular delirium at first caught his enthusiastic mind, and he was captivated by the political and philosophical theories of the day, but the scenes of blood which followed shocked his sensitive nature; disgusted him with society and the world, and made him more than ever a recluse. He shut himself up in a solitary apartment in the *Pays Latin*, the quarter of students. There, in a gloomy street not far from the monastic walls of the Sorbonne, he pursued his favorite speculations. Sometimes he spent hours together in the great libraries of Paris, those catacombs of departed authors, rummaging among their hoards of dusty and obsolete works in quest of food for his unhealthy appetite. He was, in a manner, a literary ghoul, feeding in the charnel-house of decayed literature.

Wolfgang, though solitary and recluse, was of an ardent temperament, but for a time it operated merely upon his imagination. He was too shy and ignorant of the world to make any advances to the fair, but he was a passionate admirer of female beauty, and in his lonely chamber would often lose himself in reveries on forms and faces which he had seen, and his fancy would deck out images of loveliness far surpassing the reality.

While his mind was in this excited and sublimated state, a dream produced an extraordinary effect upon him. It was of a female face of transcendent beauty. So strong was the impression made, that he dreamed of it again and again. It haunted his thoughts by day, his slumbers by night; in fine, he became passionately enamored of this shadow of a dream. This lasted so long that it became one of those fixed ideas which haunt the minds of melancholy men, and are at times mistaken for madness.

Such was Gottfried Wolfgang, and such his situation at the time I mentioned. He was returning home late one stormy night, through some of the old and gloomy streets of the *Marais*, the ancient part of Paris. The loud claps of thunder rattled among the high houses of the narrow streets. He came to the Place de la Grève, the square where public executions are performed. The lightning quivered about the pinnacles of the ancient Hôtel de Ville, and shed flickering gleams over the open space in front. As Wolfgang was crossing the square, he shrank back with horror at finding himself close by the guillotine. It was the height of the Reign of Terror, when this dreadful instrument of death stood ever ready, and its scaffold was continually running with the blood of the virtuous and the brave. It had that very day been actively employed in the work of carnage, and there it stood in grim array, amidst a silent and sleeping city, waiting for fresh victims.

Wolfgang's heart sickened within him, and he was turning shuddering from the horrible engine, when he beheld a shadowy form, cowering as it were at the foot of the steps which led up to the scaffold. A succession of vivid flashes of lightning revealed it more distinctly. It was a female figure, dressed in black. She was seated on one of the lower steps of the scaffold, leaning forward, her face hid in her lap; and her long dishevelled tresses hanging to the ground, streaming with the rain which fell in torrents. Wolfgang paused. There was something awful in this solitary monument of woe. The female had the appearance of being above the common order. He knew the times to be full of vicissitude, and that many a fair head, which had once been pillowed on down, now wandered houseless. Perhaps this was some poor mourner whom the dreadful axe had rendered desolate, and who sat here heartbroken on the strand of existence, from which all that was dear to her had been launched into eternity.

He approached, and addressed her in the accents of sympathy. She raised her head and gazed wildly at him. What was his astonishment at beholding, by the bright glare of the lightning, the very face which had haunted him in his dreams. It was pale and disconsolate, but ravishingly beautiful.

Trembling with violent and conflicting emotions, Wolfgang again accosted her. He spoke something of her being exposed at such an hour of the night, and to the fury of such a storm, and offered to conduct her to her friends. She pointed to the guillotine with a gesture of dreadful signification.

'I have no friend on earth!' said she.

'But you have a home,' said Wolfgang.

'Yes – in the grave!'

The heart of the student melted at the words.

'If a stranger dare make an offer,' said he, 'without danger of being misunderstood, I would offer my humble dwelling as a shelter; myself as a devoted friend. I am friendless myself in Paris, and a stranger in the land; but if my life could be of service, it is at your disposal, and should be sacrificed before harm or indignity should come to you.'

There was an honest earnestness in the young man's manner that had its effect. His foreign accent, too, was in his favor; it showed him not to be a hackneyed inhabitant of Paris. Indeed, there is an eloquence in true enthusiasm that is not to be doubted. The homeless stranger confided herself implicitly to the protection of the student.

He supported her faltering steps across the Pont Neuf, and by the place where the statue of Henry the Fourth had been overthrown by the populace. The storm had abated, and the thunder rumbled at a distance. All Paris was quiet; that great volcano of human passion slumbered for awhile, to gather fresh strength for the next day's eruption. The student conducted his charge through the ancient streets of the *Pays Latin*, and by the dusky walls of the Sorbonne, to the great dingy hotel which he inhabited. The old portress who admitted them stared with surprise at the unusual sight of the melancholy Wolfgang with a female companion.

On entering his apartment, the student, for the first time, blushed at the scantiness and indifference of his dwelling. He had but one chamber – an old-fashioned salon – heavily carved, and fantastically furnished with the remains of former magnificence, for it was of those hotels in the quarter of the Luxembourg Palace which had once belonged to nobility. It was lumbered with books and papers, and all the usual apparatus of a student, and his bed stood in a recess at one end.

When lights were brought, and Wolfgang had a better opportunity of contemplating the stranger, he was more than ever intoxicated by her beauty. Her face was pale, but of a dazzling fairness, set off by a profusion of raven hair that hung clustering about it. Her eyes were large and brilliant, with a singular expression approaching almost to wildness. As far as her black dress permitted her shape to be seen, it was of perfect symmetry. Her whole appearance was highly striking, though she was dressed in the simplest style. The only thing approaching to an ornament which she wore, was a broad black band round her neck, clasped by diamonds.

The perplexity now commenced with the student how to dispose of the helpless being thus thrown upon his protection. He thought of abandoning his chamber to her, and seeking shelter for himself elsewhere. Still he was so fascinated by her charms, there seemed to be such a spell upon his thoughts and senses, that he could not tear himself from her presence. Her manner, too, was singular and unaccountable. She spoke no more of the guillotine. Her grief had abated. The attentions of the student had first won her confidence, and then, apparently, her heart. She was evidently an enthusiast like himself, and enthusiasts soon understand each other.

In the infatuation of the moment, Wolfgang avowed his passion for her. He told her the story of his mysterious dream, and how she had possessed his heart before he had even seen her. She was strangely affected by his recital, and acknowledged to have felt an impulse toward him equally unaccountable. It was the time for wild theory and wild actions. Old prejudices and superstitions were done away; everything was under the sway of the 'Goddess of Reason'. Among other rubbish of the old times, the forms and ceremonies of marriage began to be considered superfluous bonds for honorable minds. Social compacts were the vogue. Wolfgang was too much of a theorist not to be tainted by the liberal doctrines of the day.

'Why should we separate?' said he, 'our hearts are united; in the eye of reason and honor we are as one. What need is there of sordid forms to bind high souls together?'

The stranger listened with emotion; she had evidently received illumination at the same school.

'You have no home nor family,' continued he; 'let me be everything to you, or rather let us be everything to one another. If form is necessary, form shall be observed – there is my hand. I pledge myself to you forever.'

'Forever?' said the stranger, solemnly.

'Forever!' repeated Wolfgang.

The stranger clasped the hand extended to her: 'Then I am yours,' murmured she, and sank upon his bosom.

The next morning the student left his bride sleeping, and sallied forth at an early hour to seek more spacious apartments, suitable to the change in his situation. When he returned, he found the stranger lying with her head hanging over the bed, and one arm thrown over it. He spoke to her, but received no reply. He advanced to awaken her from her uneasy posture. On taking her hand, it was cold – there was no pulsation – her face was pallid and ghastly. – In a word – she was a corpse.

Horrified and frantic, he alarmed the house. A scene of confusion ensued. The police was summoned. As the officer of police entered the room, he started back on beholding the corpse.

'Great heaven!' cried he, 'how did this woman come here?'

'Do you know anything about her?' said Wolfgang, eagerly.

'Do I?' exclaimed the police officer, 'she was guillotined yesterday.'

He stepped forward, undid the black collar round the neck of the corpse, and the head rolled on the floor!

The student burst into a frenzy. 'The fiend! the fiend has gained possession of me!' shrieked he; 'I am lost forever.'

They tried to soothe him, but in vain. He was possessed with the frightful belief that an evil spirit had reanimated the dead body to ensnare him. He went distracted, and died in a madhouse.

The Gray Champion

Nathaniel Hawthorne

There was once a time when New England groaned
under the actual pressure of heavier wrongs than those
threatened ones which brought on the Revolution.
James II, the bigoted successor of Charles the Volup-
tuous, had annulled the charters of all the colonies, and
sent a harsh and unprincipled soldier to take away our
liberties and endanger our religion. The administration
of Sir Edmund Andros lacked scarcely a single characteristic of tyranny: a Governor and Council, holding
office from the King, and wholly independent of the
country; laws made and taxes levied without concur-
rence of the people immediate or by the representa-
tives; the rights of private citizens violated, and the
titles of all landed property declared void; the voice of
complaint stifled by restrictions on the press; and,
finally, disaffection overawed by the first band of
mercenary troops that ever marched on our free soil.
For two years our ancestors were kept in sullen
submission by that filial love which had invariably
secured their allegiance to the mother country,
whether its head chanced to be a Parliament, Protec-
tor, or Popish Monarch. Till these evil times, however, such allegiance had been merely nominal, and
the colonists had ruled themselves, enjoying far more
freedom than is even yet the privilege of the native
subjects of Great Britain.

At length a rumor reached our shores that the Prince of Orange had ventured on an enterprise, the success of which would be the triumph of civil and religious rights and the salvation of New England. It was but a doubtful whisper; it might be false, or the attempt might fail; and, in either case, the man that stirred against King James would lose his head. Still the intelligence produced a marked effect. The people smiled mysteriously in the streets, and threw bold glances at their oppressors; while far and wide there was a subdued and silent agitation, as if the slightest signal would rouse the whole land from its sluggish despondency. Aware of their danger, the rulers resolved to avert it by an imposing display of strength, and perhaps to confirm their despotism by yet harsher measures. One afternoon in April, 1689, Sir Edmund Andros and his favorite councillors, being warm with wine, assembled the redcoats of the Governor's Guard, and made their appearance in the streets of Boston. The sun was near setting when the march commenced.

The roll of the drum at that unquiet crisis seemed to go through the streets, less as the martial music of the soldiers, than as a muster-call to the inhabitants themselves. A multitude, by various avenues, assembled in King Street, which was destined to be the scene, nearly a century afterward, of another encounter between the troops of Britain, and a people struggling against her tyranny. Though more than sixty years had elapsed since the pilgrims came, this crowd of their descendants still showed the strong and sombre features of their character perhaps more strikingly in such a stern emergency than on happier occasions. There were the sober garb, the general severity of mien, the gloomy but undismayed expression, the scriptural forms of speech, and the confidence in Heaven's blessing on a righteous cause, which would have marked a band of the original Puritans, when threatened by some peril of the wilderness. Indeed, it was not yet time for the old spirit to be extinct; since there were men in the street that day who had worshipped there beneath the trees, before a house was reared to the God for whom they had become exiles. Old soldiers of the Parliament were here, too, smiling grimly at the thought that their aged arms might strike another blow against the house of Stuart. Here, also, were the veterans of King Philip's war, who had burned villages and slaughtered young and old, with pious fierceness, while the godly souls throughout the land were helping them with prayer. Several ministers were scattered among the crowd, which, unlike all other mobs, regarded them with such reverence, as if there were sanctity in their very garments. These holy men exerted their influence to quiet the people, but not to disperse them. Meantime, the purpose of the Governor, in disturbing the peace of the town at a period when the slightest commotion might throw the country into a ferment, was almost the universal subject of inquiry, and variously explained.

'Satan will strike his master-stroke presently,' cried some, 'because he knoweth that his time is short. All our godly pastors are to be dragged to prison! We shall see them at a Smithfield fire in King Street!'

Hereupon the people of each parish gathered closer round their minister, who looked calmly upward and assumed a more apostolic dignity, as well befitted a candidate for the highest honor of his profession, the crown of martyrdom. It was actually fancied, at that period, that New England might have a John Rogers of her own to take the place of that worthy in the Primer.

'The Pope of Rome has given orders for a new St. Bartholomew!' cried others. 'We are to be massacred, man and male child!'

Neither was this rumor wholly discredited, although the wiser class believed the Governor's object somewhat less atrocious. His predecessor under the old charter, Bradstreet, a venerable companion of the first settlers, was known to be in town. There were grounds for conjecturing that Sir Edmund Andros intended at once to strike terror by a parade of military force, and to confound the opposite faction by possessing himself of their chief.

'Stand firm for the old charter, Governor!' shouted the crowd, seizing upon the idea. 'The good old Governor Bradstreet!'

While this cry was at the loudest, the people were surprised by the well-known figure of Governor Bradstreet himself, a patriarch of nearly ninety, who appeared on the elevated steps of a door, and, with characteristic mildness, besought them to submit to the constituted authorities.

'My children,' concluded this venerable person, 'do nothing rashly. Cry not aloud, but pray for the welfare of New England, and expect patiently what the Lord will do in this matter!'

The event was soon to be decided. All this time, the roll of the drum had been approaching through Cornhill, louder and deeper, till with reverberations from house to house, and the regular tramp of martial footsteps, it burst into the street. A double rank of soldiers made their appearance, occupying the whole breadth of the passage, with shouldered matchlocks, and matches burning, so as to present a row of fires in the dusk. Their steady march was like the progress of a machine, that would roll

irresistibly over everything in its way. Next, moving
slowly, with a confused clatter of hoofs on the pavement,
rode a party of mounted gentlemen, the central figure
being Sir Edmund Andros, elderly, but erect and soldier-
like. Those around him were his favorite councillors,
and the bitterest foes of New England. At his right hand
rode Edward Randolph, our arch-enemy, that 'blasted
wretch', as Cotton Mather calls him, who achieved the
downfall of our ancient government, and was followed
with a sensible curse, through life and to his grave. On
the other side was Bullivant, scattering jests and mockery
as he rode along. Dudley came behind, with a downcast
look, dreading, as well he might, to meet the indignant
gaze of the people, who beheld him, their only country-
man by birth, among the oppressors of his native land.
The captain of a frigate in the harbor, and two or three
civil officers under the Crown, were also there. But the
figure which most attracted the public eye, and stirred up
the deepest feeling, was the Episcopal clergyman of
King's Chapel, riding haughtily among the magistrates
in his priestly vestments, the fitting representative of
prelacy and persecution, the union of church and state,
and all those abominations which had driven the Puritans
to the wilderness. Another guard of soldiers, in double
rank, brought up the rear.

The whole scene was a picture of the condition of
New England, and its moral, the deformity of any
government that does not grow out of the nature of
things and the character of the people. On one side the
religious multitude, with their sad visages and dark attire,
and on the other the group of despotic rulers, with the
high churchman in the midst, and here and there a
crucifix at their bosoms, all magnificently clad, flushed
with wine, proud of unjust authority, and scoffing at the

universal groan. And the mercenary soldiers, waiting but the word to deluge the street with blood, showed the only means by which obedience could be secured.

'O Lord of Hosts,' cried a voice among the crowd, 'provide a Champion for thy people!'

This ejaculation was loudly uttered, and served as a herald's cry, to introduce a remarkable personage. The crowd had rolled back, and were now huddled together nearly at the extremity of the street, while the soldiers had advanced no more than a third of its length. The intervening space was empty – a paved solitude, between lofty edifices, which threw almost a twilight shadow over it. Suddenly, there was seen the figure of an ancient man, who seemed to have emerged from among the people, and was walking by himself along the centre of the street, to confront the armed band. He wore the old Puritan dress, a dark cloak and a steeple-crowned hat, in the fashion of at least fifty years before, with a heavy sword upon his thigh, but a staff in his hand to assist the tremulous gait of age.

When at some distance from the multitude, the old man turned slowly round, displaying a face of antique majesty, rendered doubly venerable by the hoary beard that descended on his breast. He made a gesture at once of encouragement and warning, then turned again, and resumed his way.

'Who is this gray patriarch?' asked the young men of their sires.

'Who is this venerable brother?' asked the old men among themselves.

But none could make reply. The fathers of the people, those of fourscore years and upward, were disturbed, deeming it strange that they should forget one of such evident authority, whom they must have known in their early days, the associate of Winthrop, and all the old councillors, giving laws, and making prayers, and leading them against the savage. The elderly men ought to have remembered him, too, with locks as gray in their youth, as their own were now. And the young! How could he have passed so utterly from their memories – that hoary sire, the relic of long-departed times, whose awful benediction had surely been bestowed on their uncovered heads, in childhood?

'Whence did he come? What is his purpose? Who can this old man be?' whispered the wondering crowd.

Meanwhile, the venerable stranger, staff in hand, was pursuing his solitary walk along the centre of the street. As he drew near the advancing soldiers, and as the roll of their drum came full upon his ear, the old man raised himself to a loftier mien, while the decrepitude of age seemed to fall from his shoulders, leaving him in gray but unbroken dignity. Now he marched onward with a warrior's step, keeping time to the military music. Thus the aged form advanced on one side, and the whole parade of soldiers and magistrates on the other, till, when scarcely twenty yards remained between, the old man grasped his staff by the middle, and held it before him like a leader's truncheon.

'Stand!' cried he.

The eye, the face, and attitude of command; the solemn yet warlike peal of that voice, fit either to rule a host in the battle-field or be raised to God in prayer, were irresistible. At the old man's word and outstretched arm, the roll of the drum was hushed at once, and the advancing line stood still. A tremulous enthusiasm seized upon the multitude. That stately form, combining the leader and the saint, so gray, so dimly seen, in such an ancient garb, could only belong to some old champion of

the righteous cause, whom the oppressor's drum had
summoned from his grave. They raised a shout of awe
and exultation, and looked for the deliverance of New
England.

The Governor, and the gentlemen of his party,
perceiving themselves brought to an unexpected stand,
rode hastily forward, as if they would have pressed their
snorting and affrighted horses right against the hoary
apparition. He, however, blenched not a step, but
glancing his severe eye round the group, which half
encompassed him, at last bent it sternly on Sir Edmund
Andros. One would have thought that the dark old man
was chief ruler there, and that the Governor and
Council, with soldiers at their back, representing the
whole power and authority of the Crown, had no
alternative but obedience.

'What does this old fellow here?' cried Edward
Randolph, fiercely. 'On, Sir Edmund! Bid the soldiers
forward, and give the dotard the same choice that you
give all his countrymen – to stand aside or be trampled
on!'

'Nay, nay, let us show respect to the good grandsire,'
said Bullivant, laughing. 'See you not, he is some old
round-headed dignitary, who hath lain asleep these thirty
years, and knows nothing of the change of times?
Doubtless, he thinks to put us down with a proclama-
tion in Old Noll's name!'

'Are you mad, old man?' demanded Sir Edmund
Andros, in loud and harsh tones. 'How dare you stay
the march of King James's Governor?'

'I have stayed the march of a King himself, ere now,'
replied the gray figure, with stern composure. 'I am here,
Sir Governor, because the cry of an oppressed people
hath disturbed me in my secret place; and beseeching this

favor earnestly of the Lord, it was vouchsafed me to
appear once again on earth, in the good old cause of his
saints. And what speak ye of James? There is no longer a
Popish tyrant on the throne of England, and by to-
morrow noon, his name shall be a byword in this very
street, where ye would make it a word of terror. Back,
thou that wast a Governor, back! With this night thy
power is ended – to-morrow, the prison! – back, lest I
foretell the scaffold!'

The people had been drawing nearer and nearer, and
drinking in the words of their champion, who spoke in
accents long disused, like one unaccustomed to converse,
except with the dead of many years ago. But his voice
stirred their souls. They confronted the soldiers, not
wholly without arms, and ready to convert the very
stones of the street into deadly weapons. Sir Edmund
Andros looked at the old man; then he cast his hard and
cruel eye over the multitude, and beheld them burning
with that lurid wrath, so difficult to kindle or to quench;
and again he fixed his gaze on the aged form, which
stood obscurely in an open space, where neither friend
nor foe had thrust himself. What were his thoughts, he
uttered no word which might discover. But whether the
oppressor were overawed by the Gray Champion's look,
or perceived his peril in the threatening attitude of the
people, it is certain that he gave back, and ordered his
soldiers to commence a slow and guarded retreat. Before
another sunset, the Governor, and all that rode so
proudly with him, were prisoners, and long ere it was
known that James had abdicated, King William was
proclaimed throughout New England.

But where was the Gray Champion? Some reported
that, when the troops had gone from King Street, and
the people were thronging tumultuously in their rear,

Bradstreet, the aged Governor, was seen to embrace a form more aged than his own. Others soberly affirmed, that while they marvelled at the venerable grandeur of his aspect, the old man had faded from their eyes, melting slowly into the hues of twilight, till, where he stood, there was an empty space. But all agreed that the hoary shape was gone. The men of that generation watched for his reappearance, in sunshine and in twilight, but never saw him more, nor knew when his funeral passed, nor where his gravestone was.

And who was the Gray Champion? Perhaps his name might be found in the records of that stern Court of Justice, which passed a sentence, too mighty for the age, but glorious in all after-times, for its humbling lesson to the monarch and its high example to the subject. I have heard, that whenever the descendants of the Puritans are to show the spirit of their sires, the old man appears again. When eighty years had passed, he walked once more in King Street. Five years later, in the twilight of an April morning, he stood on the green, beside the meeting-house, at Lexington, where now the obelisk of granite, with a slab of slate inlaid, commemorates the first fallen of the Revolution. And when our fathers were toiling at the breastwork on Bunker's Hill, all through that night the old warrior walked his rounds. Long, long may it be, ere he comes again! His hour is one of darkness, and adversity, and peril. But should domestic tyranny oppress us, or the invader's step pollute our soil, still may the Gray Champion come, for he is the type of New England's hereditary spirit; and his shadowy march, on the eve of danger, must ever be the pledge, that New England's sons will vindicate their ancestry.

No. 1 Branch Line: The Signalman

Charles Dickens

'Halloa! Below there!'

When he heard a voice thus calling to him, he was standing at the door of his box, with a flag in his hand, furled round its short pole. One would have thought, considering the nature of the ground, that he could not have doubted from what quarter the voice came; but, instead of looking up to where I stood on the top of the steep cutting nearly over his head, he turned himself about and looked down the Line. There was something remarkable in his manner of doing so, though I could not have said for my life, what. But, I know it was remarkable enough to attract my notice, even though his figure was foreshortened and shadowed, down in the deep trench, and mine was high above him, so steeped in the glow of an angry sunset that I had shaded my eyes with my hand before I saw him at all.

'Halloa! Below!'

From looking down the Line, he turned himself about again, and, raising his eyes, saw my figure high above him.

'Is there any path by which I can come down and speak to you?'

He looked up at me without replying, and I looked down at him without pressing him too soon with a repetition of my idle question. Just then, there came a vague vibration in the earth and air, quickly changing into a violent pulsation, and an oncoming rush that caused me to start back, as though it had force to draw me down. When such vapour as rose to my height from this rapid train, had passed me and was skimming away over the landscape, I looked down again, and saw him re-furling the flag he had shown while the train went by.

I repeated my inquiry. After a pause, during which he seemed to regard me with fixed attention, he motioned with his rolled-up flag towards a point on my level, some two or three hundred yards distant. I called down to him, 'All right!' and made for that point. There, by dint of looking closely about me, I found a rough zig-zag descending path notched out: which I followed.

The cutting was extremely deep, and unusually precipitate. It was made through a clammy stone that became oozier and wetter as I went down. For these reasons, I found the way long enough to give me time to recall a singular air of reluctance or compulsion with which he had pointed out the path.

When I came down low enough upon the zig-zag descent, to see him again, I saw that he was standing between the rails on the way by which the train had lately passed, in an attitude as if he were waiting for me to appear. He had his left hand at his chin, and that left elbow rested on his right hand crossed over his breast. His attitude was one of such expectation and watch-fulness, that I stopped a moment, wondering at it.

I resumed my downward way, and, stepping out upon the level of the railroad and drawing nearer to him, saw that he was a dark sallow man, with a dark beard and rather heavy eyebrows. His post was in as solitary and dismal a place as ever I saw. On either side, a dripping-wet wall of jagged stone, excluding all view but a strip of sky; the perspective one way, only a crooked prolongation of this great dungeon; the shorter perspective in the other direction, terminating in a gloomy red light, and the gloomier entrance to a black tunnel, in whose massive architecture there was a barbarous, depressing, and forbidding air. So little sunlight ever found its way to this spot, that it had an earthy deadly smell; and so much cold wind rushed through it, that it struck chill to me, as if I had left the natural world.

Before he stirred, I was near enough to him to have touched him. Not even then removing his eyes from mine, he stepped back one step, and lifted his hand.

This was a lonesome post to occupy (I said), and it had riveted my attention when I looked down from up yonder. A visitor was a rarity, I should suppose; not an unwelcome rarity, I hoped? In me, he merely saw a man who had been shut up within narrow limits all his life, and who, being at last set free, had a newly-awakened interest in these great works. To such purpose I spoke to him; but I am far from sure of the terms I used, for, besides that I am not happy in opening any conversation, there was something in the man that daunted me.

He directed a most curious look towards the red light near the tunnel's mouth, and looked all about it, as if something were missing from it, and then looked at me.

That light was part of his charge? Was it not?

He answered in a low voice: 'Don't you know it is?'

The monstrous thought came into my mind as I perused the fixed eyes and the saturnine face, that this was a spirit, not a man. I have speculated since, whether there may have been infection in his mind.

In my turn, I stepped back. But in making the action, I detected in his eyes some latent fear of me. This put the monstrous thought to flight.

'You look at me,' I said, forcing a smile, 'as if you had a dread of me.'

'I was doubtful,' he returned, 'whether I had seen you before.'

'Where?'

He pointed to the red light he had looked at.

'There?' I said.

Intently watchful of me, he replied (but without sound), Yes.

'My good fellow, what should I do there? However, be that as it may, I never was there, you may swear.'

'I think I may,' he rejoined. 'Yes. I am sure I may.'

His manner cleared, like my own. He replied to my remarks with readiness, and in well-chosen words. Had he much to do there? Yes; that was to say, he had enough responsibility to bear; but exactness and watchfulness were what was required of him, and of actual work – manual labour – he had next to none. To change that signal, to trim those lights, and to turn this iron handle now and then, was all he had to do under that head. Regarding those many long and lonely hours of which I seemed to make so much, he could only say that the routine of his life had shaped itself into that form, and he had grown used to it. He had taught himself a language down here – if only to know it by sight, and to have formed his own crude ideas of its pronunciation, could be called learning it. He had also worked at fractions and decimals, and tried a little algebra; but he was, and had been as a boy, a poor hand at figures. Was it necessary for him when on duty, always to remain in that channel of damp air, and could he never rise into the sunshine from between those high stone walls? Why, that depended upon times and circumstances. Under some conditions there would be less upon the Line than under others, and the same held good as to certain hours of the day and night. In bright weather, he did choose occasions for getting a little above these lower shadows; but, being at all times liable to be called by his electric bell, and at such times listening for it with redoubled anxiety, the relief was less than I would suppose.

He took me into his box, where there was a fire, a desk for an official book in which he had to make certain entries, a telegraphic instrument with its dial face and needles, and the little bell of which he had spoken. On my trusting that he would excuse the remark that he had been well educated, and (I hoped I might say without offence), perhaps educated above that station, he observed that instances of slight incongruity in such-wise would rarely be found wanting among large bodies of men; that he had heard it was so in workhouses, in the police force, even in that last desperate resource, the army; and that he knew it was so, more or less, in any great railway staff. He had been, when young (if I could believe it, sitting in that hut; he scarcely could), a student of natural philosophy, and had attended lectures; but he had run wild, misused his opportunities, gone down, and never risen again. He had no complaint to offer about that. He had made his bed, and he lay upon it. It was far too late to make another.

All that I have here condensed, he said in a quiet manner, with his grave dark regards divided between me and the fire. He threw in the word 'Sir', from time to time, and especially when he referred to his youth: as though to request me to understand that he claimed to be nothing but what I found him. He was several times interrupted by the little bell, and had to read of messages, and send replies. Once, he had to stand without the door, and display a flag as a train passed, and make some verbal communication to the driver. In the discharge of his duties I observed him to be remarkably exact and vigilant, breaking off his discourse at a syllable, and remaining silent until what he had to do was done.

In a word, I should have set this man down as one of the safest of men to be employed in that capacity, but for the circumstance that while he was speaking to me he twice broke off with a fallen colour, turned his face towards the little bell when it did NOT ring, opened the door of the hut (which was kept shut to exclude the unhealthy damp), and looked out towards the red light near the mouth of the tunnel. On both of those occasions, he came back to the fire with the inexplicable air upon him which I had remarked, without being able to define, when we were so far asunder.

Said I when I rose to leave him: 'You almost make me think that I have met with a contented man.'

(I am afraid I must acknowledge that I said it to lead him on.)

'I believe I used to be so,' he rejoined, in the low voice in which he had first spoken; 'but I am troubled, sir, I am troubled.'

He would have recalled the words if he could. He had said them, however, and I took them up quickly.

'With what? What is your trouble?'

'It is very difficult to impart, sir. It is very, very difficult to speak of. If ever you make me another visit, I will try to tell you.'

'But I expressly intend to make you another visit. Say, when shall it be?'

'I go off early in the morning, and I shall be on again at ten tomorrow night, sir.'

'I will come at eleven.'

He thanked me, and went out at the door with me. 'I'll show my white light, sir,' he said, in his peculiar low voice, 'till you have found the way up. When you have found it, don't call out! And when you are at the top, don't call out!'

His manner seemed to make the place strike colder to me, but I said no more than 'Very well'.

'And when you come down to-morrow night, don't call out! Let me ask you a parting question. What made you cry "Halloa! Below there!" to-night?'

'Heaven knows,' said I. 'I cried something to that effect –'

'Not to that effect, sir. Those were the very words. I know them well.'

'Admit those were the very words. I said them, no doubt, because I saw you below.'

'For no other reason?'

'What other reason could I possibly have!'

'You have no feeling that they were conveyed to you in any supernatural way?'

'No.'

He wished me good night, and held up his light. I walked by the side of the down Line of rails (with a very disagreeable sensation of a train coming behind me), until I found the path. It was easier to mount than to descend, and I got back to my inn without any adventure.

Punctual to my appointment, I placed my foot on the first notch of the zig-zag next night, as the distant clocks were striking eleven. He was waiting for me at the bottom, with his white light on. 'I have not called out,' I said, when we came close together; 'may I speak now?' 'By all means, sir.' 'Good night then, and here's my hand.' 'Good night, sir, and here's mine.' With that, we walked side by side to his box, entered it, closed the door, and sat down by the fire.

'I have made up my mind, sir,' he began, bending forward as soon as we were seated, and speaking in a tone but a little above a whisper, 'that you shall not have to ask me twice what troubles me. I took you for some one else yesterday evening. That troubles me.'

'That mistake?'

'No. That some one else.'

'Who is it?'

'I don't know.'

'Like me?'

'I don't know. I never saw the face. The left arm is across the face, and the right arm is waved. Violently waved. This way.'

I followed his action with my eyes, and it was the action of an arm gesticulating with the utmost passion and vehemence: 'For God's sake clear the way!'

'One moonlight night,' said the man, 'I was sitting here, when I heard a voice cry, "Halloa! Below there!" I started up, looked from that door, and saw this Some one else standing by the red light near the tunnel, waving as I just now showed you. The voice seemed hoarse with shouting, and it cried, "Look out! Look out!" And then again, "Halloa! Below there! Look out!" I caught up my lamp, turned it on red, and ran towards the figure, calling, "What's wrong? What has happened? Where?" It stood just outside the blackness of the tunnel. I advanced so close upon it that I wondered at its keeping the sleeve across its eyes. I ran right up at it, and had my hand stretched out to pull the sleeve away, when it was gone.'

'Into the tunnel,' said I.

'No. I ran on into the tunnel, five hundred yards. I stopped and held my lamp above my head, and saw the figures of the measured distance, and saw the wet stains stealing down the walls and trickling through the arch. I ran out again, faster than I had run in (for I had a mortal abhorrence of the place upon me), and I looked all round the red light with my own red light, and I went up the iron ladder to the gallery atop of it, and I came down again, and ran back here. I telegraphed both ways: "An alarm has been given. Is anything, wrong?" The answer came back, both ways: "All well.'"

Resisting the slow touch of a frozen finger tracing out my spine, I showed him how that this figure must be a deception of his sense of sight, and how that figures, originating in disease of the delicate nerves that minister to the functions of the eye, were known to have often troubled patients, some of whom had become conscious of the nature of their affliction, and had even proved it by experiments upon themselves. 'As to an imaginary cry,' said I, 'do but listen for a moment to the wind in this unnatural valley while we speak so low, and to the wild harp it makes of the telegraph wires!'

That was all very well, he returned, after we had sat listening for a while, and he ought to know something of the wind and the wires, he who so often passed long winter nights there, alone and watching. But he would beg to remark that he had not finished.

I asked his pardon, and he slowly added these words, touching my arm:

'Within six hours after the Appearance, the memorable accident on this Line happened, and within ten hours the dead and wounded were brought along through the tunnel over the spot where the figure had stood.'

A disagreeable shudder crept over me, but I did my best against it. It was not to be denied, I rejoined, that this was a remarkable coincidence, calculated deeply to impress his mind. But, it was unquestionable that remarkable coincidences did continually occur, and they must be taken into account in dealing with such a subject. Though to be sure I must admit, I added (for I thought I saw that he was going to bring the objection to bear upon me), men of common sense did not allow much for coincidences in making the ordinary calculations of life.

He again begged to remark that he had not finished.

I again begged his pardon for being betrayed into interruptions.

'This,' he said, again laying his hand upon my arm, and glancing over his shoulder with hollow eyes, 'was just a year ago. Six or seven months passed, and I had recovered from the surprise and shock, when one morning, as the day was breaking, I, standing at that door, looked towards the red light, and saw the spectre again.' He stopped, with a fixed look at me.

'Did it cry out?'

'No. It was silent.'

'Did it wave its arm?'

'No. It leaned against the shaft of the light, with both hands before the face. Like this.'

Once more, I followed his action with my eyes. It was an action of mourning. I have seen such an attitude in stone figures on tombs.

'Did you go up to it?'

'I came in and sat down, partly to collect my thoughts, partly because it had turned me faint. When I went to the door again, daylight was above me, and the ghost was gone.'

'But nothing followed? Nothing came of this?'

He touched me on the arm with his forefinger twice or thrice, giving a ghastly nod each time:

'That very day, as a train came out of the tunnel, I noticed, at a carriage window on my side, what looked like a confusion of hands and heads, and something waved. I saw it, just in time to signal the driver, Stop! He shut off, and put his brake on, but the train drifted past here a hundred and fifty yards or more. I ran after it, and, as I went along, heard terrible screams and cries. A beautiful young lady had died instantaneously in one of the compartments, and was brought in here, and laid down on this floor between us.'

Involuntarily, I pushed my chair back, as I looked from the boards at which he pointed, to himself.

'True, sir. True. Precisely as it happened, so I tell it you.'

I could think of nothing to say, to any purpose, and my mouth was very dry. The wind and the wires took up the story with a long lamenting wail.

He resumed. 'Now, sir, mark this, and judge how my mind is troubled. The spectre came back, a week ago. Ever since, it has been there, now and again, by fits and starts.'

'At the light?'

'At the Danger-light.'

'What does it seem to do?'

He repeated, if possible with increased passion and vehemence, that former gesticulation of 'For God's sake clear the way!'.

Then, he went on. 'I have no peace or rest for it. It calls to me, for many minutes together, in an agonized manner, "Below there! Look out! Look out!" It stands waving to me. It rings my little bell –'

I caught at that. 'Did it ring your bell yesterday evening when I was here, and you went to the door?'

'Twice.'

'Why, see,' said I, 'how your imagination misleads you. My eyes were on the bell, and my ears were open to the bell, and if I am a living man, it did NOT ring at those times. No, nor at any other time, except when it was rung in the natural course of physical things by the station communicating with you.'

He shook his head. 'I have never made a mistake as to that, yet, sir. I have never confused the spectre's ring with the man's. The ghost's ring is a strange vibration in the bell that it derives from nothing else, and I have not asserted that the bell stirs to the eye. I don't wonder that you failed to hear it. But *I* heard it.'

'And did the spectre seem to be there, when you looked out?'

'It WAS there.'

'Both times?'

He repeated firmly: 'Both times.'

'Will you come to the door with me, and look for it now?'

He bit his under-lip as though he were somewhat unwilling, but arose. I opened the door, and stood on the step, while he stood in the doorway. There, was the Danger-light. There, was the dismal mouth of the tunnel. There, were the high wet stone walls of the cutting. There, were the stars above them.

'Do you see it?' I asked him, taking particular note of his face. His eyes were prominent and strained; but not very much more so, perhaps, than my own had been when I had directed them earnestly towards the same spot.

'No,' he answered. 'It is not there.'

'Agreed,' said I.

We went in again, shut the door, and resumed our seats. I was thinking how best to improve this advantage,

if it might be called one, when he took up the
conversation in such a matter of course way, so assum-
ing that there could be no serious question of fact
between us, that I felt myself in the weakest of positions.

'By this time you will fully understand, sir,' he said,
'that what troubles me so dreadfully, is the question,
What does the spectre mean?'

I was not sure, I told him, that I did fully understand.

'What is its warning against?' he said, ruminating, with
his eyes on the fire, and only by times turning them on
me. 'What is the danger? Where is the danger? There is
danger overhanging, somewhere on the Line. Some
dreadful calamity will happen. It is not to be doubted
this third time, after what has gone before. But surely this
is a cruel haunting of *me*. What can *I* do!'

He pulled out his handkerchief, and wiped the drops
from his heated forehead.

'If I telegraph Danger, on either side of me, or on
both, I can give no reason for it,' he went on, wiping the
palms of his hands. 'I should get into trouble, and do no
good. They would think I was mad. This is the way it
would work: Message: "Danger! Take care!" Answer:
"What Danger? Where?" Message: "Don't know. But
for God's sake take care!" They would displace me.
What else could they do?'

His pain of mind was most pitiable to see. It was the
mental torture of a conscientious man, oppressed beyond
endurance by an unintelligible responsibility involving
life.

'When it first stood under the Danger-light,' he went
on, putting his dark hair back from his head, and drawing
his hands outward across and across his temples in an
extremity of feverish distress, 'why not tell me where that
accident was to happen – if it must happen? Why not tell

me how it could be averted – if it could have been
averted? When on its second coming it hid its face, why
not tell me instead: "She is going to die. Let them keep
her at home"? If it came, on those two occasions, only to
show me that its warnings were true, and so to prepare
me for the third, why not warn me plainly now? And I,
Lord help me! A mere poor signalman on this solitary
station! Why not go to somebody with credit to be
believed, and power to act!'

When I saw him in this state, I saw that for the poor
man's sake, as well as for the public safety, what I had to
do for the time was, to compose his mind. Therefore,
setting aside all question of reality or unreality between
us, I represented to him that whoever thoroughly
discharged his duty, must do well, and that at least it
was his comfort that he understood his duty, though he
did not understand these confounding Appearances. In
this effort I succeeded far better than in the attempt to
reason him out of his conviction. He became calm; the
occupations incidental to his post as the night advanced,
began to make larger demands on his attention; and I left
him at two in the morning. I had offered to stay through
the night, but he would not hear of it.

That I more than once looked back at the red light as I
ascended the pathway, that I did not like the red light,
and that I should have slept but poorly if my bed had
been under it, I see no reason to conceal. Nor, did I like
the two sequences of the accident and the dead girl. I see
no reason to conceal that, either.

But, what ran most in my thoughts was the consideration how ought I to act, having become the recipient of
this disclosure? I had proved the man to be intelligent,
vigilant, painstaking, and exact; but how long might he
remain so, in his state of mind? Though in a subordinate

position, still he held a most important trust, and would I (for instance) like to stake my own life on the chances of his continuing to execute it with precision?

Unable to overcome a feeling that there would be something treacherous in my communicating what he had told me, to his superiors in the Company, without first being plain with himself and proposing a middle course to him, I ultimately resolved to offer to accompany him (otherwise keeping his secret for the present) to the wisest medical practitioner we could hear of in those parts, and to take his opinion. A change in his time of duty would come round next night, he had appraised me, and he would be off an hour or two after sunrise, and on again soon after sunset. I had appointed to return accordingly.

Next evening was a lovely evening, and I walked out early to enjoy it. The sun was not yet quite down when I traversed the field-path near the top of the deep cutting. I would extend my walk for an hour, I said to myself, half an hour on and half an hour back, and it would then be time to go to my signalman's box.

Before pursuing my stroll, I stepped to the brink, and mechanically looked down, from the point from which I had first seen him. I cannot describe the thrill that seized upon me, when, close at the mouth of the tunnel, I saw the appearance of a man, with his left sleeve across his eyes, passionately waving his right arm.

The nameless horror that oppressed me, passed in a moment, for in a moment I saw that this appearance of a man was a man indeed, and that there was a little group of other men standing at a short distance, to whom he seemed to be rehearsing the gesture he made. The Danger-light was not yet lighted. Against its shaft, a little low hut, entirely new to me, had been made of some wooden supports and tarpaulin. It looked no bigger than a bed.

With an irresistible sense that something was wrong – with a flashing self-reproachful fear that fatal mischief had come of my leaving the man there, and causing no one to be sent to overlook or correct what he did – I descended the notched path with all the speed I could make.

'What is the matter?' I asked the men.

'Signalman killed this morning, sir.'

'Not the man belonging to that box?'

'Yes, sir.'

'Not the man I know?'

'You will recognize him, sir, if you knew him,' said the man who spoke for the others, solemnly uncovering his own head and raising an end of the tarpaulin, 'for his face is quite composed.'

'O! how did this happen, how did this happen?' I asked, turning from one to another as the hut closed in again.

'He was cut down by an engine, sir. No man in England knew his work better. But somehow he was not clear of the outer rail. It was just at broad day. He had struck the light, and had the lamp in his hand. As the engine came out of the tunnel, his back was towards her, and she cut him down. That man drove her, and was showing how it happened. Show the gentleman, Tom.'

The man, who wore a rough dark dress, stepped back to his former place at the mouth of the tunnel:

'Coming round the curve in the tunnel, sir,' he said, 'I saw him at the end, like as if I saw him down a perspective-glass. There was no time to check speed, and I knew him to be very careful. As he didn't seem to take heed of the whistle, I shut it off when we were running down upon him, and called to him as loud as I could call.'

'What did you say?'

'I said, Below there! Look out! Look out! For God's sake clear the way!'

I started.

'Ah! it was a dreadful time, sir. I never left off calling to him. I put this arm before my eyes, not to see, and I waved this arm to the last; but it was no use.'

Without prolonging the narrative to dwell on any one of its curious circumstances more than on any other, I may, in closing it, point out the coincidence that the warning of the Engine-Driver included, not only the words which the unfortunate Signalman had repeated to me as haunting him, but also the words which I myself – not he – had attached, and that only in my own mind, to the gesticulation he had imitated.

The Dream Woman

Wilkie Collins

Some years ago there lived in the suburbs of a large seaport town on the west coast of England a man in humble circumstances, by name Isaac Scatchard. His means of subsistence were derived from any employment that he could get as an ostler, and occasionally when times went well with him, from temporary engagements in service as stable-helper in private houses. Though a faithful, steady, and honest man, he got on badly in his calling. His ill-luck was proverbial among his neighbors. He was always missing good opportunities by no fault of his own, and always living longest in service with amiable people who were not punctual payers of wages. 'Unlucky Isaac' was his nickname in his own neighborhood, and no one could say that he did not richly deserve it.

With far more than one man's share of adversity to endure, Isaac had but one consolation to support him, and that was of the dreariest and most negative kind. He had no wife and children to increase his anxieties and add to the bitterness of his various failures in life. It might have been from mere insensibility, or it might have been from generous unwillingness to involve another in his own unlucky destiny; but the fact undoubtedly was, that he had arrived at the midlife term of life without marrying, and, what is much more remarkable, without once exposing himself from eighteen to eight-and-thirty, to the genial imputation of ever having had a sweetheart.

When he was out of service he lived alone with his widowed mother. Mrs Scatchard was a woman above the average in her lowly station as to capacity and manners. She had seen better days, as the phrase is, but she never referred to them in the presence of curious visitors; and, though perfectly polite to every one who approached her, never cultivated any intimacies among her neighbors. She contrived to provide hardly enough for her simple wants by doing rough work for the tailors, and always managed to keep a decent home for her son to return to whenever his ill-luck drove him out helpless into the world.

One bleak autumn, when Isaac was getting on fast toward forty, and when he was, as usual, out of place through no fault of his own, he set forth from his mother's cottage on a long walk inland to a gentleman's seat, where he had heard that a stable-helper was required.

It wanted then but two days of his birthday; and Mrs. Scatchard, with her usual fondness, made him promise before he started that he would be back in time to keep that anniversary with her, in as festive a way as their poor means would allow. It was easy for him to comply with this request, even supposing he slept a night each way on the road.

He was to start from home on Monday morning, and whether he got the new place or not, he was to be back for his birthday dinner on Wednesday at two o'clock.

Arriving at his destination too late on the Monday night to make application for the stable-helper's place, he slept at the village inn, and in good time on the Tuesday morning presented himself at the gentlemen's house to fill the vacant situation. Here again his ill-luck pursued him as inexorably as ever. The excellent written testimonials to his character which he was able to procure availed him nothing; his long walk had been taken in vain; only the day before the stable-helper's place had been given to another man.

Isaac accepted this new disappointment resignedly and as a matter of course. Naturally slow in capacity he had the bluntness of sensibility and phlegmatic patience of disposition which frequently distinguish men with sluggishly working mental powers. He thanked the gentleman's steward with his usual quiet civility for granting him an interview, and took his departure with no appearance of unusual depression in his face or manner.

Before starting on his homeward walk he made some inquiries at the inn, and ascertained that he might save a few miles on his return by following a new road. Furnished with full instructions, several times repeated as to the various turnings he was to take, he set forth on his homeward journey and walked on all day with only one stoppage for bread and cheese. Just as it was getting toward dark, the rain came on and the wind began to rise, and he found himself, to make matters worse, in a part of the country with which he was entirely unacquainted, though he knew himself to be some fifteen miles from home. The first house he found to inquire at was a lonely roadside inn, standing on the outskirts of a thick wood. Solitary as the place looked, it was welcome to a lost man; he was also hungry, thirsty, foot-sore, and wet. The landlord was civil and respectable looking, and the price he asked for a bed was reasonable enough. Isaac therefore decided on stopping comfortably at the inn for the night.

He was constitutionally a temperate man. His supper

consisted of two rashers of bacon, a slice of home-made bread, and a pint of ale. He did not go to bed immediately after his moderate meal, but sat up with the landlord, talking about his bad prospects and his long run of ill-luck, and diverging from these topics to the subject of horseflesh and racing. Nothing was said either by himself, his host, or the few laborers who strayed into the taproom, which could, in the slightest degree, excite the very small and very dull imaginative faculty which Isaac Scatchard possessed.

At a little after eleven the house was closed. Isaac went round with the landlord and held the candle while the doors and lower windows were being secured. He noticed with surprise the strength of the bolts and bars, and iron-sheathed shutters.

'You see we are rather lonely here,' said the landlord. 'We never have had any attempts made to break in yet, but it's always as well to be on the safe side. When nobody is sleeping here, I am the only man in the house. My wife and children are timid, and the servant-girl takes after her missuses. Another glass of ale before you turn in? No! Well, how such a sober man as you come to be out of a place is more than I can make out, for one. Here's where you're to sleep. You're our only lodger to-night, and I think you'll say my missus has done her best to make you comfortable. You're quite sure you won't have another glass of ale? Very well. Good night.'

It was half-past eleven by the clock in the passage as they went upstairs to the bedroom, the window of which looked out on the wood at the back of the house.

Isaac locked the door, set his candle on the chest of drawers, and wearily got ready for bed. The bleak autumn wind was still blowing, and the solemn, monotonous, surging moan of it in the wood was dreary and awful to hear through the night-silence. Isaac felt strangely wakeful. He resolved, as he lay down in bed, to keep the candle alight until he began to grow sleepy, for there was something unendurably depressing in the bare idea of laying awake in the darkness, listening to the dismal, ceaseless moaning of the wind in the wood.

Sleep stole on him before he was aware of it. His eyes closed and he fell off insensibly to rest without having so much as thought of extinguishing the light.

The first sensation of which he was conscious after sinking into slumber was a strange shivering that ran through him suddenly from head to foot, and a dreadful sinking pain at the heart, such as he had never felt before. The shivering only disturbed his slumbers; the pain woke him instantly. In one moment he passed from a state of sleep to a state of wakefulness – his eyes wide open – his mental perceptions cleared on a sudden as if by a miracle.

The candle had burned down nearly to the last morsel of tallow, but the top of the unsnuffed wick had just fallen off, and the light in the little room was, for the moment, fair and full.

Between the foot of the bed and the closed door there stood a woman with a knife in her hand, looking at him.

He was stricken speechless with terror, but he did not lose the preternatural clearness of his faculties, and he never took his eyes off the woman. She said not a word as they stared each other in the face, but she began to move slowly toward the left-hand side of the bed.

His eyes followed her. She was a fair, fine woman with yellowish flaxen hair and light-gray eyes, with a droop in the left eyelid. He noticed those things, and fixed them on his mind before she was round at the side of the bed. Speechless, with no expression in her face, with no noise following her footfall, she came closer and closer –

stopped and slowly raised the knife. He laid his right arm
over his throat to save it; but as he saw the knife coming
down, threw his hand across the bed to the right side,
and jerked his body over that way as the knife descended
on the mattress within an inch of his shoulder.

His eyes fixed on her arm and hand as she slowly drew
her knife out of the bed; a white, well-shaped arm, with
a pretty down lying lightly over the fair skin – a delicate
lady's hand; with the crowning beauty of a pink flush
under and round the finger nails.

She drew the knife out, and passed again slowly to the
foot of the bed; stopped there for a moment looking at
him; then came on – still speechless, still with no sound
following the stealthy footfalls – came on to the right side
of the bed where he now lay.

As she approached, she raised the knife again, and he
drew himself away to the left side. She struck, as before,
right into the mattress, with a deliberate, perpendicularly
downward action of the arm. This time his eyes
wandered from her to the knife. It was like the large
clasp-knives which he had often seen laboring men use
to cut their bread and bacon with. Her delicate little
fingers did not conceal more than two-thirds of the
handle; he noticed that it was made of buckhorn, clean
and shining the blade was, and looking like new.

For the second time she drew the knife out, concealed
it in the wide sleeve of her gown, then stopped by the
bedside, watching him. For an instant he saw her
standing in that position, then the wick of the spent
candle fell over into the socket, the flame diminished to
the little blue point, and the room was dark.

A moment, or less, if possible, passed so, and then the
wick flamed up, smokingly, for the last time. His eyes
were still looking eagerly over the right-hand side of the

bed when the final flash of the candle came, but he discerned nothing. The fair woman with the knife was gone.

The conviction that he was alone again weakened the hold of the terror that had struck him dumb up to this time. The preternatural sharpness which the very intensity of his panic had mysteriously imparted to his faculties left them suddenly. His brain grew confused – his heart beat wildly – his ears opened for the first time since the appearance of the woman to a sense of woeful, ceaseless moaning of the wind among the trees. With the dreadful conviction of the reality of what he had seen still strong within him, he leaped out of bed, and screaming, 'Murder! Wake up there! wake up!', dashed headlong through the darkness to the door.

It was fast locked, exactly as he had left it on going to bed.

His cries on starting up had alarmed the house. He heard the terrified, confused exclamations of women; he saw the master of the house approaching along the passage with his burning rush-candle in one hand and his gun in the other.

'What is it?' asked the landlord, breathlessly.

Isaac could only answer in a whisper. 'A woman, with a knife in her hand,' he gasped out. 'In my room – a fair, yellow-haired woman; she jabbed at me with the knife twice over.'

The landlord's pale cheeks grew paler. He looked at Isaac eagerly by the flickering light of his candle, and his face began to get red again; his voice altered too, as well as his complexion.

'She seems to have missed you twice,' he said.

'I dodged the knife as it came down,' Isaac went on, in the same scared whisper. 'It struck the bed each time.'

The landlord took the candle into the bedroom immediately. In less than a minute he came out again into the passage in a violent passion.

'The devil fly away with you and your woman with the knife! There isn't a mark in the bedclothes anywhere. What do you mean by coming into a man's place, and frightening his family out of their wits about a dream?'

'I'll leave your house,' said Isaac, faintly. 'Better out on the road, in rain and dark, on my road home, than back again in that room, after what I've seen in it. Lend me a light to get my clothes by, and tell me what I'm to pay.'

'Pay!' cried the landlord, leading the way with his light sulkily into the bedroom. 'You'll find your score on the slate when you go downstairs. I wouldn't have taken you in for all the money you've got about you if I'd known your dreaming, screeching ways beforehand. Look at the bed. Where's the cut of a knife in it? Look at the window – is the lock bursted? Look at the door (which I heard you fasten yourself) – is it broke in? A murdering woman with a knife in my house! You ought to be ashamed of yourself!'

Isaac answered not a word. He huddled on his clothes, and they went downstairs together.

'Nigh on twenty minutes past two!' said the landlord, as they passed a clock. 'A nice time in the morning to frighten honest people out of their wits!'

Isaac paid his bill, and the landlord let him out at the front door, asking, with a grin of contempt, as he undid the strong fastenings, whether 'the murdering woman got in that way'.

They parted without a word on either side. The rain had ceased, but the night was dark, and the wind bleaker than ever. Little did the darkness or the cold or the uncertainty about the way home matter to Isaac. If he had been turned out into the wilderness in a thunderstorm, it would have been a relief after what he had suffered in the bedroom of the inn.

What was the fair woman with the knife? The creature of a dream, or that other creature from the unknown world called among men by the name of ghost? He could make nothing of the mystery – had made nothing of it, even when it was midday on Wednesday, and when he stood, at last, after many times missing his road, once more on the doorstep of home.

His mother came out eagerly to receive him. His face told her in a moment that something was wrong.

'I've lost the place; but that's my luck. I dreamed an ill dream last night, mother – or maybe I saw a ghost. Take it either way, it scared me out of my senses, and I am not my own man again yet.'

'Isaac, your face frightens me. Come in to the fire – come in, and tell mother all about it.'

He was as anxious to tell as she was to hear; for it had been his hope, all the way home, that his mother, with her quicker capacity and superior knowledge, might be able to throw some light on the mystery which he could not clear up for himself. His memory of the dream was still mechanically vivid, though his thoughts were entirely confused by it.

His mother's face grew paler and paler as he went on. She never interrupted him by so much as a single word; but when he had done, she moved her chair close to his, put her arms around his neck, and said to him:

'Isaac, you dreamed your ill dream on this Wednesday morning. What time was it when you saw the fair woman with a knife in her hand?'

Isaac reflected on what the landlord had said when they had passed by the clock on his leaving the inn;

allowed as nearly as he could for the time that must have elapsed between the unlocking of his bedroom door and the paying of his bill just before going away, and answered:

'Somewhere about two o'clock in the morning.'

His mother suddenly quitted her hold of his neck, and struck her hands together with a gesture of despair.

'This Wednesday is your birthday, Isaac, and two o'clock in the morning was the time when you were born.'

Isaac's capacities were not quick enough to catch the infection of his mother's superstitious dread. He was amazed, and a little startled also, when she suddenly rose from her chair, opened her old writing-desk, took pen, ink, and paper, and then said to him:

'Your memory is but a poor one, Isaac, and now I'm an old woman mine's not much better. I want all about this dream of yours to be as well known to both of us, years hence, as it is now. Tell me over again all you told me a minute ago, when you spoke of what the woman with the knife looked like.'

Isaac obeyed, and marveled much as he saw his mother carefully set down on paper the very words that he was saying.

'Light-gray eyes,' she wrote, as they came to the descriptive part, 'with a droop in the left eyelid; flaxen hair, with a gold-yellow streak in it; white arms, with a down upon them; little lady's hand, with a reddish look about the finger nails; clasp-knife with a buckhorn handle, that seemed as good as new.' To these particulars Mrs. Scratchard added the year, month, day of the week, and time in the morning when the woman of the dream appeared to her son. She then locked up the paper carefully in the writing-desk.

Neither on that day nor on any day after could her son induce her to return to the matter of the dream. She obstinately kept her thoughts about it to herself, and even refused to refer again to the paper in her writing-desk. Ere long Isaac grew weary of attempting to make her break her resolute silence; and time, which sooner or later wears out all things, gradually wore out the impression produced on him by the dream. He began by thinking of it carelessly, and he ended by not thinking of it at all.

The result was the more easily brought about by the advent of some important changes for the better in his prospects, which commenced not long after his terrible night's experience at the inn. He reaped at last the reward of his long and patient suffering under adversity by getting an excellent place, keeping it for seven years, and leaving it, on the death of his master, not only with an excellent character, but also with a comfortable annuity bequeathed to him as a reward for saving his mistress's life in a carriage accident. Thus it happened that Isaac Scatchard returned to his old mother, seven years after the time of the dream of the inn, with an annual sum of money at his disposal sufficient to keep them both in ease and independence for the rest of their lives.

The mother, whose health had been bad of late years, profited so much by the care bestowed on her and by freedom from money anxieties, that when Isaac's birthday came round she was able to sit up comfortably at table and dine with him.

On that day, as the evening drew on, Mrs. Scatchard discovered that a bottle of tonic medicine which she was accustomed to take, and in which she had fancied that a dose or more was still left, happened to be empty. Isaac immediately volunteered to go to the chemist's and get it filled again. It was as rainy and bleak an autumn night as on the memorable past occasion when he lost his way and slept at the roadside inn.

On going into the chemist's shop he was passed hurriedly by a poorly dressed woman coming out of it. The glimpse he had of her face struck him, and he looked back after her as she descended the door steps.

'You're noticing that woman?' said the chemist's apprentice behind the counter. 'It's my opinion there's something wrong with her. She's been asking for laudanum to put to a bad tooth. Master's out for half an hour, and I told her I wasn't allowed to sell poison to strangers in his absence. She laughed in a queer way, and said she would come back in half an hour. If she expects master to serve her, I think she'll be disappointed. It's a case of suicide, sir, if ever there was one yet.'

These words added immeasurably to the sudden interest in the woman which Isaac had felt at the first sight of her face. After he had got the medicine-bottle filled, he looked about anxiously for her as soon as he was out in the street. She was walking slowly up and down on the opposite side of the road. With his heart, very much to his own surprise, beating fast, Isaac crossed over and spoke to her.

He asked her if she was in any distress. She pointed to her torn shawl, her scanty dress, her crushed, dirty bonnet; then moved under a lamp so as to let the light fall on her stern, pale, but still most beautiful face.

'I look like a comfortable, happy woman, don't I?' she said, with a bitter laugh.

She spoke with a purity of intonation which Isaac had never before heard from other lips than lady's lips. Her slightest action seemed to have the easy, negligent grace of a thoroughbred woman. Her skin, for all its poverty-stricken paleness, was as delicate as if her life had been passed in the enjoyment of every social comfort that wealth can purchase. Even her small, finely shaped hands, gloveless as they were, had not lost their whiteness.

Little by little, in answer to his questions, the sad story of the woman came out. There is no need to relate it here; it is told over and over again in police reports and paragraphs about attempted suicides.

'My name is Rebecca Murdoch,' said the woman, as she ended. 'I have ninepence left, and I thought of spending it at the chemist's over the way in securing a passage to the other world. Whatever it is, it can't be worse to me than this; so why should I stop here?'

Besides the natural compassion and sadness moved in his heart by what he heard, Isaac felt within him some mysterious influence at work all the time the woman was speaking which utterly confused his ideas and almost deprived him of his powers of speech. All that he could say in answer to her reckless words was that he would prevent her from attempting her own life, if he followed her about all night to do it. His rough, trembling earnestness seemed to impress her.

'I won't occasion you that trouble,' she answered when he repeated his threat. 'You have given me a fancy for living by speaking kindly to me. No need for the mockery of protestations and promises. You may believe me without them. Come to Fuller's Meadow to-morrow at twelve, and you will find me alive, to answer for myself – No! – no money. My ninepence will do to get me as good a night's lodging as I want.'

She nodded and left him. He made no attempt to follow – he felt no suspicion that she was deceiving him.

'It's strange, but I can't help believing her,' he said to himself, and walked away, bewildered, toward home.

On entering the house his mind was still so completely absorbed by its new subject of interest that he took no notice of what his mother was doing when he came in with the bottle of medicine. She had opened her old writing-desk in his absence, and was now reading a paper attentively that lay inside it. On every birthday of Isaac's since she had written down the particulars of his dream from his own lips, she had been accustomed to read that same paper, and ponder over it in private.

The next day he went to Fuller's Meadow.

He had done only right in believing her so implicitly. She was there, punctual to a minute, to answer for herself. The last-left faint defenses in Isaac's heart against the fascination which a word or look from her began inscrutably to exercise over him sank down and vanished before her forever on that memorable morning.

When a man previously insensible to the influence of woman forms an attachment in middle life, the instances are rare indeed, let the warning circumstances be what they may, in which he is found capable of freeing himself from the tyranny of the new ruling passion. The charm of being spoken to familiarly, fondly, and gratefully by a woman whose language and manners still retained enough of their early refinement to hint at the high social station that she had lost, would have been a dangerous luxury to a man of Isaac's rank at the age of twenty. But it was far more than that – it was certain ruin to him – now that his heart was opening unworthily to a new influence at that middle time of life when strong feelings of all kinds, once implanted, strike root most stubbornly in a man's moral nature. A few more stolen interviews after that first morning in Fuller's Meadow completed his infatuation. In less than a month from the time when he first met her, Isaac Scatchard had consented to give Rebecca Murdoch a new interest in existence and a chance of recovering the character she had lost by promising to make her his wife.

She had taken possession, not of his passions only, but of his faculties as well. All the mind he had he put into her keeping. She directed him on every point – even instructing him how to break the news of his approaching marriage in the safest manner to his mother.

'If you tell her how you met me and who I am at first,' said the cunning woman, 'she will move heaven and earth to prevent our marriage. Say I am the sister of one of your fellow-servants – ask her to see me before you go into any more particulars – and leave it to me to do the rest. I mean to make her love me next best to you, Isaac, before she knows anything of who I really am.'

The motive of the deceit was sufficient to sanctify it to Isaac. The stratagem proposed relieved him of his one great anxiety, and quieted his uneasy conscience on the subject of his mother. Still, there was something wanting to perfect his happiness, something that he could not realize, something mysteriously untraceable, and yet something that perpetually made itself felt, not when he was absent from Rebecca Murdoch, but, strange to say, when he was actually in her presence! She was kindness itself with him. She never made him feel his inferior capacities and inferior manners. She showed the sweetest anxiety to please him in his smallest trifles! but, in spite of all these attractions, he never could feel quite at his ease with her. At their first meeting there had mingled with his admiration, when he looked in her face, a faint, involuntary feeling of doubt whether that face was entirely strange to him. No after familiarity had the slightest effect on this inexplicable wearisome uncertainty.

Concealing the truth as he had been directed, he announced his engagement to his mother on the day when he contracted it. Poor Mrs. Scatchard showed her perfect confidence in her son by flinging her arms round his neck, and giving evidence of her joy at his having found at last, in the sister of one of his fellow-servants, a woman to comfort, and care for him after his mother was gone. She was all eagerness to see the woman of her son's choice, and the next day was fixed for the introduction.

It was a bright sunny morning, and the little cottage parlor was full of light as Mrs. Scatchard, happy and expectant, dressed for the occasion in her Sunday gown, sat waiting for her son and her future daughter-in-law.

Punctual to the appointed time, Isaac hurriedly and nervously led his promised wife into the room. His mother rose to receive her – advanced a few steps smiling – looked Rebecca full in the eyes, and suddenly stopped. Her face, which had been flushed the moment before, turned white in an instant; her eyes lost their expression of softness and kindness, and assumed a blank look of terror; her out-stretched hands fell to her sides, and she staggered back a few steps and with a low cry to her son.

'Isaac,' she whispered, clutching him fast by the arm when he asked alarmedly if she was taken ill, 'Isaac, does that woman's face remind you of nothing?'

Before he could answer – before he could look round to where Rebecca stood, astonished and angered by her reception, at the lower end of the room – his mother pointed impatiently to her writing-desk, and gave him the key.

'Open it,' she said, in a quick, breathless whisper.

'What does this mean? Why am I treated as if I had no business here? Does your mother want to insult me?' asked Rebecca, angrily.

'Open it, and give me the paper in the left-hand drawer. Quick! quick, for Heaven's sake!' said Mrs. Scatchard, shrinking further back in terror.

Isaac gave her the paper. She looked it over eagerly for a moment, then followed Rebecca, who was now turning away haughtily to leave the room, and caught her by the shoulder – abruptly raised the long, loose sleeve of her gown, and glanced at her hand and arm. Something like fear began to steal over the angry expression of Rebecca's face as she shook herself free from the old woman's grasp. 'Mad!' she said to herself, 'and Isaac never told me.' With these few words she left the room.

Isaac was hastening after her when his mother turned and stopped his further progress. It wrung his heart to see the misery and terror in her face as she looked at him.

'Light-gray eyes,' she said, in low, mournful, awe-struck tones, pointing toward the open door; 'a droop in the left eyelid; flaxen hair, with a gold-yellow streak in it; white arms, with a down upon them; little lady's hand, with a reddish look under the finger nails – the Dream Woman, Isaac, the Dream Woman!'

That faint cleaving doubt which he had never been able to shake off in Rebecca Murdoch's presence was fatally set at rest forever. He had seen her face, then, before – seven years before, on his birthday, in the bedroom of the lonely inn.

'Be warned! oh, my son, be warned! Isaac, Isaac, let her go, and do you stop with me!'

Something darkened the parlor window as these words were said. A sudden chill ran through him, and he glanced sidelong at the shadow. Rebecca Murdoch had come back. She was peering in curiously at them over the low window-blind.

'I have promised to marry, mother,' he said, 'and marry I must.'

The tears came into his eyes as he spoke and dimmed his sight, but he could just discern the fatal form outside moving away again from the window.

His mother's head sank lower.

'Are you faint?' he whispered.

'Broken-hearted, Isaac.'

He stooped down and kissed her. The shadow, as he did so, returned to the window, and the fatal face peered in curiously once more.

Three weeks after that day Isaac and Rebecca were man and wife. All that was hopelessly dogged and stubborn in the man's moral nature seemed to have closed round his fatal passion, and to have fixed it unassailably in his heart.

After that first interview in the cottage parlor no consideration would induce Mrs. Scatchard to see her son's wife again, or even to talk of her when Isaac tried hard to plead her cause after their marriage.

This course of conduct was not in any degree occasioned by a discovery of the degradation in which Rebecca had lived. There was no question of that between mother and son. There was no question of anything but the fearfully exact resemblance between the living, breathing woman and the specter-woman of Isaac's dream.

Rebecca, on her side, neither felt nor expressed the slightest sorrow at the estrangement between herself and her mother-in-law. Isaac, for the sake of peace, had never contradicted her first idea that age and long illness

had affected Mrs. Scatchard's mind. He even allowed his
wife to upbraid him for not having confessed this to her
at the time of their marriage engagement rather than risk
anything by hinting at the truth. The sacrifice of his
integrity before his one all-mastering delusion seemed
but a small thing, and cost his conscience but little after
the sacrifices he had already made.

The time of waking from his delusion – the cruel and
the rueful time – was not far off. After some quiet
months of married life, as the summer was ending, and
the year was getting on toward the month of his
birthday, Isaac found his wife altering toward him. She
grew sullen and contemptuous; she formed acquaintances of the most dangerous kind in defiance of his
objections, his entreaties, and his commands; and, worst
of all, she learned, erelong, after every fresh difference
with her husband, to seek the deadly self-oblivion of
drink. Little by little, after the first miserable discovery
that his wife was keeping company with drunkards, the
shocking certainty forced itself on Isaac that she had
grown to be a drunkard herself.

He had been in a sadly desponding state for some time
before the occurrence of these domestic calamities. His
mother's health, as he could but too plainly discern every
time he went to see her at the cottage, was failing fast,
and he upbraided himself in secret as the cause of the
bodily and mental suffering she endured. When to his
remorse on his mother's account was added the shame
and misery occasioned by the discovery of his wife's
degradation, he sank under the double trial – his face
began to alter fast and he looked what he was, a spirit-
broken man.

His mother, still struggling bravely against the illness
that was hurrying her to the grave, was the first to notice

the sad alteration in him, and the first to hear of his last worst trouble with his wife. She could only weep bitterly on the day when he made his humiliating confession, but on the next occasion when he went to see her she had taken a resolution in reference to his domestic afflictions which astonished and even alarmed him. He found her dressed to go out, and on asking the reason received this answer:

'I am not long for this world, Isaac,' she said, 'and I shall not feel easy on my death-bed unless I have done my best to the last to make my son happy. I mean to put my own fears and my own feelings out of the question, and to go with you to your wife, and try what I can do to reclaim her. Give me your arm, Isaac, and let me do the last thing I can in this world to help my son before it is too late.'

He could not disobey her, and they walked together slowly toward his miserable home.

It was only one o'clock in the afternoon when they reached the cottage where he lived. It was their dinner-hour, and Rebecca was in the kitchen. He was thus able to take his mother quietly into the parlor, and then prepare his wife for the interview. She had fortunately drunk but little at that early hour, and she was less sullen and capricious than usual.

He returned to his mother with his mind tolerably at ease. His wife soon followed him into the parlor, and the meeting between her and Mrs. Scatchard passed off better than he had ventured to anticipate, though he observed with secret apprehension that his mother, resolutely as she controlled herself in other respects, could not look his wife in the face when she spoke to her. It was a relief to him, therefore, when Rebecca began to lay the cloth.

She laid the cloth, brought in the bread-tray, and cut a slice from the loaf for her husband, then returned to the kitchen. At that moment, Isaac, still anxiously watching his mother, was startled by seeing the same ghastly change pass over her face which had altered it so awfully on the morning when Rebecca and she first met. Before he could say a word, she whispered, with a look of horror:

'Take me back – home, home again, Isaac. Come with me, and never go back again.'

He was afraid to ask for an explanation; he could only sign to her to be silent, and help her quickly to the door. As they passed the bread-tray on the table she stopped and pointed to it.

'Did you see what your wife cut your bread with?' she asked, in a low whisper.

'No, mother – I was not noticing – what was it?'

'Look!'

He did look. A new clasp-knife, with a buckhorn handle, lay with the loaf in the bread-tray. He stretched out his hand shudderingly to possess himself of it; but, at the same time, there was a noise in the kitchen, and his mother caught at his arm.

'The knife of the dream! Isaac, I'm faint with fear. Take me away before she comes back.'

He was hardly able to support her. The visible, tangible reality of the knife struck him with a panic, and utterly destroyed any faint doubts that he might have entertained up to this time in relation to the mysterious dream-warning of nearly eight years before. By a last desperate effort, he summoned self-possession enough to help his mother out of the house – so quietly that the 'Dream Woman' (he thought of her by that name now) did not hear them departing from the kitchen.

'Don't go back, Isaac — don't go back!' implored Mrs. Scatchard, as he turned to go away, after seeing her safely seated again in her own room.

'I must get the knife,' he answered, under his breath. His mother tried to stop him again, but he hurried out without another word.

On his return he found that the wife had discovered their secret departure from the house. She had been drinking and was in a fury of passion. The dinner in the kitchen was flung under the grate; the cloth was off the parlor table. Where was the knife?

Unwisely, he asked for it. She was only too glad of the opportunity of irritating him which the request afforded her. He wanted the knife, did he? Could he give her a reason why? No! Then he should not have it — not if he went down on his knees to ask for it. Further recrimination elicited the fact that she had bought it at a bargain, and that she considered it her own special property. Isaac saw the uselessness of attempting to get the knife by fair means, and determined to search for it, later in the day, in secret. The search was unsuccessful. Night came on, and he left the house to walk about the streets. He was afraid now to sleep in the same room with her.

Three weeks passed. Still sullenly enraged with him, she would not give up the knife; and still that fear of sleeping in the same room with her possessed him. He walked about at night, or dozed in the parlor, or sat watching by his mother's bedside. Before the expiration of the first week in the new month his mother died. It wanted then but ten days of her son's birthday. She had longed to live till that anniversary. Isaac was present at her death, and her last words in this world were addressed to him:

'Don't go back, my son, don't go back!'

He was obliged to go back, if it were only to watch his wife. Exasperated to the last degree by his distrust in her, she had revengefully sought to add a sting to his grief, during the last days of his mother's illness, by declaring that she would assert her right to attend the funeral. In spite of all that he could do or say, she held with wicked pertinacity to her word, and on the day appointed for the burial forced herself – inflamed and shameless with drink – into her husband's presence, and declared that she would walk in the funeral procession to his mother's grave.

This last worst outrage, accompanied by all that was most insulting in word and look, maddened him for the moment. He struck her.

The instant the blow was dealt he repented it. She crouched down, silent, in a corner of the room, and eyed him steadily; it was a look that cooled his hot blood and made him tremble. But there was no time now to think of the worst till the funeral was over. There was but one way of making sure of her. He locked her in her bedroom.

When he came back some hours after, he found her sitting very much altered in look and bearing, by the bedside, with a bundle on her lap. She rose and faced him quietly, and spoke with a strange stillness in her voice, a strange repose in her eyes, a strange composure in her manner.

'No man has ever struck me twice,' she said, 'and my husband shall have no second opportunity. Set the door open and let me go. From this day forth we see each other no more.'

Before he could answer she passed him and left the room. He saw her walk away up the street.

Would she return?

All that night he watched and waited, but no footstep came near the house. The next night, overpowered by fatigue, he lay down in bed in his clothes, with the door locked, the key on the table, and the candle burning. His slumber was not disturbed. The third night, the fourth, the fifth, the sixth passed, and nothing happened. He lay down on the seventh, still in his clothes, still with the door locked, the key on the table, and the candle burning, but easier in his mind.

Easier in his mind, and in perfect health of body when he fell off to sleep. But his rest was disturbed. He woke twice without any sensation of uneasiness. But the third time it was that never-to-be-forgotten shivering of the night at the lonely inn, that dreadful sinking pain at the heart which once more aroused him in an instant.

His eyes opened toward the left-hand side of the bed, and there stood –

The Dream Woman again? No! his wife; the living reality, with the dream-specter's face, in the dream-specter's attitude; the fair arm up, the knife clasped in the delicate white hand.

He sprang upon her almost at the instant of seeing her, and yet not quickly enough to prevent her from hiding the knife. Without a word from him – without a cry from her – he pinioned her in a chair. With one hand he felt up her sleeve, and there, where the Dream Woman had hidden the knife, his wife had hidden it – the knife with the buckhorn handle, that looked like new.

In the despair of that fearful moment his brain was steady, his heart was calm. He looked at her fixedly with the knife in his hand, and said these last words:

'You have told me we should see each other no more, and you have come back. It is now my turn to go, and to go forever. I say that we shall see each other no more, and *my* word shall not be broken.'

He left her, and set forth into the night. There was a bleak wind abroad, and the smell of recent rain was in the air. The distant church-clocks chimed the quarter as he walked rapidly beyond the last houses in the suburb. He asked the first policeman he met what hour that was of which the quarter past had struck.

The man referred sleepily to his watch, and answered, 'Two o'clock.' Two in the morning. What day of the month was this day that had just begun? He reckoned it up from the date of his mother's funeral. The fatal parallel was complete; it was his birthday!

Had he escaped the mortal peril which his dream foretold? or had he only received a second warning?

As that ominous doubt forced itself on his head, he stopped, reflected, and turned back again toward the city. He was still resolute to hold to his word, and never to let her see him more; but there was a thought now in his mind of having her watched and followed. The knife was in his possession; the world was before him; but a new distrust of her – a vague, unspeakable, superstitious dread – had come over him.

'I must know where she goes, now she thinks I have left her,' he said to himself, as he stole back wearily to the precincts of his house.

It was still dark. He had left the candle burning in the bed-chamber; but when he looked up to the window of the room now, there was no light in it. He crept cautiously to the house door. On going away, he remembered to have closed it; on trying it now, he found it open.

He waited outside, never losing sight of the house, till daylight. Then he ventured indoors – listened, and heard nothing – looked into kitchen, scullery, parlor, and found nothing; went up, at last into the bedroom – it was empty. A picklock lay on the floor; betraying how she had gained entrance in the night, and that was the only trace of her.

Whither had she gone? That no mortal tongue could tell him. The darkness had covered her flight; and when the day broke no man could say where the light found her.

Before leaving the house and the town forever, he gave instructions to a friend and neighbor to sell his furniture for anything that it would fetch, and apply the proceeds to employing the police to trace her. The directions were honestly followed, and the money was all spent, but the inquiries led to nothing. The picklock on the bedroom floor remained the one last useless trace of the Dream Woman.

A Horseman in the Sky

Ambrose Bierce

One sunny afternoon in the autumn of the year 1861, a soldier lay in a clump of laurel by the side of a road in Western Virginia. He lay at full length, upon his stomach, his feet resting upon the toes, his head upon the left forearm. His extended right hand loosely grasped his rifle. But for the somewhat methodical disposition of his limbs and a slight rhythmic movement of the cartridge box at the back of his belt, he might have been thought to be dead. He was asleep at his post of duty. But if detected he would be dead shortly afterward, that being the just and legal penalty of his crime.

The clump of laurel in which the criminal lay was in the angle of a road which, after ascending, southward, a steep acclivity to that point, turned sharply to the west, running along the summit for perhaps one hundred yards. There it turned southward again and went zigzagging downward through the forest. At the salient of that second angle was a large flat rock, jutting out from the ridge to the northward, overlooking the deep valley from which the road ascended. The rock capped a high cliff; a stone dropped from its outer edge would have fallen sheer downward one thousand feet to the tops of the pines. The angle where the soldier lay was on another spur of the same cliff. Had he been awake he would have commanded a view, not only of the short arm of the road and the jutting rock but of the entire profile of the cliff below it. It might well have made him giddy to look.

The country was wooded everywhere except at the bottom of the valley to the northward, where there was a small natural meadow, through which flowed a stream scarcely visible from the valley's rim. This open ground looked hardly larger than an ordinary door-yard, but was really several acres in extent. Its green was more vivid than that of the enclosing forest. Away beyond it rose a line of giant cliffs similar to those upon which we are supposed to stand in our survey of the savage scene, and through which the road had somehow made its climb to the summit. The configuration of the valley, indeed, was such that from our point of observation it seemed entirely shut in, and one could not but have wondered how the road which found a way out of it had found a way into it, and whence came and whither went the waters of the stream that parted the meadow two thousand feet below.

No country is so wild and difficult but men will make it a theatre of war; concealed in the forest at the bottom of that military rat-trap, in which half a hundred men in possession of the exits might have starved an army to submission, lay five regiments of Federal infantry. They had marched all the previous day and night and were resting. At nightfall they would take to the road again, climb to the place where their unfaithful sentinel now slept, and, descending the other slope of the ridge, fall upon a camp of the enemy at about midnight. Their hope was to surprise it, for the road led to the rear of it. In case of failure their position would be perilous in the extreme; and fail they surely would should accident or vigilance apprise the enemy of the movement.

The sleeping sentinel in the clump of laurel was a young Virginian named Carter Druse. He was the son of wealthy parents, an only child, and had known such ease and cultivation and high living as wealth and taste were able to command in the mountain country of Western Virginia. His home was but a few miles from where he now lay. One morning he had risen from the breakfast table and said, quietly and gravely: 'Father, a Union regiment has arrived at Grafton. I am going to join it.'

The father lifted his leonine head, looked at the son a moment in silence, and replied: 'Go, Carter, and, whatever may occur, do what you conceive to be your duty. Virginia, to which you are a traitor, must get on without you. Should we both live to the end of the war, we will speak further of the matter. Your mother, as the physician has informed you, is in a most critical condition; at the best she cannot be with us longer than a few weeks, but that time is precious. It would be better not to disturb her.'

So Carter Druse, bowing reverently to his father, who returned the salute with a stately courtesy which masked a breaking heart, left the home of his childhood to go soldiering. By conscience and courage, by deeds of devotion and daring, he soon commended himself to his fellows and his officers; and it was to these qualities and to some knowledge of the country that he owed his selection for his present perilous duty at the extreme outpost. Nevertheless, fatigue had been stronger than resolution, and he had fallen asleep. What good or bad angel came in a dream to rouse him from his state of crime who shall say? Without a movement, without a sound, in the profound silence and the languor of the late afternoon, some invisible messenger of fate touched with unsealing finger the eyes of his consciousness –

whispered into the ear of his spirit the mysterious
awakening word which no human lips have ever
spoken, no human memory ever has recalled. He
quietly raised his forehead from his arm and looked
between the masking stems of the laurels, instinctively
closing his right hand about the stock of his rifle.

His first feeling was a keen artistic delight. On a colossal
pedestal, the cliff, motionless at the extreme edge of the
capping rock and sharply outlined against the sky, was an
equestrian statue of impressive dignity. The figure of the
man sat the figure of the horse, straight and soldierly, but
with the repose of a Grecian god carved in the marble
which limits the suggestion of activity. The grey costume
harmonized with its aerial background; the metal of
accoutrement and caparison was softened and subdued
by the shadow; the animal's skin had no points of high
light. A carbine, strikingly foreshortened, lay across the
pommel of the saddle, kept in place by the right hand
grasping it at the 'grip'; the left hand, holding the bridle
rein, was invisible. In silhouette against the sky, the profile
of the horse was cut with the sharpness of a cameo; it
looked across the heights of air to the confronting cliffs
beyond. The face of the rider, turned slightly to the left,
showed only an outline of temple and beard; he was
looking downward to the bottom of the valley. Magnified
by its lift against the sky and by the soldier's testifying sense
of the formidableness of a near enemy, the group appeared
of heroic, almost colossal, size.

For an instant Druse had a strange, half-defined feeling
that he had slept to the end of the war and was looking
upon a noble work of art reared upon that commanding
eminence to commemorate the deeds of an heroic past of
which he had been an inglorious part. The feeling was
dispelled by a slight movement of the group; the horse,

without moving its feet, had drawn its body slightly backward from the verge; the man remained immobile as before. Broad awake and keenly alive to the significance of the situation, Druse now brought the butt of his rifle against his cheek by cautiously pushing the barrel forward through the bushes, cocked the piece, and, glancing through the sights, covered a vital spot of the horseman's breast. A touch upon the trigger and all would have been well with Carter Druse. At that instant the horseman turned his head and looked in the direction of his concealed foeman – seemed to look into his very face, into his eyes, into his brave compassionate heart.

Is it, then, so terrible to kill an enemy in war – an enemy who has surprised a secret vital to the safety of one's self and comrades – an enemy more formidable for his knowledge than all his army for its numbers? Carter Druse grew deathly pale; he shook in every limb, turned faint, and saw the statuesque group before him as black figures, rising, falling, moving unsteadily in arcs of circles in a fiery sky. His hand fell away from his weapon, his head slowly dropped until his face rested on the leaves in which he lay. This courageous gentleman and hardy soldier was near swooning from intensity of emotion.

It was not for long; in another moment his face was raised from earth, his hands resumed their places on the rifle, his forefinger sought the trigger; mind, heart, and eyes were clear, conscience and reason sound. He could not hope to capture that enemy; to alarm him would but send him dashing to his camp with his fatal news. The duty of the soldier was plain: the man must be shot dead from ambush – without warning, without a moment's spiritual preparation, with never so much as an unspoken prayer, he must be sent to his account. But no – there is a hope; he may have discovered nothing – perhaps he is but admiring the sublimity of the landscape. If permitted he may turn and ride carelessly away in the direction whence he came. Surely it will be possible to judge at the instant of his withdrawing whether he knows. It may well be that his fixity of attention – Druse turned his head and looked below, through the deeps of air downward, as from the surface to the bottom of a translucent sea. He saw creeping across the green meadow a sinuous line of figures of men and horses – some foolish commander was permitting the soldiers of his escort to water their beasts in the open, in plain view from a hundred summits!

Druse withdrew his eyes from the valley and fixed them again upon the group of man and horse in the sky, and again it was through the sights of his rifle. But this time his aim was at the horse. In his memory, as if they were a divine mandate, rang the words of his father at their parting. 'Whatever may occur, do what you conceive to be your duty.' He was calm now. His teeth were firmly but not rigidly closed; his nerves were as tranquil as a sleeping babe's – not a tremor affected any muscle of his body; his breathing until suspended in the act of taking aim, was regular and slow. Duty had conquered; the spirit had said to the body: 'Peace, be still.' He fired.

At that moment an officer of the Federal force, who, in a spirit of adventure or in quest of knowledge, had left the hidden bivouac in the valley, and, with aimless feet, had made his way to the lower edge of a small open space near the foot of the cliff, was considering what he had to gain by pushing his exploration further. At a distance of a quarter-mile before him, but apparently at a stone's throw, rose from its fringe of pines the gigantic face of rock, towering to so great a height above him that it made him giddy to look up to where its edge cut a sharp, rugged line against the sky. At some distance away to his right it presented a clean, vertical profile against a background of blue sky to a point half of the way down, and of distant hills hardly less blue thence to the tops of the trees at its base. Lifting his eyes to the dizzy altitude of its summit, the officer saw an astonishing sight – a man on horseback riding down into the valley through the air!

Straight upright sat the rider, in military fashion, with a firm seat in the saddle, a strong clutch upon the rein to hold his charger from too impetuous a plunge. From his bare head his long hair streamed upward, waving like a plume. His right hand was concealed in the cloud of the horse's lifted mane. The animal's body was as level as if every hoof stroke encountered the resistant earth. Its motions were those of a wild gallop, but even as the officer looked they ceased, with all the legs thrown sharply forward as in the act of alighting from a leap. But this was a flight!

Filled with amazement and terror by this apparition of a horseman in the sky – half believing himself the chosen scribe of some new Apocalypse, the officer was overcome by the intensity of his emotions; his legs failed him and he fell. Almost at the same instant he heard a crashing sound in the trees – a sound that died without an echo, and all was still.

The officer rose to his feet, trembling. The familiar sensation of an abraded shin recalled his dazed faculties. Pulling himself together, he ran rapidly obliquely away from the cliff to a point a half-mile from its foot; thereabout he expected to find his man; and thereabout he naturally failed. In the fleeting instant of his vision his imagination had been so wrought upon by the apparent grace and ease and intention of the marvellous performance that it did not occur to him that the line of march of aerial cavalry is directed downward, and that he could find the objects of his search at the very foot of the cliff. A half-hour later he returned to camp.

This officer was a wise man; he knew better than to tell an incredible truth. He said nothing of what he had seen. But when the commander asked him if in his scout he had learned anything of advantage to the expedition, he answered:

'Yes, sir; there is no road leading down into this valley from the southward.'

The commander, knowing better, smiled.

After firing his shot Private Carter Druse reloaded his rifle and resumed his watch. Ten minutes had hardly passed when a Federal sergeant crept cautiously to him on hands and knees. Druse neither turned his head nor looked at him, but lay without motion or sign of recognition.

'Did you fire?' the sergeant whispered.

'Yes.'

'At what?'

'A horse. It was standing on yonder rock – pretty far out. You see it is no longer there. It went over the cliff.'

The man's face was white, but he showed no other sign of emotion. Having answered, he turned away his face and said no more. The sergeant did not understand.

'See here, Druse,' he said, after a moment's silence, 'it's no use making a mystery. I order you to report. Was there anybody on the horse?'

'Yes.'

'Who?'

'My father.'

The sergeant rose to his feet and walked away. 'Good God!' he said.

The Jolly Corner

Henry James

I

'Every one asks me what I "think" of everything,' said Spencer Brydon; 'and I make answer as I can – begging or dodging the question, putting them off with any nonsense. It wouldn't matter to any of them really,' he went on, 'for, even were it possible to meet in that stand-and-deliver way so silly a demand on so big a subject, my "thoughts" would still be almost altogether about something that concerns only myself.' He was talking to Miss Staverton, with whom for a couple of months now he had availed himself of every possible occasion to talk; this disposition and this resource, this comfort and support, as the situation in fact presented itself, having promptly enough taken the first place in the considerable array of rather unattenuated surprises attending his so strangely belated return to America. Everything was somehow a surprise; and that might be natural when one had so long and so consistently neglected everything, taken pains to give surprises so much margin for play. He had given them more than thirty years – thirty-three, to be exact; and they now seemed to him to have organised their performance quite on the scale of that license. He had been twenty-three on leaving New York – he was fifty-six today: unless indeed he were to reckon as he had sometimes, since his repatriation, found himself feeling;

in which case he would have lived longer than is often allotted to man. It would have taken a century, he repeatedly said to himself, and said also to Alice Staverton, it would have taken a longer absence and a more averted mind than those even of which he had been guilty, to pile up the differences, the newnesses, the queernesses, above all the bignesses, for the better or the worse, that at present assaulted his vision wherever he looked.

The great fact all the while however had been the incalculability; since he *had* supposed himself, from decade to decade, to be allowing, and in the most liberal and intelligent manner, for brilliancy of change. He actually saw that he had allowed for nothing; he missed what he would have been sure of finding, he found what he would never have imagined. Proportions and values were upside-down; the ugly things he had expected, the ugly things of his far-away youth, when he had too promptly waked up to a sense of the ugly – these uncanny phenomena placed him rather, as it happened, under the charm; whereas the 'swagger' things, the modern, the monstrous, the famous things, those he had more particularly, like thousands of ingenuous enquirers every year, come over to see, were exactly his sources of dismay. They were as so many set traps for displeasure, above all for reaction, of which his restless tread was constantly pressing the spring. It was interesting, doubtless, the whole show, but it would have been too disconcerting hadn't a certain finer truth saved the situation. He had distinctly not, in this steadier light, come over *all* for the monstrosities; he had come, not only in the last analysis but quite on the face of the act, under an impulse with which they had nothing to do. He had come – putting the thing pompously – to look at his 'property', which he had thus for a third of a century not been within four thousand miles of; or, expressing it less sordidly, he had yielded to the humour of seeing again his house on the jolly corner, as he usually, and quite fondly, described it – the one in which he had first seen the light, in which various members of his family had lived and had died, in which the holidays of his overschooled boyhood had been passed and the few social flowers of his chilled adolescence gathered, and which, alienated then for so long a period had, through the successive deaths of his two brothers and the termination of old arrangements, come wholly into his hands. He was the owner of another, not quite so 'good' – the jolly corner having been, from far back, super-latively extended and consecrated; and the value of the pair represented his main capital, with an income consisting, in these later years, of their respective rents which (thanks precisely to their original excellent type) had never been depressingly low. He could live in 'Europe', as he had been in the habit of living, on the product of these flourishing New York leases, and all the better since, that of the second structure, the mere number in its long row, having within a twelvemonth fallen in, renovation at a high advance had proved beautifully possible.

These were items of property indeed, but he had found himself since his arrival distinguishing more than ever between them. The house within the street, two bristling blocks westward, was already in course of reconstruction as a tall mass of flats; he had acceded, some time before, to overtures for this conversion – in which, now that it was going forward, it had been not the least of his astonishments to find himself able, on the spot, and though without a previous ounce of such experience, to participate with a certain intelligence, almost with a certain authority. He had lived his life with his back so turned to such concerns and his face addressed to those of so different an order that he scarce knew what to make of this lively stir, in a compartment of his mind never yet penetrated, of a capacity for business and a sense for construction. These virtues, so common all round him now, had been dormant in his own organism – where it might be said of them perhaps that they had slept the sleep of the just. At present, in the splendid autumn weather – the autumn at least was a pure boon in the terrible place – he loafed about his 'work' undeterred, secretly agitated; not in the least 'minding' that the whole proposition, as they said, was vulgar and sordid, and ready to climb ladders, to walk the plank, to handle materials and look wise about them, to ask questions, in fine, and challenge explanations and really 'go into' figures.

It amused, it verily quite charmed him; and, by the same stroke, it amused, and even more, Alice Staverton, though perhaps charming her perceptibly less. She wasn't however going to be better off for it, as *he* was – and so astonishingly much: nothing was now likely, he knew, even to make her better-off than she found herself, in the afternoon of life, as the delicately frugal possessor and tenant of the small house in Irving Place to which she had subtly managed to cling through her almost un-broken New York career. If he knew the way to it now better than to any other address among the dreadful multiplied numberings which seemed to him to reduce the whole place to some vast ledger-page, overgrown, fantastic, of ruled and criss-crossed lines and figures – if he had formed, for his consolation, that habit, it was really not a little because of the charm of his having

encountered and recognised, in the vast wilderness of the
wholesale, breaking through the mere gross general-
isation of wealth and force and success, a small still
scene where items and shades, all delicate things, kept
the sharpness of the notes of a high voice perfectly
trained, and where economy hung about like the scent
of a garden. His old friend lived with one maid and
herself dusted her relics and trimmed her lamps and
polished her silver; she stood off, in the awful modern
crush, when she could, but she sallied forth and did battle
when the challenge was really to 'spirit', the spirit she
after all confessed to, proudly and a little shyly, as to that
of the better time, that of *their* common, their quite far-
away and antediluvian social period and order. She made
use of the street-cars when need be, the terrible things
that people scrambled for as the panic-stricken at sea
scramble for the boats; she affronted, inscrutably, under
stress, all the public concussions and ordeals; and yet,
with that slim mystifying grace of her appearance, which
defied you to say if she were a fair young woman who
looked older through trouble, or a fine smooth older one
who looked young through successful indifference; with
her precious reference, above all, to memories and
histories into which he could enter, she was as exquisite
for him as some pale pressed flower (a rarity to begin
with), and, failing other sweetnesses, she was a sufficient
reward of his effort. They had communities of knowledge, 'their' knowledge (this discriminating possessive
was always on her lips) of presences of the other age,
presences all overlaid, in his case, by the experience of a
man and the freedom of a wanderer, overlaid by
pleasure, by infidelity, by passages of life that were
strange and dim to her, just by 'Europe' in short, but
still unobscured, still exposed and cherished, under that

pious visitation of the spirit from which she had never been diverted.

She had come with him one day to see how his 'apartment-house' was rising; he had helped her over gaps and explained to her plans, and while they were there had happened to have, before her, a brief but lively discussion with the man in charge, the representative of the building-firm that had undertaken his work. He had found himself quite 'standing-up' to this personage over a failure on the latter's part to observe some detail of one of their noted conditions, and had so lucidly argued his case that, besides ever so prettily flushing, at the time, for sympathy in his triumph, she had afterwards said to him (though to a slightly greater effect of irony) that he had clearly for too many years neglected a real gift. If he had but stayed at home he would have anticipated the inventor of the sky-scraper. If he had but stayed at home he would have discovered his genius in time really to start some new variety of awful architectural hare and run it till it burrowed in a gold-mine. He was to remember these words, while the weeks elapsed, for the small silver ring they had sounded over the queerest and deepest of his own lately most disguised and most muffled vibrations.

It had begun to be present to him after the first fortnight, it had broken out with the oddest abruptness, this particular wanton wonderment: it met him there – and this was the image under which he himself judged the matter, or at least, not a little, thrilled and flushed with it – very much as he might have been met by some strange figure, some unexpected occupant, at a turn of one of the dim passages of an empty house. The quaint analogy quite hauntingly remained with him, when he didn't indeed rather improve it by a still

intenser form: that of his opening a door behind which
he would have made sure of finding nothing, a door into
a room shuttered and void, and yet so coming, with a
great suppressed start, on some quite erect confronting
presence, sometimes planted in the middle of the place
and facing him through the dusk. After that visit to the
house in construction he walked with his companion to
see the other and always so much the better one, which
in the eastward direction formed one of the corners, the
'jolly' one precisely, of the street now so generally
dishonoured and disfigured in its westward reaches,
and of the comparatively conservative Avenue. The
Avenue still had pretensions, as Miss Staverton said, to
decency; the old people had mostly gone, the old names
were unknown, and here and there an old association
seemed to stray, all vaguely, like some very aged person,
out too late, whom you might meet and feel the impulse
to watch or follow, in kindness, for safe restoration to
shelter.

They went in together, our friends; he admitted
himself with his key, as he kept no one there, he
explained, preferring, for his reasons, to leave the place
empty, under a simple arrangement with a good woman
living in the neighbourhood and who came for a daily
hour to open windows and dust and sweep. Spencer
Brydon had his reasons and was growingly aware of
them; they seemed to him better each time he was there,
though he didn't name them all to his companion, any
more than he told her as yet how often, how quite
absurdly often, he himself came. He only let her see for
the present, while they walked through the great blank
rooms, that absolute vacancy reigned and that, from top
to bottom, there was nothing but Mrs. Muldoon's
broomstick, in a corner, to tempt the burglar.

Mrs. Muldoon was then on the premises, and she loquaciously attended the visitors, preceding them from room to room and pushing back shutters and throwing up sashes – all to show them, as she remarked, how little there was to see. There was little indeed to see in the great gaunt shell where the main dispositions and the general apportionment of space, the style of an age of ampler allowances, had nevertheless for its master their honest pleading message, affecting him as some good old servant's, some lifelong retainer's appeal for a character, or even for a retiring-pension; yet it was also a remark of Mrs. Muldoon's that, glad as she was to oblige him by her noonday round, there was a request she greatly hoped he would never make of her. If he should wish her for any reason to come in after dark she would just tell him, if he 'plased', that he must ask it of somebody else.

The fact that there was nothing to see didn't militate for the worthy woman against what one *might* see, and she put it frankly to Miss Staverton that no lady could be expected to like, could she? 'scraping up to thim top storeys in the ayvil hours'. The gas and electric light were off the house, and she fairly evoked a gruesome vision of her march through the great grey rooms – so many of them as there were too! – with her glimmering taper. Miss Staverton met her honest glare with a smile and the profession that she herself certainly would recoil from such an adventure. Spencer Brydon meanwhile held his peace – for the moment; the question of the 'evil' hours in his old home had already become too grave for him. He had begun some time since to 'crape', and he knew just why a packet of candles addressed to that pursuit had been stowed by his own hand, three weeks before, at the back of a drawer of the fine old sideboard that occupied, as a 'fixture,' the deep recess in the dining-room. Just now he laughed at his companions – quickly however changing the subject; for the reason that, in the first place, his laugh struck him even at that moment as starting the odd echo, the conscious human resonance (he scarce knew how to qualify it) that sounds made while he was there alone sent back to his ear or his fancy; and that, in the second, he imagined Alice Staverton for the instant on the point of asking him, with a divination, if he ever so prowled. There were divinations he was unprepared for, and he had at all events averted enquiry by the time Mrs. Muldoon had left them, passing on to other parts.

There was happily enough to say, on so consecrated a spot, that could be said freely and fairly; so that a whole train of declarations was precipitated by his friend's having herself broken out, after a yearning look round: 'But I hope you don't mean they want you to pull *this* to pieces!' His answer came, promptly, with his re-awakened wrath: it was of course exactly what they wanted, and what they were 'at' him for, daily, with the iteration of people who couldn't for their life understand a man's liability to decent feelings. He had found the place, just as it stood and beyond what he could express, an interest and a joy. There were values other than the beastly rent-values, and in short, in short –! But it was thus Miss Staverton took him up. 'In short you're to make so good a thing of your sky-scraper that, living in luxury on *those* ill-gotten gains, you can afford for a while to be sentimental here!' Her smile had for him, with the words, the particular mild irony with which he found half her talk suffused; an irony without bitterness and that came, exactly, from her having so much imagination – not, like the cheap sarcasms with which one heard most

people, about the world of 'society,' bid for the reputation of cleverness, from nobody's really having any. It
was agreeable to him at this very moment to be sure that
when he had answered, after a brief demur, 'Well yes: so,
precisely you may put it!' her imagination would still do
him justice. He explained that even if never a dollar were
to come to him from the other house he would nevertheless cherish this one; and he dwelt, further, while they
lingered and wandered, on the fact of the stupefaction he
was already exciting, the positive mystification he felt
himself create.

He spoke of the value of all he read into it, into the
mere sight of the walls, mere shapes of the rooms, mere
sound of the floors, mere feel, in his hand, of the old
silver-plated knobs of the several mahogany doors,
which suggested the pressure of the palms of the dead;
the seventy years of the past in fine that these things
represented, the annals of nearly three generations,
counting his grandfather's, the one that had ended
there, and the impalpable ashes of his long-extinct
youth, afloat in the very air like microscopic motes.
She listened to everything; she was a woman who
answered intimately but who utterly didn't chatter. She
scattered abroad therefore no cloud of words; she could
assent, she could agree, above all she could encourage,
without doing that. Only at the last she went a little
further than he had done himself. 'And then how do you
know? You may still, after all, want to live here.' It rather
indeed pulled him up, for it wasn't what he had been
thinking, at least in her sense of the words. 'You mean I
may decide to stay on for the sake of it?'

'Well, *with* such a home –!' But, quite beautifully, she
had too much tact to dot so monstrous an *i*, and it was
precisely an illustration of the way she didn't rattle. How

could any one – of any wit – insist on any one else's 'wanting' to live in New York?

'Oh,' he said, 'I *might* have lived here (since I had my opportunity early in life); I might have put in here all these years. Then everything would have been different enough – and, I dare say, "funny" enough. But that's another matter. And then the beauty of it – I mean of my perversity, of my refusal to agree to a "deal" – is just in the total absence of a reason. Don't you see that if I had a reason about the matter at all it would *have* to be the other way, and would then be inevitably a reason of dollars? There are no reasons here *but* of dollars. Let us therefore have none whatever – not the ghost of one.'

They were back in the hall then for departure, but from where they stood the vista was large, through an open door, into the great square main saloon, with its almost antique felicity of brave spaces between windows. Her eyes came back from that reach and met his own a moment. 'Are you very sure the "ghost" of one doesn't, much rather, serve –?'

He had a positive sense of turning pale. But it was as near as they were then to come. For he made answer, he believed, between a glare and a grin: 'Oh ghosts – of course the place must swarm with them! I should be ashamed of it if it didn't. Poor Mrs. Muldoon's right, and it's why I haven't asked her to do more than look in.'

Miss Staverton's gaze again lost itself, and things she didn't utter, it was clear, came and went in her mind. She might even for the minute, off there in the fine room, have imagined some element dimly gathering. Simplified like the death-mask of a handsome face, it perhaps produced for her just then an effect akin to the stir of an expression in the 'set' commemorative plaster. Yet whatever her impression may have been she produced instead a vague platitude. 'Well, if it were only furnished and lived in – !'

She appeared to imply that in case of its being still furnished he might have been a little less opposed to the idea of a return. But she passed straight into the vestibule, as if to leave her words behind her, and the next moment he had opened the house-door and was standing with her on the steps. He closed the door and, while he re-pocketed his key, looking up and down, they took in the comparatively harsh actuality of the Avenue, which reminded him of the assault of the outer light of the Desert on the traveller emerging from an Egyptian tomb. But he risked before they stepped into the street his gathered answer to her speech. 'For me it *is* lived in. For me it *is* furnished.' At which it was easy for her to sigh 'Ah yes –!' all vaguely and discreetly; since his parents and his favourite sister, to say nothing of other kin, in numbers, had run their course and met their end there. That represented, within the walls, ineffaceable life.

It was a few days after this that, during an hour passed with her again, he had expressed his impatience of the too flattering curiosity – among the people he met – about his appreciation of New York. He had arrived at none at all that was socially producible, and as for that matter of his 'thinking' (thinking the better or the worse of anything there) he was wholly taken up with one subject of thought. It was mere vain egoism, and it was moreover, if she liked, a morbid obsession. He found all things come back to the question of what he personally might have been, how he might have led his life and 'turned out', if he had not so, at the outset, given it up. And confessing for the first time to the intensity within him of this absurd speculation – which but proved also, no doubt, the habit of too selfishly thinking – he affirmed the impotence there of any other source of interest, any other native appeal. 'What would it have made of me, what would it have made of me? I keep for ever wondering, all idiotically; as if I could possibly know! I see what it has made of dozens of others, those I meet, and it positively aches within me, to the point of exasperation, that it would have made something of me as well. Only I can't make out *what*, and the worry of it, the small rage of curiosity never to be satisfied, brings back what I remember to have felt, once or twice, after judging best, for reasons, to burn some important letter unopened. I've been sorry, I've hated it — I've never known what was in the letter. You may of course say it's a trifle —!'

'I don't say it's a trifle,' Miss Staverton gravely interrupted.

She was seated by her fire, and before her, on his feet and restless, he turned to and fro between this intensity of his idea and a fitful and unseeing inspection, through his single eye-glass, of the dear little old objects on her chimney-piece. Her interruption made him for an instant look at her harder. 'I shouldn't care if you did!' he laughed, however; 'and it's only a figure, at any rate, for the way I now feel. *Not* to have followed my perverse young course — and almost in the teeth of my father's curse, as I may say; not to have kept it up, so, "over there", from that day to this, without a doubt or a pang; not, above all, to have liked it, to have loved it, so much, loved it, no doubt, with such an abysmal conceit of my own preference: some variation from *that*, I say, must have produced some different effect for my life and for my "form". I should have stuck here — if it had been possible; and I was too young, at twenty-three, to judge, *pour deux sous*, whether it *were* possible. If I had waited I might have seen it was, and then I might have been, by staying here, something nearer to one of these types who have been hammered so hard and made so keen by their conditions. It isn't that I admire them so much – the question of any charm in them, or of any charm, beyond that of the rank money-passion, exerted by their conditions *for* them, has nothing to do with the matter: it's only a question of what fantastic, yet perfectly possible, development of my own nature I mayn't have missed. It comes over me that I had then a strange *alter ego* deep down somewhere within me, as the full-blown flower is in the small tight bud, and that I just took the course, I just transferred him to the climate, that blighted him for once and for ever.'

'And you wonder about the flower,' Miss Staverton said. 'So do I, if you want to know; and so I've been wondering these several weeks. I believe in the flower,' she continued, 'I felt it would have been quite splendid, quite huge and monstrous.'

'Monstrous above all!' her visitor echoed; 'and I imagine, by the same stroke, quite hideous and offensive.'

'You don't believe that,' she returned; 'if you did you wouldn't wonder. You'd know, and that would be enough for you. What you feel – and what I feel *for* you – is that you'd have had power.'

'You'd have liked me that way?' he asked.

She barely hung fire. 'How should I not have liked you?'

'I see. You'd have liked me, have preferred me, a billionaire!'

'How should I not have liked you?' she simply again asked.

He stood before her still – her question kept him
motionless. He took it in, so much there was of it; and
indeed his not otherwise meeting it testified to that. 'I
know at least what I am,' he simply went on; 'the other
side of the medal's clear enough. I've not been edifying –
I believe I'm thought in a hundred quarters to have been
barely decent. I've followed strange paths and worshipped strange gods; it must have come to you again
and again – in fact you've admitted to me as much – that
I was leading, at any time these thirty years, a selfish
frivolous scandalous life. And you see what it has made of
me.'

She just waited, smiling at him. 'You see what it has
made of *me*.'

'Oh you're a person whom nothing can have altered.
You were born to be what you are, anywhere, anyway:
you've the perfection nothing else could have blighted.
And don't you see how, without my exile, I shouldn't
have been waiting till now –?' But he pulled up for the
strange pang.

'The great thing to see,' she presently said, 'seems to
me to be that it has spoiled nothing. It hasn't spoiled your
being here at last. It hasn't spoiled this. It hasn't spoiled
your speaking –' She also however faltered.

He wondered at everything her controlled emotion
might mean. 'Do you believe then – too dreadfully! –
that I *am* as good as I might ever have been?'

'Oh no! Far from it!' With which she got up from her
chair and was nearer to him. 'But I don't care,' she
smiled.

'You mean I'm good enough?'

She considered a little. 'Will you believe it if I say so? I
mean will you let that settle your question for you?' And
then as if making out in his face that he drew back from

this, that he had some idea which, however absurd, he couldn't yet bargain away: 'Oh you don't care either – but very differently: you don't care for anything but yourself.'

Spencer Brydon recognised it – it was in fact what he had absolutely professed. Yet he importantly qualified. '*He* isn't myself. He's the just so totally other person. But I do want to see him,' he added. 'And I can. And I shall.'

Their eyes met for a minute while he guessed from something in hers that she divined his strange sense. But neither of them otherwise expressed it, and her apparent understanding, with no protesting shock, no easy derision, touched him more deeply than anything yet, constituting for his stifled perversity, on the spot, an element that was like breathable air. What she said however was unexpected. 'Well, *I've* seen him.'

'You –?'

'I've see him in a dream.'

'Oh a "dream" –!' It let him down.

'But twice over,' she continued. 'I saw him as I see you now.'

'You've dreamed the same dream –?'

'Twice over,' she repeated. 'The very same.'

This did somehow a little speak to him, as it also gratified him. 'You dream about me at that rate?'

'Ah about *him*!' she smiled.

His eyes again sounded her. 'Then you know all about him.' And as she said nothing more: 'What's the wretch like?'

She hesitated, and it was as if he were pressing her so hard that, resisting for reasons of her own, she had to turn away. 'I'll tell you some other time!'

II

It was after this that there was most of a virtue for him, most of a cultivated charm, most of a preposterous secret thrill, in the particular form of surrender to his obsession and of address to what he more and more believed to be his privilege. It was what in these weeks he was living for – since he really felt life to begin but after Mrs. Muldoon had retired from the scene and, visiting the ample house from attic to cellar, making sure he was alone, he knew himself in safe possession and, as he tacitly expressed it, let himself go. He sometimes came twice in the twenty-four hours; the moments he liked best were those of gathering dusk, of the short autumn twilight; this was the time of which, again and again, he found himself hoping most. Then he could, as seemed to him, most intimately wander and wait, linger and listen, feel his fine attention, never in his life before so fine, on the pulse of the great vague place: he preferred the lampless hour and only wished he might have prolonged each day the deep crepuscular spell. Later – rarely much before midnight, but then for a considerable vigil – he watched with his glimmering light; moving slowly, holding it high, playing it far, rejoicing above all, as much as he might, in open vistas, reaches of communication between rooms and by passages; the long straight chance or show, as he would have called it, for the revelation he pretended to invite. It was a practice he found he could perfectly 'work' without exciting remark; no one was in the least the wiser for it; even Alice Staverton, who was moreover a well of discretion, didn't quite fully imagine.

He let himself in and let himself out with the assurance of calm proprietorship; and accident so far favoured him that, if a fat Avenue 'officer' had happened on occasion to see him entering at eleven-thirty, he had never yet, to the best of his belief, been noticed as emerging at two. He walked there on the crisp November nights, arrived regularly at the evening's end; it was as easy to do this after dining out as to take his way to a club or to his hotel. When he left his club, if he hadn't been dining out, it was ostensibly to go to his hotel; and when he left his hotel, if he had spent a part of the evening there, it was ostensibly to go to his club. Everything was easy in fine; everything conspired and promoted: there was truly even in the strain of his experience something that glossed over, something that salved and simplified, all the rest of consciousness. He circulated, talked, renewed, loosely and pleasantly, old relations — met indeed, so far as he could, new expectations and seemed to make out on the whole that in spite of the career, of such different contacts, which he had spoken of to Miss Staverton as ministering so little, for those who might have watched it, to edification, he was positively rather liked than not. He was a dim secondary social success — and all with people who had truly not an idea of him. It was all mere surface sound, this murmur of their welcome, this popping of their corks — just as his gestures of response were the extravagant shadows, emphatic in proportion as they meant little, of some game of *ombres chinoises*. He projected himself all day, in thought, straight over the bristling line of hard unconscious heads and into the other, the real, the waiting life; the life that, as soon as he had heard behind him the click of his great house-door, began for him, on the jolly corner, as beguilingly as the slow opening bars of some rich music follows the tap of the conductor's wand.

He always caught the first effect of the steel point of his stick on the old marble of the hall pavement, large black-and-white squares that he remembered as the admiration of his childhood and that had then made in him, as he now saw, for the growth of an early conception of style. This effect was the dim reverberating tinkle as of some far-off bell hung who should say where? – in the depths of the house, of the past, of that mystical other world that might have flourished for him had he not, for weal or woe, abandoned it. On this impression he did ever the same thing; he put his stick noiselessly away in a corner – feeling the place once more in the likeness of some great glass bowl, all precious concave crystal, set delicately humming by the play of a moist finger round its edge. The concave crystal held, as it were, this mystical other world, and the indescribably fine murmur of its rim was the sigh there, the scarce audible pathetic wail to his strained ear, of all the old baffled forsworn possibilities. What he did therefore by this appeal of his hushed presence was to wake them into such measure of ghostly life as they might still enjoy. They were shy, all but unappeasably shy, but they weren't really sinister; at least they weren't as he had hitherto felt them – before they had taken the Form he so yearned to make them take, the Form he at moments saw himself in the light of fairly hunting on tiptoe, the points of his evening-shoes, from room to room and from storey to storey.

That was the essence of his vision – which was all rank folly, if one would, while he was out of the house and otherwise occupied, but which took on the last verisimilitude as soon as he was placed and posted. He knew what he meant and what he wanted; it was as clear as the figure on a cheque presented in demand for cash. His *alter ego* 'walked' – that was the note of his image of him, while his image of his motive for his own odd pastime was the desire to waylay him and meet him. He roamed, slowly, warily, but all restlessly, he himself did – Mrs. Muldoon had been right, absolutely, with her figure of their 'craping'; and the presence he watched for would roam restlessly too. But it would be as cautious and as shifty; the conviction of its probable, in fact its already quite sensible, quite audible evasion of pursuit grew for him from night to night, laying on him finally a rigour to which nothing in his life had been comparable. It had been the theory of many superficially-judging persons, he knew, that he was wasting that life in a surrender to sensations, but he had tasted of no pleasure so fine as his actual tension, had been introduced to no sport that demanded at once the patience and the nerve of this stalking of a creature more subtle, yet at bay perhaps more formidable, than any beast of the forest. The terms, the comparisons, the very practices of the chase positively came again into play; there were even moments when passages of his occasional experience as a sportsman, stirred memories, from his younger time, of moor and mountain and desert, revived for him – and to the increase of his keenness – by the tremendous force of analogy. He found himself at moments – once he had placed his single light on some mantel-shelf or in some recess – stepping back into shelter or shade, effacing himself behind a door or in an embrasure, as he had sought of old the vantage of rock and tree; he found himself holding his breath and living in the joy of the instant, the supreme suspense created by big game alone.

He wasn't afraid (though putting himself the question as he believed gentlemen on Bengal tiger-shoots or in close quarters with the great bear of the Rockies had been known to confess to having put it); and this indeed – since here at least he might be frank! – because of the

impression, so intimate and so strange, that he himself
produced as yet a dread, produced certainly a strain,
beyond the liveliest he was likely to feel. They fell for
him into categories, they fairly became familiar, the signs,
for his own perception, of the alarm his presence and his
vigilance created; though leaving him always to remark,
portentously, on his probably having formed a relation,
his probably enjoying a consciousness, unique in the
experience of man. People enough, first and last, had
been in terror of apparitions, but who had ever before so
turned the tables and become himself, in the apparitional
world, an incalculable terror? He might have found this
sublime had he quite dared to think of it; but he didn't
too much insist, truly, on that side of his privilege. With
habit and repetition he gained to an extraordinary degree
the power to penetrate the dusk of distances and the
darkness of corners, to resolve back into their innocence
the treacheries of uncertain light, the evil-looking forms
taken in the gloom by mere shadows, by accidents of the
air, by shifting effects of perspective; putting down his
dim luminary he could still wander on without it, pass
into other rooms and, only knowing it was there behind
him in case of need, see his way about, visually project
for his purpose a comparative clearness. It made him feel,
this acquired faculty, like some monstrous stealthy cat; he
wondered if he would have glared at these moments
with large shining yellow eyes, and what it mightn't
verily be, for the poor hard-pressed *alter ego*, to be
confronted with such a type.

He liked however the open shutters; he opened
everywhere those Mrs. Muldoon had closed, closing
them as carefully afterwards, so that she shouldn't
notice: he liked – oh this he did like, and above all in
the upper rooms! – the sense of the hard silver of the

autumn stars through the window-panes, and scarcely less the flare of the street-lamps below, the white electric lustre which it would have taken curtains to keep out. This was human actual social; this was of the world he had lived in, and he was more at his ease certainly for the countenance, coldly general and impersonal, that all the while and in spite of his detachment it seemed to give him. He had support of course mostly in the rooms at the wide front and the prolonged side; it failed him considerably in the central shades and the parts at the back. But if he sometimes, on his rounds, was glad of his optical reach, so none the less often the rear of the house affected him as the very jungle of his prey. The place was there more subdivided; a large 'extension' in particular, where small rooms for servants had been multiplied, abounded in nooks and corners, in closets and passages, in the ramifications especially of an ample back staircase over which he leaned, many a time, to look far down – not deterred from his gravity even while aware that he might, for a spectator, have figured some solemn simpleton playing at hide-and-seek. Outside in fact he might himself make that ironic *rapprochement*; but within the walls, and in spite of the clear windows, his consistency was proof against the cynical light of New York.

It had belonged to that idea of the exasperated consciousness of his victim to become a real test for him; since he had quite put it to himself from the first that, oh distinctly! he could 'cultivate' his whole perception. He had felt it as above all open to cultivation – which indeed was but another name for his manner of spending his time. He was bringing it on, bringing it to perfection, by practice; in consequence of which it had grown so fine that he was now aware of impressions, attestations of his general postulate, that couldn't have broken upon him at once. This was the case more specifically with a phenomenon at last quite frequent for him in the upper rooms, the recognition – absolutely unmistakeable, and by a turn dating from a particular hour, his resumption of his campaign after a diplomatic drop, a calculated absence of three nights – of his being definitely followed, tracked at a distance carefully taken and to the express end that he should the less confidently, less arrogantly, appear to himself merely to pursue. It worried, it finally quite broke him up, for it proved, of all the conceivable impressions, the one least suited to his book. He was kept in sight while remaining himself – as regards the essence of his position – sightless, and his only recourse then was in abrupt turns, rapid recoveries of ground. He wheeled about, retracing his steps, as if he might so catch in his face at least the stirred air of some other quick revolution. It was indeed true that his fully dislocalised thought of these manoeuvres recalled to him Pantaloon, at the Christmas farce, buffeted and tricked from behind by ubiquitous Harlequin; but it left intact the influence of the conditions themselves each time he was re-exposed to them, so that in fact this association, had he suffered it to become constant, would on a certain side have but ministered to his intenser gravity. He had made, as I have said, to create on the premises the baseless sense of a reprieve, his three absences; and the result of the third was to confirm the after-effect of the second.

On his return, that night – the night succeeding his last intermission – he stood in the hall and looked up the staircase with a certainty more intimate than any he had yet known. 'He's *there*, at the top, and waiting – not, as in general, falling back for disappearance. He's holding his ground, and it's the first time – which is a proof, isn't it?

that something has happened for him.' So Brydon argued
with his hand on the banister and his foot on the lowest
stair; in which position he felt as never before the air
chilled by his logic. He himself turned cold in it, for he
seemed of a sudden to know what now was involved.
'Harder pressed? – yes, he takes it in, with its thus making
clear to him that I've come, as they say, "to stay". He
finally doesn't like and can't bear it, in the sense, I mean,
that his wrath, his menaced interest, now balances with
his dread. I've hunted him till he has "turned": that, up
there, is what has happened – he's the fanged or the
antlered animal brought at last to bay.' There came to
him, as I say – but determined by an influence beyond
my notation! – the acuteness of this certainty; under
which however the next moment he had broken into a
sweat that he would as little have consented to attribute
to fear as he would have dared immediately to act upon it
for enterprise. It marked none the less a prodigious thrill,
a thrill that represented sudden dismay, no doubt, but
also represented, and with the selfsame throb, the
strangest, the most joyous, possibly the next minute
almost the proudest, duplication of consciousness.

'He has been dodging, retreating, hiding, but now,
worked up to anger, he'll fight!' – this intense impression
made a single mouthful, as it were, of terror and applause.
But what was wondrous was that the applause, for the felt
fact, was so eager, since, if it was his other self he was
running to earth, this ineffable identity was thus in the
last resort not unworthy of him. It bristled there –
somewhere near at hand, however unseen still – as the
hunted thing, even as the trodden worm of the adage
must at last bristle; and Brydon at this instant tasted
probably of a sensation more complex than had ever
before found itself consistent with sanity. It was as if it

would have shamed him that a character so associated with his own should triumphantly succeed in just skulking, should to the end not risk the open, so that the drop of this danger was, on the spot, a great lift of the whole situation. Yet with another rare shift of the same subtlety he was already trying to measure by how much more he himself might now be in peril of fear; so rejoicing that he could, in another form, actively inspire that fear, and simultaneously quaking for the form in which he might passively know it.

The apprehension of knowing it must after a little have grown in him, and the strangest moment of his adventure perhaps, the most memorable or really most interesting, afterwards, of his crisis, was the lapse of certain instants of concentrated conscious *combat*, the sense of a need to hold on to something, even after the manner of a man slipping and slipping on some awful incline; the vivid impulse, above all, to move, to act, to charge, somehow and upon something – to show himself, in a word, that he wasn't afraid. The state of 'holding-on' was thus the state to which he was momentarily reduced; if there had been anything, in the great vacancy, to seize, he would presently have been aware of having clutched it as he might under a shock at home have clutched the nearest chair-back. He had been surprised at any rate – of this he *was* aware – into something unprecedented since his original appropria-tion of the place; he had closed his eyes, held them tight, for a long minute, as with that instinct of dismay and that terror of vision. When he opened them the room, the other contiguous rooms, extraordinarily, seemed lighter – so light, almost, that at first he took the change for day. He stood firm, however that might be, just where he had paused; his resistance had helped him – it was as if there

were something he had tided over. He knew after a little
what this was – it had been in the imminent danger of
flight. He had stiffened his will against going; without
this he would have made for the stairs, and it seemed to
him that, still with his eyes closed, he would have
descended them, would have known how, straight and
swiftly, to the bottom.

Well, as he had held out, here he was – still at the top,
among the more intricate upper rooms and with the
gauntlet of the others, of all the rest of the house, still to
run when it should be his time to go. He would go at his
time – only at his time: didn't he go every night very
much at the same hour? He took out his watch – there
was light for that: it was scarcely a quarter past one, and
he had never withdrawn so soon. He reached his
lodgings for the most part at two – with his walk of a
quarter of an hour. He would wait for the last quarter –
he wouldn't stir till then; and he kept his watch there
with his eyes on it, reflecting while he held it that this
deliberate wait, a wait with an effort, which he recognised, would serve perfectly for the attestation he desired
to make. It would prove his courage – unless indeed the
latter might most be proved by his budging at last from
his place. What he mainly felt now was that, since he
hadn't originally scuttled, he had his dignities – which
had never in his life seemed so many – all to preserve and
to carry aloft. This was before him in truth as a physical
image, an image almost worthy of an age of greater
romance. That remark indeed glimmered for him only to
glow the next instant with a finer light; since what age of
romance, after all, could have matched either the state of
his mind or, 'objectively', as they said, the wonder of his
situation? The only difference would have been that,
brandishing his dignities over his head as in a parchment

scroll, he might then – that is in the heroic time – have proceeded downstairs with a drawn sword in his other grasp.

At present, really, the light he had set down on the mantel of the next room would have to figure his sword; which utensil, in the course of a minute, he had taken the requisite number of steps to possess himself of. The door between the rooms was open, and from the second another door opened to a third. These rooms, as he remembered, gave all three upon a common corridor as well, but there was a fourth, beyond them, without issue save through the preceding. To have moved, to have heard his step again, was appreciably a help; though even in recognising this he lingered once more a little by the chimney-piece on which his light had rested. When he next moved, just hesitating where to turn, he found himself considering a circumstance that, after his first and comparatively vague apprehension of it, produced in him the start that often attends some pang of recollection, the violent shock of having ceased happily to forget. He had come into sight of the door in which the brief chain of communication ended and which he now surveyed from the nearer threshold, the one not directly facing it. Placed at some distance to the left of this point, it would have admitted him to the last room of the four, the room without other approach or egress, had it not, to his intimate conviction, been closed *since* his former visitation, the matter probably of a quarter of an hour before. He stared with all his eyes at the wonder of the fact, arrested again where he stood and again holding his breath while he sounded its sense. Surely it had been *subsequently* closed – that is it had been on his previous passage indubitably open!

He took it full in the face that something had happened between – that he couldn't not have noticed before (by which he meant on his original tour of all the rooms that evening) that such a barrier had exceptionally presented itself. He had indeed since that moment undergone an agitation so extraordinary that it might have muddled for him any earlier view; and he tried to convince himself that he might perhaps then have gone into the room and, inadvertently, automatically, on coming out, have drawn the door after him. The difficulty was that this exactly was what he never did; it was against his whole policy, as he might have said, the essence of which was to keep vistas clear. He had them from the first, as he was well aware, quite on the brain: the strange apparition, at the far end of one of them, of his baffled 'prey' (which had become by so sharp an irony so little the term now to apply!) was the form of success his imagination had most cherished, projecting into it always a refinement of beauty. He had known fifty times the start of perception that had afterwards dropped; had fifty times gasped to himself 'There!' under some fond brief hallucination. The house, as the case stood, admirably lent itself; he might wonder at the taste, the native architecture of the particular time, which could rejoice so in the multiplication of doors – the opposite extreme to the modern, the actual almost complete proscription of them; but it had fairly contributed to provoke this obsession of the presence encountered telescopically, as he might say, focussed and studied in diminishing perspective and as by a rest for the elbow.

It was with these considerations that his present attention was charged – they perfectly availed to make what he saw portentous. He *couldn't*, by any lapse, have blocked that aperture; and if he hadn't, if it was unthinkable, why what else was clear but that there had been another agent? Another agent? – he had been catching, as he felt, a moment back, the very breath of him; but when had he been so close as in this simple, this logical, this completely personal act? It was so logical, that is, that one might have *taken* it for personal; yet for what did Brydon take it, he asked himself, while, softly panting, he felt his eyes almost leave their sockets. Ah this time at last they *were*, the two, the opposed projections of him, in presence; and this time, as much as one would, the question of danger loomed. With it rose, as not before, the question of courage – for what he knew the blank face of the door to say to him was 'Show us how much you have!' It stared, it glared back at him with that challenge; it put to him the two alternatives: should he just push it open or not? Oh to have this consciousness was to *think* – and to think, Brydon knew, as he stood there, was, with the lapsing moments, not to have acted! Not to have acted – that was the misery and the pang – was even still not to act; was in fact *all* to feel the thing in another, in a new and terrible way. How long did he pause and how long did he debate? There was presently nothing to measure it; for his vibration had already changed – as just by the effect of its intensity. Shut up there, at bay, defiant, and with the prodigy of the thing palpably proveably *done*, thus giving notice like some stark signboard – under that accession of accent the situation itself had turned; and Brydon at last remarkably made up his mind on what it had turned to.

It had turned altogether to a different admonition; to a supreme hint, for him, of the value of Discretion! This slowly dawned, no doubt – for it could take its time; so perfectly, on his threshold, had he been stayed, so little as yet had he either advanced or retreated. It was the

strangest of all things that now when, by his taking ten
steps and applying his hand to a latch, or even his
shoulder and his knee, if necessary, to a panel, all the
hunger of his prime need might have been met, his high
curiosity crowned, his unrest assuaged – it was amazing,
but it was also exquisite and rare, that insistence should
have, at a touch, quite dropped from him. Discretion –
he jumped at that; and yet not, verily, at such a pitch,
because it saved his nerves or his skin, but because, much
more valuably, it saved the situation. When I say he
'jumped' at it I feel the consonance of this term with the
fact that – at the end indeed of I know not how long – he
did move again, he crossed straight to the door. He
wouldn't touch it – it seemed now that he might *if* he
would: he would only just wait there a little, to show, to
prove, that he wouldn't. He had thus another station,
close to the thin partition by which revelation was
denied him; but with his eyes bent and his hands held
off in a mere intensity of stillness. He listened as if there
had been something to hear, but this attitude, while it
lasted, was his own communication. 'If you won't then –
good: I spare you and I give up. You affect me as by the
appeal positively for pity: you convince me that for
reasons rigid and sublime – what do I know? – we
both of us should have suffered. I respect them then, and,
though moved and privileged as, I believe, it has never
been given to man, I retire, I renounce – never, on my
honour, to try again. So rest for ever – and let *me*!'

That, for Brydon was the deep sense of this last
demonstration – solemn, measured, directed, as he felt
it to be. He brought it to a close, he turned away; and
now verily he knew how deeply he had been stirred. He
retraced his steps, taking up his candle, burnt, he
observed, well-nigh to the socket, and marking again,

lighten it as he would, the distinctness of his footfall; after which, in a moment, he knew himself at the other side of the house. He did here what he had not yet done at these hours – he opened half a casement, one of those in the front, and let in the air of the night; a thing he would have taken at any time previous for a sharp rupture of his spell. His spell was broken now, and it didn't matter – broken by his concession and his surrender, which made it idle henceforth that he should ever come back. The empty street – its other life so marked even by the great lamplit vacancy – was within call, within touch; he stayed there as to be in it again, high above it though he was still perched; he watched as for some comforting common fact, some vulgar human note, the passage of a scavenger or a thief, some night-bird however base. He would have blessed that sign of life; he would have welcomed positively the slow approach of his friend the policeman, whom he had hitherto only sought to avoid, and was not sure that if the patrol had come into sight he mightn't have felt the impulse to get into relation with it, to hail it, on some pretext, from his fourth floor.

The pretext that wouldn't have been too silly or too compromising, the explanation that would have saved his dignity and kept his name, in such a case, out of the papers, was not definite to him: he was so occupied with the thought of recording his Discretion – as an effect of the vow he had just uttered to his intimate adversary – that the importance of this loomed large and something had overtaken all ironically his sense of proportion. If there had been a ladder applied to the front of the house, even one of the vertiginous perpendiculars employed by painters and roofers and sometimes left standing over-night, he would have managed somehow, astride of the window-sill, to compass by outstretched leg and arm that

mode of descent. If there had been some such uncanny
thing as he had found in his room at hotels, a workable
fire-escape in the form of notched cable or a canvas
shoot, he would have availed himself of it as a proof –
well, of his present delicacy. He nursed that sentiment, as
the question stood, a little in vain, and even – at the end
of he scarce knew, once more, how long – found it, as by
the action on his mind of the failure of response of the
outer world, sinking back to vague anguish. It seemed to
him he had waited an age for some stir of the great grim
hush; the life of the town was itself under a spell – so
unnaturally, up and down the whole prospect of known
and rather ugly objects, the blankness and the silence
lasted. Had they ever, he asked himself, the hard-faced
houses, which had begun to look livid in the dim dawn,
had they ever spoken so little to any need of his spirit?
Great builded voids, great crowded stillnesses put on,
often, in the heart of cities, for the small hours, a sort of
sinister mask, and it was of this large collective negation
that Brydon presently became conscious – all the more
that the break of day was, almost incredibly, now at
hand, proving to him what a night he had made of it.

He looked again at his watch, saw what had become of
his time-values (he had taken hours for minutes – not, as
in other tense situations, minutes for hours) and the
strange air of the streets was but the weak, the sullen flush
of a dawn in which everything was still locked up. His
choked appeal from his own open window had been the
sole note of life, and he could but break off at last as for a
worse despair. Yet while so deeply demoralised he was
capable again of an impulse denoting – at least by his
present measure – extraordinary resolution; of retracing
his steps to the spot where he had turned cold with the
extinction of his last pulse of doubt as to there being in

the place another presence than his own. This required
an effort strong enough to sicken him; but he had his
reason, which overmastered for the moment everything
else. There was the whole of the rest of the house to
traverse, and how should he screw himself to that if the
door he had seen closed were at present open? He could
hold to the idea that the closing had practically been for
him an act of mercy, a chance offered him to descend,
depart, get off the ground and never again profane it.
This conception held together, it worked; but what it
meant for him depended now clearly on the amount of
forbearance his recent action, or rather his recent
inaction, had engendered. The image of the 'presence',
whatever it was, waiting there for him to go – this image
had not yet been so concrete for his nerves as when he
stopped short of the point at which certainty would have
come to him. For, with all his resolution, or more exactly
with all his dread, he did stop short – he hung back from
really seeing. The risk was too great and his fear too
definite: it took at this moment an awful specific form.

He knew – yes, as he had never known anything –
that, *should* he see the door open, it would all too abjectly
be the end of him. It would mean that the agent of his
shame – for his shame was the deep abjection – was once
more at large and in general possession; and what glared
him thus in the face was the act that this would
determine for him. It would send him straight about to
the window he had left open, and by that window, be
long ladder and dangling rope as absent as they would, he
saw himself uncontrollably insanely fatally take his way to
the street. The hideous chance of this he at least could
avert; but he could only avert it by recoiling in time from
assurance. He had the whole house to deal with, this fact
was still there; only he now knew that uncertainty alone

could start him. He stole back from where he had checked himself – merely to do so was suddenly like safety – and, making blindly for the greater staircase, left gaping rooms and sounding passages behind. Here was the top of the stairs, with a fine large dim descent and three spacious landings to mark off. His instinct was all for mildness, but his feet were harsh on the floors, and, strangely, when he had in a couple of minutes become aware of this, it counted somehow for help. He couldn't have spoken, the tone of his voice would have scared him, and the common conceit or resource of 'whistling in the dark' (whether literally or figuratively) have appeared basely vulgar; yet he liked none the less to hear himself go, and when he had reached his first landing – taking it all with no rush, but quite steadily – that stage of success drew from him a gasp of relief.

The house, withal, seemed immense, the scale of space again inordinate; the open rooms, to no one of which his eyes deflected, gloomed in their shuttered state like mouths of caverns; only the high skylight that formed the crown of the deep well created for him a medium in which he could advance, but which might have been, for queerness of colour, some watery under-world. He tried to think of something noble, as that his property was really grand, a splendid possession; but this nobleness took the form too of the clear delight with which he was finally to sacrifice it. They might come in now, the builders, the destroyers – they might come as soon as they would. At the end of two flights he had dropped to another zone, and from the middle of the third, with only one more left, he recognised the influence of the lower windows, of half-drawn blinds, of the occasional gleam of street-lamps, of the glazed spaces of the vestibule. This was the bottom of the sea, which

showed an illumination of its own and which he even
saw paved – when at a given moment he drew up to sink
a long look over the banisters – with the marble squares
of his childhood. By that time indubitably he felt, as he
might have said in a commoner cause, better; it had
allowed him to stop and draw breath, and the ease
increased with the sight of the old black-and-white
slabs. But what he most felt was that now surely, with
the element of impunity pulling him as by hard firm
hands, the case was settled for what he might have seen
above had he dared that last look. The closed door,
blessedly remote now, was still closed – and he had only
in short to reach that of the house.

He came down further, he crossed the passage
forming the access to the last flight; and if here again
he stopped an instant it was almost for the sharpness of
the thrill of assured escape. It made him shut his eyes –
which opened again to the straight slope of the remainder of the stairs. Here was impunity still, but impunity
almost excessive; inasmuch as the side-lights and the high
fan-tracery of the entrance were glimmering straight into
the hall; an appearance produced, he the next instant
saw, by the fact that the vestibule gaped wide, that the
hinged halves of the inner door had been thrown far
back. Out of that again the *question* sprang at him,
making his eyes, as he felt, half-start from his head, as
they had done, at the top of the house, before the sign of
the other door. If he had left that one open, hadn't he left
this one closed, and wasn't he now in *most* immediate
presence of some inconceivable occult activity? It was as
sharp, the question, as a knife in his side, but the answer
hung fire still and seemed to lose itself in the vague
darkness to which the thin admitted dawn, glimmering
archwise over the whole outer door, made a semicircular

margin, a cold silvery nimbus that seemed to play a little
as he looked – to shift and expand and contract.

It was as if there had been something within it,
protected by indistinctness and corresponding in extent
with the opaque surface behind, the painted panels of the
last barrier to his escape, of which the key was in his
pocket. The indistinctness mocked him even while he
stared, affected him as somehow shrouding or challeng-
ing certitude, so that after faltering an instant on his step
he let himself go with the sense that here *was* at last
something to meet, to touch, to take, to know –
something all unnatural and dreadful, but to advance
upon which was the condition for him either of
liberation or of supreme defeat. The penumbra, dense
and dark, was the virtual screen of a figure which stood
in it as still as some image erect in a niche or as some
black-vizored sentinel guarding a treasure. Brydon was
to know afterwards, was to recall and make out, the
particular thing he had believed during the rest of his
descent. He saw, in its great grey glimmering margin, the
central vagueness diminish, and he felt it to be taking the
very form toward which, for so many days, the passion of
his curiosity had yearned. It gloomed, it loomed, it was
something, it was somebody, the prodigy of a personal
presence.

Rigid and conscious, spectral yet human, a man of his
own substance and stature waited there to measure
himself with his power to dismay. This only could it
be – this only till he recognised, with his advance, that
what made the face dim was the pair of raised hands that
covered it and in which, so far from being offered in
defiance, it was buried as for dark deprecation. So
Brydon, before him, took him in; with every fact of
him now, in the higher light, hard and acute – his

planted stillness, his vivid truth, his grizzled bent head and white masking hands, his queer actuality of evening-dress, of dangling double eye-glass, of gleaming silk lappet and white linen, of pearl button and gold watch-guard and polished shoe. No portrait by a great modern master could have presented him with more intensity, thrust him out of his frame with more art, as if there had been 'treatment', of the consummate sort, in his every shade and salience. The revulsion, for our friend, had become, before he knew it, immense – this drop, in the act of apprehension, to the sense of his adversary's inscrutable manœuvre. That meaning at least, while he gaped, it offered him; for he could but gape at his other self in this other anguish, gape as a proof that *he*, standing there for the achieved, the enjoyed, the triumphant life, couldn't be faced in his triumph. Wasn't the proof in the splendid covering hands, strong and completely spread? – so spread and so intentional that, in spite of a special verity that surpassed every other, the fact that one of these hands had lost two fingers, which were reduced to stumps, as if accidentally shot away, the face was effectually guarded and saved.

'Saved', though, would it be? – Brydon breathed his wonder till the very impunity of his attitude and the very insistence of his eyes produced, as he felt, a sudden stir which showed the next instant as a deeper portent, which the head raised itself, the betrayal of a braver purpose. The hands, as he looked, began to move, to open; then, as if deciding in a flash, dropped from the face and left it uncovered and presented. Horror, with the sight, had leaped into Brydon's throat, gasping there in a sound he couldn't utter; for the bared identity was too hideous as *his*, and his glare was the passion of his protest. The face, *that* face, Spencer Brydon's? – he searched it still, but looking away from it in dismay and denial, falling straight from his height of sublimity. It was unknown, inconceivable, awful, disconnected from any possibility −! He had been 'sold', he inwardly moaned, stalking such game as this: the presence before him was a presence, the horror within him a horror, but the waste of his nights had been only grotesque and the success of his adventure an irony. Such an identity fitted his at *no* point, made its alternative monstrous. A thousand times yes, as it came upon him nearer now − the face was the face of a stranger. It came upon him nearer now, quite as one of those expanding fantastic images projected by the magic lantern of childhood; for the stranger, whoever he might be, evil, odious, blatant, vulgar, had advanced as for aggression, and he knew himself give ground. Then harder pressed still, sick with the force of his shock, and falling back as under the hot breath and the roused passion of a life larger than his own, a rage of personality before which his own collapsed, he felt the whole vision turn to darkness and his very feet give way. His head went round; he was going; he had gone.

III

What had next brought him back, clearly − though after how long? − was Mrs. Muldoon's voice, coming to him from quite near, from so near that he seemed presently to see her as kneeling on the ground before him while he lay looking up at her; himself not wholly on the ground, but half-raised and upheld − conscious, yes, of tenderness of support and, more particularly, of a head pillowed in extraordinary softness and faintly refreshing fragrance. He considered, he wondered, his wit but half at his service; then another face intervened, bending more directly over him, and he finally knew that Alice Staverton had made her lap an ample and perfect cushion to him, and that she had to this end seated herself on the lowest degree of the staircase, the rest of his long person remaining stretched on his old black and white slabs. They were cold, these marble squares of his youth; but *he* somehow was not, in this rich return of consciousness – the most wonderful hour, little by little, that he had ever known, leaving him, as it did, so gratefully, so abysmally passive, and yet as with a treasure of intelligence waiting all round him for quiet appropriation; dissolved, he might call it, in the air of the place and producing the golden glow of a late autumn afternoon. He had come back, yes – come back from further away than any man but himself had ever travelled; but it was strange how with this sense what he had come back *to* seemed really the great thing, and as if his prodigious journey had been all for the sake of it. Slowly but surely his consciousness grew, his vision of his state thus completing itself: he had been miraculously *carried* back – lifted and carefully borne as from where he had been picked up, the uttermost end of an interminable grey passage. Even with this he was suffered to rest, and what had now brought him to knowledge was the break in the long mild motion.

It had brought him to knowledge, to knowledge – yes, this was the beauty of his state; which came to resemble more and more that of a man who has gone to sleep on some news of a great inheritance, and then, after dreaming it away, after profaning it with matters strange to it, has waked up again to serenity of certitude and has only to lie and watch it grow. This was the drift of his patience – that he had only to let it shine on him. He must moreover, with intermissions, still have been lifted and borne; since why and how else should he have known himself, later on, with the afternoon glow intenser, no longer at the foot of his stairs – situated as these now seemed at that dark other end of his tunnel – but on a deep window-bench of his high saloon, over which had been spread, couch-fashion, a mantle of soft stuff lined with grey fur that was familiar to his eyes and that one of his hands kept fondly feeling as for its pledge of truth. Mrs. Muldoon's face had gone, but the other, the second he had recognised, hung over him in a way that showed how he was still propped and pillowed. He took it all in, and the more he took it the more it seemed to suffice: he was as much at peace as if he had had food and drink. It was the two women who had found him, on Mrs. Muldoon's having plied, at her usual hour, her latch-key – and on her having above all arrived while Miss Staverton still lingered near the house. She had been turning away, all anxiety, from worrying the vain bell-handle – her calculation having been of the hour of the good woman's visit; but the latter, blessedly, had come up while she was still there, and they had entered together. He had then lain, beyond the vestibule, very much as he was lying now – quite, that is, as he appeared to have fallen, but all so wondrously without bruise or gash; only in a depth of stupor. What he most took in, however, at present, with the steadier clearance, was that Alice Staverton had for a long unspeakable moment not doubted he was dead.

'It must have been that I *was*.' He made it out as she held him. 'Yes – I can only have died. You brought me literally to life. Only,' he wondered, his eyes rising to her, 'only, in the name of all the benedictions, how?'

It took her but an instant to bend her face and kiss

him, and something in the manner of it, and in the way her hands clasped and locked his head while he felt the cool charity and virtue of her lips, something in all this beatitude somehow answered everything. 'And now I keep you,' she said.

'Oh keep me, keep me!' he pleaded while her face still hung over him: in response to which it dropped again and stayed close, clingingly close. It was the seal of their situation – of which he tasted the impress for a long blissful moment in silence. But he came back. 'Yet how did you know –?'

'I was uneasy. You were to have come, you remember – and you had sent no word.'

'Yes, I remember – I was to have gone to you at one today.' It caught on to their 'old' life and relation – which were so near and so far. 'I was still out there in my strange darkness – where was it, what was it? I must have stayed there so long.' He could but wonder at the depth and the duration of his swoon.

'Since last night?' she asked with a shade of fear for her possible indiscretion.

'Since this morning – it must have been: the cold dim dawn of today. Where have I been,' he vaguely wailed, 'where have I been?' He felt her hold him close, and it was as if this helped him now to make in all security his mild moan. 'What a long dark day!'

All in her tenderness she had waited a moment. 'In the cold dim dawn?' she quavered.

But he had already gone on piecing together the parts of the whole prodigy. 'As I didn't turn up you came straight –?'

She barely cast about. 'I went first to your hotel – where they told me of your absence. You had dined out last evening and hadn't been back since. But they appeared to know you had been at your club.'

'So you had the idea of *this* –?'

'Of what?' she asked in a moment.

'Well – of what has happened.'

'I believed at least you'd have been here. I've known, all along,' she said, 'that you've been coming.'

'"Known" it –?'

'Well, I've believed it. I said nothing to you after that talk we had a month ago – but I felt sure. I knew you *would*,' she declared.

'That I'd persist, you mean?'

'That you'd see him.'

'Ah but I didn't!' cried Brydon with his long wail. 'There's somebody – an awful beast; whom I brought, too horribly, to bay. But it's not me.'

At this she bent over him again, and her eyes were in his eyes. 'No – it's not you.' And it was as if, while her face hovered, he might have made out in it, hadn't it been so near, some particular meaning blurred by a smile. 'No, thank heaven,' she repeated – 'it's not you! Of course it wasn't to have been.'

'Ah but it *was*,' he gently insisted. And he stared before him now as he had been staring for so many weeks. 'I was to have known myself.'

'You couldn't!' she returned consolingly. And then reverting, and as if to account further for what she had herself done, 'But it wasn't only *that*, that you hadn't been at home,' she went on. 'I waited till the hour at which we had found Mrs. Muldoon that day of my going with you; and she arrived, as I've told you, while, failing to bring any one to the door, I lingered in my despair on the steps. After a little, if she hadn't come, by such a mercy, I should have found means to hunt her up. But it wasn't,' said Alice Staverton, as if once more with her fine intention – 'it wasn't only that.'

His eyes, as he lay, turned back to her. 'What more then?'

She met it, the wonder she had stirred. 'In the cold dim dawn, you say? Well, in the cold dim dawn of this morning I too saw you.'

'*Saw me* –?'

'*Saw him*,' said Alice Staverton. 'It must have been at the same moment.'

He lay an instant taking it in – as if he wished to be quite reasonable. 'At the same moment?'

'Yes – in my dream again, the same one I've named to you. He came back to me. Then I knew it for a sign. He had come to you.'

At this Brydon raised himself; he had to see her better. She helped him when she understood his movement, and he sat up, steadying himself beside her there on the window-bench and with his right hand grasping her left. '*He* didn't come to me.'

'You came to yourself,' she beautifully smiled.

'Ah I've come to myself now – thanks to you, dearest. But this brute, with his awful face – this brute's a black stranger. He's none of *me*, even as I *might* have been,' Brydon sturdily declared.

But she kept the clearness that was like the breath of infallibility. 'Isn't the whole point that you'd have been different?'

He almost scowled for it. 'As different as *that* –?'

Her look again was more beautiful to him than the things of this world. 'Haven't you exactly wanted to know *how* different? So this morning,' she said, 'you appeared to me.'

'Like *him*?'

'A black stranger!'

'Then how did you know it was I?'

'Because, as I told you weeks ago, my mind, my imagination, had worked so over what you might, what you mightn't have been – to show you, you see, how I've thought of you. In the midst of that you came to me – that my wonder might be answered. So I knew,' she went on; 'and believed that, since the question held you too so fast, as you told me that day, you too would see for yourself. And when this morning I again saw I knew it would be because you had – and also then, from the first moment, because you somehow wanted me. *He* seemed to tell me of that. So why,' she strangely smiled, 'shouldn't I like him?'

It brought Spencer Brydon to his feet. 'You "like" that horror –?'

'I *could* have liked him. And to me,' she said, 'he was no horror. I had accepted him.'

'"Accepted" –?' Brydon oddly sounded.

'Before, for the interest of his difference – yes. And as *I* didn't disown him, as *I* knew him – which you at last, confronted with him in his difference, so cruelly didn't, my dear – well, he must have been, you see, less dreadful to me. And it may have pleased him that I pitied him.'

She was beside him on her feet, but still holding his hand – still with her arm supporting him. But though it all brought for him thus a dim light, 'You "pitied" him?' he grudgingly, resentfully asked.

'He has been unhappy; he has been ravaged,' she said.

'And haven't I been unhappy? Am not I – you've only to look at me! – ravaged?'

'Ah I don't say I like him *better*,' she granted after a thought. 'But he's grim, he's worn – and things have happened to him. He doesn't make shift, for sight, with your charming monocle.'

'No' – it struck Brydon: 'I couldn't have sported mine "down-town". They'd have guyed me there.'

'His great convex pince-nez – I saw it, I recognised the kind – is for his poor ruined sight. And his poor right hand –!'

'Ah!' Brydon winced – whether for his proved identity or for his lost fingers. Then, 'He has a million a year,' he lucidly added. 'But he hasn't you.'

'And he isn't – no, he isn't – *you*!' she murmured as he drew her to his breast.

The Stalls of Barchester Cathedral

Montague Rhodes James

This matter began, as far as I am concerned, with the reading of a notice in the obituary section of the *Gentleman's Magazine* for an early year in the nineteenth century:

'On February 26th, at his residence in the Cathedral Close of Barchester, the Venerable John Benwell Haynes, D.D., aged 57, Archdeacon of Sowerbridge and Rector of Pickhill and Candley. He was of ———— College, Cambridge, and where, by talent and assiduity, he commanded the esteem of his seniors; when, at the usual time, he took his first degree, his name stood high in the list of *wranglers*. These academical honors procured for him within a short time a Fellowship of his College. In the year 1873 he received Holy Orders, and was shortly afterwards presented to the perpetual Curacy of Ranxton-sub-Ashe by his friend and patron the late truly venerable Bishop of Lichfield . . . His speedy preferments, first to a Prebend, and subsequently to the dignity of Precentor in the Cathedral of Barchester, form an eloquent testimony to the respect in which he was held and to his eminent qualifications. He succeeded to the Archdeaconry upon the sudden decease of Archdeacon Pulteney in 1810. His sermons, ever conformable to the principles of the

religion and Church which he adorned, displayed in
no ordinary degree, without the least trace of
enthusiasm, the refinement of the scholar united
with the graces of the Christian. Free from sectarian
violence, and informed by the spirit of the truest
charity, they will long dwell in the memories of his
hearers. (Here a further omission.) The productions
of his pen include an able defense of Episcopacy,
which, though often perused by the author of this
tribute to his memory, afford but one additional
instance of the want of liberality and enterprise
which is a too common characteristic of the publish-
ers of our generation. His published works are,
indeed confined to a spirited and elegant version of
the "Argonautica" of Valerius Flaccus, a volume of
"Discourses upon the Several Events in the Life of
Joshua", delivered in his Cathedral, and a number of
the charges which he pronounced at various visita-
tions to the clergy of his Archdeaconry. These are
distinguished by etc., etc. The urbanity and hospitality of the subject of these lines will not readily be
forgotten by those who enjoyed his acquaintance. His
interest in the venerable and awful pile under whose
hoary vault he was so punctual an attendant, and
particularly in the musical portion of its rites, might be
termed filial, and formed a strong and delightful
contrast to the polite indifference displayed by too
many of our Cathedral dignitaries at the present time.'

The final paragraph, after informing us that Dr. Haynes
died a bachelor, says:

'It might have been augured that an existence so
placid and benevolent would have been terminated

in a ripe old age by a dissolution equally gradual and calm. But how unsearchable are the workings of Providence! The peaceful and retired seclusion amid which the honored evening of Dr. Haynes' life was mellowing to its close was destined to be disturbed, nay, shattered, by a tragedy as appalling as it was unexpected. The morning of the 26th of February –'

But perhaps I shall do better to keep back the remainder of the narrative until I have told the circumstances which led up to it. These, as far as they are now accessible, I have derived from another source.

I had read the obituary notice which I have been quoting, quite by chance, along with a great many others of the same period. It had excited some little speculation in my mind, but, beyond thinking that, if I ever had the opportunity of examining the local records of the period indicated, I would try to remember Dr. Haynes, I made no effort to pursue his case.

Quite lately I was cataloguing the manuscripts in the library of the college to which he belonged. I had reached the end of the numbered volumes on the shelves, and I proceeded to ask the librarian whether there were any more books which he thought I ought to include in my description. 'I don't think there are,' he said, 'but we had better come and look at the manuscript class and make sure. Have you time to do that now?' I had time. We went to the library, checked off the manuscripts, and, at the end of our survey arrived at a shelf of which I had seen nothing. Its contents consisted for the most part of sermons, bundles of fragmentary papers, college exercises, *Cyrus*, an epic poem in several cantos, the product of a country clergyman's leisure, mathematical tracts by a deceased professor, and other similar material of a kind with which I am only too familiar. I took brief notes of these. Lastly, there was a tin box, which was pulled out and dusted. Its label, much faded, was thus inscribed: 'Papers of the Ven. Archdeacon Haynes. Bequeathed in 1834 by his sister, Miss Letitia Haynes.'

I knew at once that the name was one which I had somewhere encountered, and could very soon locate it. 'That must be the Archdeacon Haynes who came to a very odd end at Barchester. I've read his obituary in the *Gentleman's Magazine*. May I take the box home? Do you know if there is anything interesting in it?'

The librarian was very willing that I should take the box and examine it at leisure. 'I never looked inside it myself,' he said, 'but I've always been meaning to. I am pretty sure that is the box which our old Master once said ought never to have been accepted by the college. He said that to Martin years ago; and he said also that as long as he had control over the library it should never be opened. Martin told me about it, and said that he wanted terribly to know what was in it; but the Master was librarian, and always kept the box in the lodge, so there was no getting at it in his time, and when he died it was taken away by mistake by his heirs, and only returned a few years ago. I can't think why I haven't opened it; but, as I have to go away from Cambridge this afternoon, you had better have first go at it. I think I can trust you not to publish anything undesirable in our catalogue.'

I took the box home and examined its contents, and thereafter consulted the librarian as to what should be done about publication, and, since I have his leave to make a story out of it, provided I disguise the identity of the people concerned, I will try what can be done.

The materials are, of course, mainly journals and letters. How much I shall quote and how much epitomize must

be determined by considerations of space. The proper
understanding of the situation has necessitated a little – not
very arduous – research, which has been greatly facilitated
by the excellent illustrations and text of the Barchester
volume in Bell's *Cathedral Series*.

When you enter the choir of Barchester Cathedral now,
you pass through a screen of metal and colored marbles,
designed by Sir Gilbert Scott, and find yourself in what I
must call a very bare and odiously furnished place. The
stalls are modern, without canopies. The places of the
dignitaries and the names of the prebends have fortunately
been allowed to survive, and are inscribed on small brass
plates affixed to the stalls. The organ is in the triforium, and
what is seen of the case is Gothic. The reredos and its
surroundings are like every other.

Careful engravings of a hundred years ago show a very
different state of things. The organ is on a massive
classical screen. The stalls are also classical and very
massive. There is a baldacchino of wood over the altar,
with urns upon its corners. Further east is a solid altar
screen, classical in design, of wood, with a pediment, in
which is a triangle surrounded by rays, enclosing certain
Hebrew letters in gold. Cherubs contemplate these.
There is a pulpit with a great sounding-board at the
eastern end of the stalls on the north side, and there is a
black and white marble pavement. Two ladies and a
gentleman are admiring the general effect. From other
sources I gather that the archdeacon's stall then, as now,
was next to the bishop's throne at the south-eastern end
of the stalls. His house almost faces the western part of
the church, and is a fine red-brick building of William
the Third's time.

Here Dr. Haynes, already a mature man, took up his
abode with his sister in the year 1810. The dignity had

long been the object of his wishes, but his predecessor refused to depart until he had attained the age of ninety-two. About a week after he had held a modest festival in celebration of that ninety-second birthday, there came a morning, late in the year, when Dr. Haynes, hurrying cheerfully into his breakfast-room, rubbing his hands and humming a tune, was greeted, and checked in his genial flow of spirits, by the sight of his sister, seated, indeed, in her usual place behind the tea-urn, but bowed forward and sobbing unrestrainedly into her handkerchief. 'What – what is the matter? What bad news?' he began. 'Oh, Johnny, you've not heard? The poor dear archdeacon!' 'The archdeacon, yes? What is it – ill, is he?' 'No, no; they found him on the staircase this morning; it is so shocking.' 'Is it possible! Dear, dear, poor Pulteney! Had there been any seizure?' They don't think so, and that is almost the worst thing about it. It seems to have been all the fault of that stupid maid of theirs, Jane.' Dr. Haynes paused. 'I don't quite understand, Letitia. How was the maid at fault?' 'Why, as far as I can make out, there was a stair-rod missing, and she never mentioned it, and the poor archdeacon set his foot quite on the edge of the step – you know how slippery that oak is – and it seems he must have fallen almost the whole flight and broken his neck. It *is* so sad for poor Miss Pulteney. Of course, they will get rid of the girl at once. I never liked her.' Miss Haynes's grief resumed its sway, but eventually relaxed so far as to permit of her taking some breakfast. Not so her brother, who, after standing in silence before the window for some minutes, left the room, and did not appear again that morning.

I need only add that the careless maid-servant was dismissed forthwith, but that the missing stair-rod was very shortly afterwards found *under* the stair-carpet – an additional proof, if any were needed, of extreme stupidity and carelessness on her part.

For a good many years Dr. Haynes had been marked out by his ability, which seems to have been really considerable, as the likely successor of Archdeacon Pulteney, and no disappointment was in store for him. He was duly installed, and entered with zeal upon the discharge of those functions which are appropriate to one in his position. A considerable space in his journals is occupied with exclamations upon the confusion in which Archdeacon Pulteney had left the business of his office and the documents appertaining to it. Dues upon Wringham and Barnswood have been uncollected for something like twelve years, and are largely irrecoverable; no visitation has been held for seven years; four chancels are almost past mending. The persons deputized by the archdeacon have been nearly as incapable as himself. It was almost a matter for thankfulness that this state of things had not been permitted to continue, and a letter from a friend confirms this view. 'ὁ κατέχων,' it says (in rather cruel allusion to the Second Epistle to the Thessalonians), 'is removed as last. My poor friend! Upon what a scene of confusion will you be entering! I give you my word that, on the last occasion of my crossing his threshold, there was no single paper that he could lay hands upon, no syllable of mine that he could hear, and no fact in connection with my business that he could remember. But now, thanks to a negligent maid and a loose stair-carpet, there is some prospect that necessary business will be transacted without a complete loss alike of voice and temper.' This letter was tucked into a pocket in the cover of one of the diaries.

There can be no doubt of the new archdeacon's zeal and enthusiasm. 'Give me but time to reduce to some

semblance of order the innumerable errors and compli-
cations with which I am confronted, and I shall gladly
and sincerely join with the aged Israelite in the canticle
which too many, I fear, pronounce but with their lips.'
This reflection I find, not in a diary, but a letter; the
doctor's friends seem to have returned his correspondence to his surviving sister. He does not confine
himself, however, to reflections. His investigation of
the rights and duties of his office are very searching
and businesslike, and there is a calculation in one place
that a period of three years will just suffice to set the
business of the Archdeaconry upon a proper footing.
The estimate appears to have been an exact one. For just
three years he is occupied in reforms; but I look in vain at
the end of that time for the promised *Nunc dimittis*. He
has now found a new sphere of activity. Hitherto his
duties have precluded him from more than an occasional
attendance at the Cathedral services. Now he begins to
take an interest in the fabric and the music. Upon his
struggles with the organist, an old gentleman who had
been in office since 1786, I have no time to dwell; they
were not attended with any marked success. More to the
purpose is his sudden growth of enthusiasm for the
Cathedral itself and its furniture. There is a draft of a
letter to Sylvanus Urban (which I do not think was ever
sent) describing the stalls in the choir. As I have said,
these were of fairly late date – of about the year 1700, in
fact.

'The archdeacon's stall, situated at the southeast end,
west of the episcopal throne (now so worthily occupied
by the truly excellent prelate who adorns the See of
Barchester), is distinguished by some curious ornamen-
tation. In addition to the arms of Dean West, by whose

efforts the whole of the internal furniture of the choir was completed, the prayer-desk is terminated at the eastern extremity by three small but remarkable statucttcs in the grotesque manner. One is an exquisitely modeled figure of a cat, whose crouching posture suggests with admirable spirit the suppleness, vigilance, and craft of the redoubted adversary of the genus *Mus*. Opposite to this is a figure seated upon a throne and invested with the attributes of royalty; but it is no earthly monarch whom the carver has sought to portray. His feet are studiously concealed by the long robe in which he is draped: but neither the crown nor the cap which he wears suffice to hide the prickears and curving horns which betray his Tartarean origin; and the hand which rests upon his knee is armed with talons of horrifying length and sharpness. Between these two figures stands a shape muffled in a long mantle. This might at first sight be mistaken for a monk or 'friar of orders gray', for the head is cowled and a knotted cord depends from somewhere about the waist. A slight inspection, however, will lead to a very different conclusion. The knotted cord is quickly seen to be a halter, held by a hand all but concealed within the draperies; while the sunken features and, horrid to relate, the rent flesh upon the cheek-bones, proclaim the King of Terrors. These figures are evidently the production of no unskilled chisel; and should it chance that any of your correspondents are able to throw light upon their origin and significance, my obligations to your valuable miscellany will be largely increased.'

There is more description in the paper, and, seeing that the woodwork in question has now disappeared, it has a considerable interest. A paragraph at the end is worth quoting:

'Some late researches among the Chapter accounts have shown me that the carving of the stalls was not, as was very usually reported, the work of Dutch artists, but was executed by a native of this city or district named Austin. The timber was procured from an oak copse in the vicinity, the property of the Dean and Chapter, known as Holywood. Upon a recent visit to the parish within whose boundaries it is situated, I learned from the aged and truly respectable incumbent that traditions still lingered amongst the inhabitants of the great size and age of the oaks employed to furnish the materials of the stately structure which has been, however imperfectly, described in the above lines. Of one in particular, which stood near the center of the grove, it is remembered that it was known as the Hanging Oak. The propriety of that title is confirmed by the fact that a quantity of human bones was found in the soil about its roots, and that at certain times of the year it was the custom for those who wished to secure a successful issue to their affairs, whether of love or the ordinary business of life, to suspend from its bough small images or puppets rudely fashioned of straw, twigs, or the like rustic materials.'

So much for the archdeacon's archæological investigations. To return to his career as it is to be gathered from his diaries. Those of his first three years of hard and careful work show him throughout in high spirits, and, doubtless, during this time, that reputation for hospitality and urbanity which is mentioned in his obituary notice was well deserved. After that, as time goes on, I see a shadow coming over him – destined to develop into utter blackness – which I cannot but think must have been reflected in his outward demeanor. He commits a good deal of his fears and troubles to his diary; there was no other outlet for them. He was unmarried, and his sister was not always with him. But I am much mistaken if he has told all that he might have told. A series of extracts shall be given:

'*Aug*. 30, 1816. – The days begin to draw in more perceptibly than ever. Now that the Archdeaconry papers are reduced to order, I must find some further employment for the evening hours of autumn and winter. It is a great blow that Letitia's health will not allow her to stay through these months. Why not go on with my "Defence of Episcopacy"? It may be useful.

'*Sept*. 15. – Letitia has left me for Brighton.

'*Oct*. 11. – Candles lit in the choir for the first time at evening prayers. It came as a shock: I find that I absolutely shrink from the dark season.

'*Nov*. 17. – Much struck by the character of the carving on my desk: I do not know that I had ever carefully noticed it before. My attention was called to it by an accident. During the *Magnificat* I was, I regret to say, almost overcome with sleep. My hand was resting on the back of the carved figure of a cat which is the nearest to me of the three figures on the end of my stall. I was not aware of this, for I was not looking in that direction, until I was startled by what seemed a softness, a feeling as of rather rough and coarse fur, a sudden movement, as if the creature were twisting round its head to bite me. I regained complete consciousness in an instant, and I have some idea that I must have uttered a suppressed exclamation, for I noticed that Mr. Treasurer turned his head quickly in my direction. The impression of the unpleasant feeling was so strong that I found myself rubbing my hand upon my surplice. This accident led me to examine the figures after prayers more carefully than I had done before, and I realized for the first time with what skill they are executed.

'*Dec.* 6. – I do indeed miss Letitia's company. The evenings, after I have worked as long as I can at my "Defence", are very trying. The house is too large for a lonely man, and visitors of any kind are too rare. I get an uncomfortable impression when going to my room that there *is* company of some kind. The fact is (I may as well formulate it to myself) that I hear voices. This, I am well aware, is a common symptom of incipient decay of the brain – and I believe that I should be less disquieted than I am if I had any suspicion that this was the cause. I have none – none whatever, nor is there anything in my family history to give color to such an idea. Work, diligent work, and a punctual attention to the duties which fall to me is my best remedy, and I have little doubt that it will prove efficacious.

'*Jan.* 1. – My trouble is, I must confess it, increasing upon me. Last night, upon my return after midnight from the Deanery, I lit my candle to go upstairs. I was nearly at the top when something whispered to me, "Let me wish you a happy New Year." I could not be mistaken: it spoke distinctly and with a peculiar emphasis. Had I dropped my candle, as I all but did, I tremble to think what the consequences must have been. As it was, I managed to get up the last flight, and was quickly in my room with the door locked, and experienced no other disturbance.

'*Jan*. 15. – I had occasion to come downstairs last night to my workroom for my watch, which I had inadvertently left on my table when I went up to bed. I think I was at the top of the last flight when I had a sudden impression of a sharp whisper in my ear, "*Take care.*" I clutched the balusters and naturally looked round at once. Of course, there was nothing. After a moment I went on – it was no good turning back – but I had as nearly as possible fallen: a cat – a large one by the feel of it – slipped between my feet, but again, of course, I saw nothing. It *may* have been the kitchen cat, but I do not think it was.

'*Feb*. 27. – A curious thing last night, which I should like to forget. Perhaps if I put it down here I may see it in its true proportion. I worked in the library from about 9 to 10. The hall and staircase seemed to be unusually full of what I can only call movement without sound: by this I mean that there seemed to be continuous going and coming, and that whenever I ceased writing to listen, or looked out into the hall, the stillness was absolutely unbroken. Nor, in going to my room at an earlier hour than usual – about half-past ten – was I conscious of anything that I could call a noise. It so happened that I had told John to come to my room for the letter to the bishop which I wished to have delivered early in the morning at the Palace. He was to sit up, therefore, and come for it when he heard me retire. This I had for the moment forgotten, though I had remembered to carry the letter with me to my room. But when, as I was winding up my watch, I heard a light tap at the door, and a low voice saying, "May I come in?" (which I most undoubtedly did hear), I recollected the fact, and took up the letter from my dressing-table, saying, "Certainly: come in." No one, however, answered my summons, and it was now that, as I strongly suspect, I committed an error for I opened the door and held the letter out. There was certainly no one at that moment in the passage, but in the instant of my standing there, the door at the end opened and John appeared carrying a candle. I asked him whether he had come to the door earlier; but am satisfied that he had not. I do not like the situation; but although my senses were very much on the alert, and though it was some time before I could sleep, I must allow that I perceived nothing further of an untoward character.'

With the return of spring, when his sister came to live with him for some months, Dr. Haynes's entries became more cheerful, and, indeed, no symptom of depression is discernible until the early part of September, when he was again left alone. And now, indeed, there is evidence that he was incommoded again, and that more pressingly. To this matter I will return in a moment, but I digress to put in a document which, rightly or wrongly, I believe to have a bearing on the thread of the story.

The account-books of Dr. Haynes, preserved along with his other papers, show, from a date but little later than that of his institution as archdeacon, a quarterly payment of £25 to J.L. Nothing could have been made of this, had it stood by itself. But I connect with it a very dirty and ill-written letter, which, like another that I have quoted, was in a pocket in the cover of a diary. Of date or postmark there is no vestige, and the decipherment was not easy. It appears to run:

'Dr. Sr.:
'I have bin expctin to her off you theis last wicks, and not Haveing done so must suppose you have not got mine witch was saying how me and my man had met in with bad times this season all seems to go cross with us on the farm and which way to look for the rent we have no knowledge of it this been the sad case with us if you would have the great [liberality *probably, but the exact spelling defies reproduction*] to send fourty pounds otherwise steps will have to be took which I should not wish. Has you was the Means of my losing my place with Dr. Pulteney I think it is only just what I am asking and you know best what I could say if I was Put to it but I do not wish anything of that unpleasant Nature being one that always wish to have everything Pleasant about me.
                                    'Your obedt Servt,
                                                'JANE LEE.'

About the time at which I suppose this letter to have been written there is, in fact, a payment of £40 to J.L.
  We return to the diary:

  '*Oct*. 22. – At evening prayers, during the Psalms, I had that same experience which I recollect from last year. I was resting my hand on one of the carved figures, as before (I usually avoid that of the cat now), and – I was going to have said – a change came over it, but that seems attributing too much importance to what must, after all, be due to some physical affection in myself: at any rate, the wood seemed to become chilly and soft as if made of wet linen. I can assign the moment at which I became sensible of this. The choir was singing the words (*Set thou an ungodly man to be ruler over him and*) *let Satan stand at his right hand*.

'The whispering in my house was more persistent tonight. I seemed not to be rid of it in my room. I have not noticed this before. A nervous man, which I am not, and hope I am not becoming, would have been much annoyed, if not alarmed, by it. The cat was on the stairs to-night. I think it sits there always. There *is* no kitchen cat.

'*Nov.* 15. – Here again I must note a matter I do not understand. I am much troubled in sleep. No definite image presented itself, but I was pursued by the very vivid impression that wet lips were whispering into my ear with great rapidity and emphasis for some time together. After this, I suppose, I fell asleep, but was awakened with a start by a feeling as if a hand were laid on my shoulder. To my intense alarm I found myself standing at the top of the lowest flight on the first staircase. The moon was shining brightly enough through the large window to let me see that there was a large cat on the second or third step. I can make no comment. I crept up to bed again, I do not know how. Yes, mine is a heavy burden. [Then follows a line or two which has been scratched out. I fancy I read something like "acted for the best".]'

Not long after this it is evident to me that the archdeacon's firmness began to give way under the pressure of these phenomena. I omit as unnecessarily

painful and distressing the ejaculations and prayers which,
in the months of December and January, appear for the
first time and become increasingly frequent. Throughout
this time, however, he is obstinate in clinging to his post.
Why he did not plead ill-health and take refuge at Bath or
Brighton I cannot tell; my impression is that it would
have done him no good; that he was a man who, if he had
confessed himself beaten by the annoyances, would have
succumbed at once, and that he was conscious of this. He
did seek to palliate them by inviting visitors to his house.
The result he has noted in this fashion:

'*Jan.* 7. – I have prevailed on my cousin Allen to
give me a few days, and he is to occupy the chamber
next to mine.

'*Jan.* 8. – A still night. Allen slept well, but
complained of the wind. My own experiences
were as before: still whispering and whispering:
what is it that he wants to say?

'*Jan.* 9. – Allen thinks this is a very noisy house.
He thinks, too, that my cat is an unusually large and
fine specimen, but very wild.

'*Jan.* 10. – Allen and I in the library until 11. He
left me twice to see what the maids were doing in
the hall: returning the second time he told me he
had seen one of them passing through the door at
the end of the passage, and said if his wife were here
she would soon get them into better order. I asked
him what colored dress the maid wore; he said gray
or white. I supposed it would be so.

'*Jan.* 11. – Allen left me to-day. I must be firm.'

These words, *I must be firm*, occur again and again on
subsequent days; sometimes they are the only entry. In

these cases they are in an unusually large hand, and dug into the paper in a way which must have broken the pen that wrote them.

Apparently the archdeacon's friends did not remark any change in his behavior, and this gives me a high idea of his courage and determination. The diary tells us nothing more than I have indicated of the last days of his life. The end of it all must be told in the polished language of the obituary notice:

'The morning of the 26th of February was cold and tempestuous. At an early hour the servants had occasion to go into the front hall of the residence occupied by the lamented subject of these lines. What was their horror upon observing the form of their beloved and respected master lying upon the landing of the principal staircase in an attitude which inspired the gravest fears. Assistance was procured, and an universal consternation was experienced upon the discovery that he had been the object of a brutal and a murderous attack. The vertebral column was fractured in more than one place. This might have been the result of a fall: it appeared that the stair-carpet was loosened at one point. But, in addition to this, there were injuries inflicted upon the eyes, nose and mouth, as if by the agency of some savage animal, which, dreadful to relate, rendered those features unrecognizable. The vital spark was, it is needless to add, completely extinct, and had been so, upon the testimony of respectable medical authorities, for several hours. The author or authors of this mysterious outrage are alike buried in mystery, and the most active

conjecture has hitherto failed to suggest a solution
of the melancholy problem afforded by this
appalling occurrence.'

The writer goes on to reflect upon the probability that
the writings of Mr. Shelley, Lord Byron, and M. Voltaire
may have been instrumental in bringing about the
disaster, and concludes by hoping, somewhat vaguely,
that this event may 'operate as an example to the rising
generation'; but this portion of his remarks need not be
quoted in full.

I had already formed the conclusion that Dr. Haynes
was responsible for the death of Dr. Pulteney. But the
incident connected with the carved figure of death upon
the archdeacon's stall was a very perplexing feature. The
conjecture that it had been cut out of the wood of the
Hanging Oak was not difficult, but seemed impossible to
substantiate. However, I paid a visit to Barchester, partly
with the view of finding out whether there were any
relics of the woodwork to be heard of. I was introduced
by one of the canons to the curator of the local museum,
who was, my friend said, more likely to be able to give
me information on the point than any one else. I told this
gentleman of the description of certain carved figures
and arms formerly on the stalls, and asked whether any
had survived. He was able to show me the arms of Dean
West and some other fragments. These, he said, had been
got from an old resident, who had also once owned a
figure – perhaps one of those which I was inquiring for.
There was a very odd thing about that figure, he said.
'The old man who had it told me that he picked it up in a
wood-yard, whence he had obtained the still extant
pieces, and had taken it home for his children. On the
way home he was fiddling about with it and it came in

two in his hands, and a bit of paper dropped out. This he picked up and, just noticing that there was writing on it, put it into his pocket, and subsequently into a vase on his mantel-piece. I was at his house not very long ago, and happened to pick up the vase and turn it over to see whether there were any marks on it, and the paper fell into my hand. The old man, on my handing it to him, told me the story I have told you, and said I might keep the paper. It was crumpled and rather torn, so I have mounted it on a card, which I have here. If you can tell me what it means I shall be very glad, and also, I may say, a good deal surprised.'

He gave me the card. The paper was quite legibly inscribed in an old hand, and this is what was on it:

'When I grew in the Wood
I was water'd wth Blood
Now in the Church I stand
Who that touches me with his Hand
If a Bloody hand be bear
I councell him to be ware
Lest he be fetcht away
Whether by night or day,
But chiefly when the wind blows high
In a night of February.'

'This I dreampt, 26 Febr. A° 1699. JOHN AUSTIN.'

'I suppose it is a charm or a spell: wouldn't you call it something of that kind?' said the curator.

'Yes,' I said, 'I suppose one might. What became of the figure in which it was concealed?'

'Oh, I forgot,' said he. 'The old man told me it was so ugly and frightened his children so much that he burnt it.'

The Phantom 'Rickshaw

Rudyard Kipling

One of the few advantages that India has over England is a great Knowability. After five years' service a man is directly or indirectly acquainted with the two or three hundred Civilians in his Province, all the Messes of ten or twelve Regiments and Batteries, and some fifteen hundred other people of the non-official caste. In ten years his knowledge should be doubled, and at the end of twenty he knows, or knows something about, every Englishman in the Empire, and may travel anywhere and everywhere without paying hotel bills.

Globe-trotters who expect entertainment as a right have, even within my memory, blunted this open-heartedness, but none the less to-day, if you belong to the Inner Circle and are neither a Bear nor a Black Sheep, all houses are open to you, and our small world is very, very kind and helpful.

Rickett of Kamartha stayed with Polder of Kumaon some fifteen years ago. He meant to stay two nights, but was knocked down by rheumatic fever, and for six weeks disorganized Polder's establishment, stopped Polder's work, and nearly died in Polder's bedroom. Polder behaves as though he had been placed under eternal obligation by Rickett, and yearly sends the little Ricketts a box of presents and toys. It is the same everywhere. The men who do not take the trouble to conceal from you their opinion that you are an incompetent ass, and women who blacken your character and misunderstand your wife's amusements, will work themselves to the bone in your behalf if you fall sick or into serious trouble.

Heatherlegh, the Doctor, kept, in addition to his regular practice, a hospital on his private account – an arrangement of loose boxes for Incurables, his friend called it – but it was really a sort of fitting-up shed for craft that had been damaged by stress of weather. The weather in India is often sultry, and since the tale of bricks is always a fixed quantity, and the only liberty allowed is permission to work overtime and get no thanks, men occasionally break down and become as mixed as the metaphors in this sentence.

Heatherlegh is the dearest doctor that ever was, and his invariable prescription to all his patients is, 'Lie low, go slow, and keep cool.' He says that more men are killed by overwork than the importance of this world justifies. He maintains that overwork slew Pansay, who died under his hands about three years ago. He has, of course, the right to speak authoritatively, and he laughs at my theory that there was a crack in Pansay's head and a little bit of the Dark World came through and pressed him to death. 'Pansay went off the handle,' says Heatherlegh, 'after the stimulus of long leave Home. He may or he may not have behaved like a blackguard to Mrs. Keith-Wessington. My notion is that the work of the Katabundi Settlement ran him off his legs, and that he took to brooding and making much of an ordinary P. & O. flirtation. He certainly was engaged to Miss Mannering, and she certainly broke off the engagement. Then he took a feverish chill and all that nonsense about ghosts developed. Overwork started his illness, kept it alight, and killed him, poor devil. Write him off to the System – one man to take the work of two and a half men.'

I do not believe this. I used to sit up with Pansay sometimes when Heatherlegh was called out to patients, and I happened to be within claim. The man would make me most unhappy by describing in a low, even voice, the procession that was always passing at the bottom of his bed. He had a sick man's command of language. When he recovered I suggested that he should write out the whole affair from beginning to end, knowing that ink might assist him to ease his mind. When little boys have learned a new bad word they are never happy till they have chalked it up on a door. And this also is Literature.

He was in a high fever while he was writing, and the blood-and-thunder Magazine diction he adopted did not calm him. Two months afterward he was reported fit for duty, but in spite of the fact that he was urgently needed to help an undermanned Commission stagger through a deficit, he preferred to die; vowing at the last that he was hag-ridden. I got his manuscript before he died, and this is his version of the affair, dated 1885:—

My doctor tells me that I need rest and change of air. It is not improbable that I shall get both ere long – rest that neither the red-coated messenger nor the midday gun can break, and change of air far beyond that which any homeward-bound steamer can give me. In the meantime I am resolved to stay where I am; and, in flat defiance of my doctor's orders, to take all the world into my confidence. You shall learn for yourselves the precise nature of my malady; and shall, too, judge for yourselves whether any man born of woman on this weary earth was ever so tormented as I.

Speaking now as a condemned criminal might speak ere the drop bolts are drawn, my story, wild and hideously improbable as it may appear, demands at least attention. That it will ever receive credence I utterly disbelieve. Two months ago I should have scouted as mad or drunk the man who had dared tell me the like. Two months ago I was the happiest man in India. To-day, from Peshawar to the sea, there is no one more wretched. My doctor and I are the only two who know this. His explanation is, that my brain, digestion, and eyesight are all slightly affected; giving rise to my frequent and persistent 'delusions'. Delusions, indeed! I call him a fool; but he attends me still with the same unwearied smile, the same bland professional manner, the same neatly trimmed red whiskers, till I begin to suspect that I am an ungrateful, evil-tempered invalid. But you shall judge for yourselves. Three years ago it was my fortune – my great misfortune – to sail from Gravesend to Bombay, on return from long leave, with one Agnes Keith-Wessington, wife of an officer on the Bombay side. It does not in the least concern you to know what manner of woman she was. Be content with the knowledge that, ere the voyage had ended, both she and I were desperately and unreasoningly in love with one another. Heaven knows that I can make the admission now without one particle of vanity. In matters of this sort there is always one who gives and another who accepts. From the first day of our ill-omened attachment, I was conscious that Agnes's passion was a stronger, a more dominant, and – if I may use the expression – a purer sentiment than mine. Whether she recognized the fact then, I do not know. Afterward it was bitterly plain to both of us.

Arrived at Bombay in the spring of the year, we went our respective ways to meet no more for the next three or four months, when my leave and her love took us both to Simla. There we spent the season together; and there my fire of straw burned itself out to a pitiful end with the closing year. I attempt no excuse. I make no apology. Mrs. Wessington had given up much for my sake, and was prepared to give up all. From my own lips, in August, 1882, she learned that I was sick of her presence, tired of her company, and weary of the sound of her voice. Ninety-nine women out of a hundred would have wearied of me as I wearied of them; seventy-five of that number would have promptly avenged themselves by active and obtrusive flirtation with other men. Mrs. Wessington was the hundredth. On her neither my openly expressed aversion nor the cutting brutalities with which I garnished our interviews had the least effect.

'Jack, darling!' was her one eternal cuckoo cry: 'I'm sure it's all a mistake – a hideous mistake; and we'll be good friends again some day. *Please* forgive me, Jack, dear.'

I was the offender, and I knew it. That knowledge transformed my pity into passive endurance, and, eventually, into blind hate – the same instinct, I suppose, which prompts a man to savagely stamp on the spider he has but half killed. And with this hate in my bosom the season of 1882 came to an end.

Next year we met again at Simla – she with her monotonous face and timid attempts at reconciliation, and I with loathing of her in every fibre of my frame. Several times I could not avoid meeting her alone; and on each occasion her words were identically the same. Still the unreasoning wail that it was all a 'mistake'; and still the hope of eventually 'making friends'. I might have seen, had I cared to look, that that hope only was keeping her alive. She grew more wan and thin month

by month. You will agree with me, at least, that such
conduct would have driven any one to despair. It was
uncalled for; childish; unwomanly. I maintain that she
was much to blame. And again, sometimes, in the black,
fever-stricken night-watches, I have begun to think that
I might have been a little kinder to her. But that really *is* a
'delusion'. I could not have continued pretending to
love her when I didn't; could I? It would have been
unfair to us both.

Last year we met again – on the same terms as
before. The same weary appeals, and the same curt
answers from my lips. At least I would make her see
how wholly wrong and hopeless were her attempts at
resuming the old relationship. As the season wore on,
we fell apart – that is to say, she found it difficult to
meet me, for I had other and more absorbing interests
to attend to. When I think it over quietly in my sick-
room, the season of 1884 seems a confused nightmare
wherein light and shade were fantastically intermingled
– my courtship of little Kitty Mannering; my hopes,
doubts, and fears; our long rides together; my trembling avowal of attachment; her reply; and now and
again a vision of a white face flitting by in the
'rickshaw with the black and white liveries I once
watched for so earnestly; the wave of Mrs. Wessington's gloved hand; and, when she met me alone,
which was but seldom, the irksome monotony of her
appeal. I loved Kitty Mannering; honestly, heartily
loved her, and with my love for her grew my hatred
for Agnes. In August Kitty and I were engaged. The
next day I met those accursed 'magpie' *jhampanies* at
the back of Jakko, and, moved by some passing
sentiment of pity, stopped to tell Mrs. Wessington
everything. She knew it already.

'So I hear you're engaged, Jack, dear.' Then, without a moment's pause:– 'I'm sure it's all a mistake – a hideous mistake. We shall be as good friends some day, Jack, as we ever were.'

My answer might have made even a man wince. It cut the dying woman before me like the blow of a whip. 'Please forgive me, Jack; I didn't mean to make you angry; but it's true, it's true!'

And Mrs. Wessington broke down completely. I turned away and left her to finish her journey in peace, feeling, but only for a moment or two, that I had been an unutterably mean hound. I looked back, and saw that she had turned her 'rickshaw with the idea, I suppose, of overtaking me.

The scene and its surroundings were photographed on my memory. The rain-swept sky (we were at the end of the wet weather), the sodden, dingy pines, the muddy road, and the black powder-riven cliffs formed a gloomy background against which the black and white liveries of the *jhampanies*, the yellow-panelled 'rickshaw and Mrs. Wessington's down-bowed golden head stood out clearly. She was holding her handkerchief in her left hand and was leaning back exhausted against the 'rickshaw cushions. I turned my horse up a by-path near the Sanjowlie Reservoir and literally ran away. Once I fancied I heard a faint call of 'Jack!'. This may have been imagination. I never stopped to verify it. Ten minutes later I came across Kitty on horseback; and, in the delight of a long ride with her, forgot all about the interview.

A week later Mrs. Wessington died, and the inexpressible burden of her existence was removed from my life. I went Plainsward perfectly happy. Before three months were over I had forgotten all about her, except that at times the discovery of some of her old letters reminded me unpleasantly of our bygone relationship. By January I had disinterred what was left of our correspondence from among my scattered belongings and had burned it. At the beginning of April of this year, 1885, I was at Simla – semi-deserted Simla – once more, and was deep in lover's talks and walks with Kitty. It was decided that we should be married at the end of June. You will understand, therefore, that, loving Kitty as I did, I am not saying too much when I pronounce myself to have been, at that time, the happiest man in India.

Fourteen delightful days passed almost before I noticed their flight. Then, aroused to the sense of what was proper among mortals circumstanced as we were, I pointed out to Kitty that an engagement ring was the outward and visible sign of her dignity as an engaged girl; and that she must forthwith come to Hamilton's to be measured for one. Up to that moment, I give you my word, we had completely forgotten so trivial a matter. To Hamilton's we accordingly went on the 15th of April, 1885. Remember that – whatever my doctor may say to the contrary – I was then in perfect health, enjoying a well-balanced mind and an *absolutely* tranquil spirit. Kitty and I entered Hamilton's shop together, and there, regardless of the order of affairs, I measured Kitty for the ring in the presence of the amused assistant. The ring was a sapphire with two diamonds. We then rode out down the slope that leads to the Combermere Bridge and Peliti's shop.

While my Waler was cautiously feeling his way over the loose shale, and Kitty was laughing and chattering at my side – while all Simla, that is to say as much of it as had then come from the Plains, was grouped round the Reading-room and Peliti's veranda, – I was aware that some one, apparently at a vast distance, was calling me by

my Christian name. It struck me that I had heard the
voice before, but when and where I could not at once
determine. In the short space it took to cover the road
between the path from Hamilton's shop and the first
plank of the Combermere Bridge I had thought over half
a dozen people who might have committed such a
solecism, and had eventually decided that it must have
been some singing in my ears. Immediately opposite
Peliti's shop my eye was arrested by the sight of four
jhampanies in 'magpie' livery, pulling a yellow-panelled,
cheap, bazaar 'rickshaw. In a moment my mind flew
back to the previous season and Mrs. Wessington with a
sense of irritation and disgust. Was it not enough that the
woman was dead and done with, without her black and
white servitors reappearing to spoil the day's happiness?
Whoever employed them now I thought I would call
upon, and ask as a personal favor to change her
jhampanies' livery. I would hire the men myself, and, if
necessary, buy their coats from off their backs. It is
impossible to say here what a flood of undesirable
memories their presence evoked.

'Kitty,' I cried, 'there are poor Mrs. Wessington's
jhampanies turned up again! I wonder who has them
now?'

Kitty had known Mrs. Wessington slightly last season,
and had always been interested in the sickly woman.

'What? Where?' she asked. 'I can't see them anywhere.'

Even as she spoke, her horse, swerving from a laden
mule, threw himself directly in front of the advancing
'rickshaw. I had scarcely time to utter a word of
warning, when, to my unutterable horror, horse and
rider passed *through* men and carriage as if they had been
thin air.

'What's the matter?' cried Kitty; 'what made you call out so foolishly, Jack? If I *am* engaged I don't want all creation to know about it. There was lots of space between the mule and the veranda; and, if you think I can't ride – There!'

Whereupon wilful Kitty set off, her dainty little head in the air, at a hand-gallop in the direction of the Bandstand; fully expecting, as she herself afterward told me, that I should follow her. What was the matter? Nothing indeed. Either that I was mad or drunk, or that Simla was haunted with devils. I reined in my impatient cob, and turned round. The 'rickshaw had turned too, and now stood immediately facing me, near the left railing of the Combermere Bridge.

'Jack! Jack, darling!' (There was no mistake about the words this time: they rang through my brain as if they had been shouted in my ear.) 'It's some hideous mistake, I'm sure. *Please* forgive me, Jack, and let's be friends again.'

The 'rickshaw-hood had fallen back, and inside, as I hope and pray daily for the death I dread by night, sat Mrs. Keith-Wessington, handkerchief in hand, and golden head bowed on her breast.

How long I stared motionless I do not know. Finally; I was aroused by my syce taking the Waler's bridle and asking whether I was ill. From the horrible to the commonplace is but a step. I tumbled off my horse and dashed, half fainting, into Peliti's for a glass of cherry-brandy. There two or three couples were gathered round the coffee-tables discussing the gossip of the day. Their trivialities were more comforting to me just then than the consolations of religion could have been. I plunged into the midst of the conversation at once; chatted, laughed, and jested with a face (when I caught a glimpse of it in a mirror) as white and drawn as that of a corpse. Three or four men noticed my condition; and, evidently setting it down to the results of over-many pegs, charitably endeavored to draw me apart from the rest of the loungers. But I refused to be led away. I wanted the company of my kind – as a child rushes into the midst of the dinner-party after a fright in the dark. I must have talked for about ten minutes or so, though it seemed an eternity to me, when I heard Kitty's clear voice outside inquiring for me. In another minute she had entered the shop, prepared to roundly upbraid me for failing so signally in my duties. Something in my face stopped her.

'Why, Jack,' she cried, 'what *have* you been doing? What *has* happened? Are you ill?' Thus driven into a direct lie, I said that the sun had been a little too much for me. It was close upon five o'clock of a cloudy April afternoon, and the sun had been hidden all day. I saw my mistake as soon as the words were out of my mouth: attempted to recover it; blundered hopelessly and followed Kitty in a regal rage, out of doors, amid the smiles of my acquaintances. I made some excuse (I have forgotten what) on the score of my feeling faint; and cantered away to my hotel, leaving Kitty to finish the ride by herself.

In my room I sat down and tried calmly to reason out the matter. Here was I, Theobald Jack Pansay, a well-educated Bengal Civilian in the year of grace 1885, presumably sane, certainly healthy, driven in terror from my sweetheart's side by the apparition of a woman who had been dead and buried eight months ago. These were facts that I could not blink. Nothing was further from my thought than any memory of Mrs. Wessington when Kitty and I left Hamilton's shop. Nothing was more utterly commonplace than the stretch of wall opposite

Peliti's. It was broad daylight. The road was full of people; and yet here, look you, in defiance of every law of probability, in direct outrage of Nature's ordinance, there had appeared to me a face from the grave.

Kitty's Arab had gone *through* the 'rickshaw: so that my first hope that some woman marvellously like Mrs. Wessington had hired the carriage and the coolies with their old livery was lost. Again and again I went round this tread-mill of thought; and again and again gave up baffled and in despair. The voice was as inexplicable as the apparition. I had originally some wild notion of confiding it all to Kitty; of begging her to marry me at once; and in her arms defying the ghostly occupant of the 'rickshaw. 'After all,' I argued, 'the presence of the 'rickshaw is in itself enough to prove the existence of a spectral illusion. One may see ghosts of men and women, but surely never of coolies and carriages. The whole thing is absurd. Fancy the ghost of a hillman!'

Next morning I sent a penitent note to Kitty, imploring her to overlook my strange conduct of the previous afternoon. My Divinity was still very wroth, and a personal apology was necessary. I explained, with a fluency born of night-long pondering over a falsehood, that I had been attacked with a sudden palpitation of the heart – the result of indigestion. This eminently practical solution had its effect; and Kitty and I rode out that afternoon with the shadow of my first lie dividing us.

Nothing would please her save a canter round Jakko. With my nerves still unstrung from the previous night I feebly protested against the notion, suggesting Observatory Hill, Jutogh, the Boileaugunge road – anything rather than the Jakko round. Kitty was angry and a little hurt: so I yielded from fear of provoking further

misunderstanding, and we set out together toward Chota
Simla. We walked a greater part of the way, and,
according to our custom, cantered from a mile or so
below the Convent to the stretch of level road by the
Sanjowlie Reservoir. The wretched horses appeared to
fly, and my heart beat quicker and quicker as we neared
the crest of the ascent. My mind had been full of
Mrs. Wessington all the afternoon; and every inch of
the Jakko road bore witness to our old-time walks and
talks. The bowlders were full of it; the pines sang it aloud
overhead; the rain-fed torrents giggled and chuckled
unseen over the shameful story; and the wind in my ears
chanted the iniquity aloud.

As a fitting climax, in the middle of the level men call
the Ladies' Mile the Horror was awaiting me. No other
'rickshaw was in sight – only the four black and white
jhampanies, the yellow-panelled carriage, and the golden
head of the woman within – all apparently just as I had
left them eight months and one fortnight ago! For an
instant I fancied that Kitty *must* see what I saw – we were
so marvellously sympathetic in all things. Her next words
undeceived me – 'Not a soul in sight! Come along, Jack,
and I'll race you to the Reservoir buildings!' Her wiry
little Arab was off like a bird, my Waler following close
behind, and in this order we dashed under the cliffs. Half
a minute brought us within fifty yards of the 'rickshaw. I
pulled my Waler and fell back a little. The 'rickshaw was
directly in the middle of the road; and once more the
Arab passed through it, my horse following. 'Jack! Jack
dear! *Please* forgive me,' rang with a wail in my ears, and,
after an interval:– 'It's all a mistake, a hideous mistake!'

I spurred my horse like a man possessed. When I
turned my head at the Reservoir works, the black and
white liveries were still waiting – patiently waiting –

under the gray hillside, and the wind brought me a
mocking echo of the words I had just heard. Kitty
bantered me a good deal on my silence throughout the
remainder of the ride. I had been talking up till then
wildly and at random. To save my life I could not speak
afterward naturally, and from Sanjowlie to the Church
wisely held my tongue.

I was to dine with the Mannerings that night, and had
barely time to canter home to dress. On the road to
Elysium Hill I overheard two men talking together in the
dusk – 'It's a curious thing,' said one, 'how completely all
trace of it disappeared. You know my wife was insanely
fond of the woman (never could see anything in her
myself), and wanted me to pick up her old 'rickshaw and
coolies if they were to be got for love or money. Morbid
sort of fancy I call it; but I've got to do what *Memsahib*
tells me. Would you believe that the man she hired it
from tells me that all four of the men – they were
brothers – died of cholera on the way to Hardwar, poor
devils; and the 'rickshaw has been broken up by the man
himself. Told me he never used a dead *Memsahib*'s
'rickshaw. Spoiled his luck. Queer notion, wasn't it?
Fancy poor little Mrs. Wessington spoiling any one's
luck except her own!' I laughed aloud at this point; and
my laugh jarred on me as I uttered it. So there *were* ghosts
of 'rickshaws after all, and ghostly employments in the
other world! How much did Mrs. Wessington give her
men? What were their hours? Where did they go?

And for visible answer to my last question I saw the
infernal Thing blocking my path in the twilight. The
dead travel fast, and by short cuts unknown to ordinary
coolies. I laughed aloud a second time and checked my
laughter suddenly, for I was afraid I was going mad. Mad
to a certain extent I must have been, for I recollect that I

reined in my horse at the head of the 'rickshaw, and politely wished Mrs. Wessington 'Good evening'. Her answer was one I knew only too well. I listened to the end; and replied that I had heard it all before, but should be delighted if she had anything further to say. Some malignant devil stronger than I must have entered into me that evening, for I have a dim recollection of talking the commonplaces of the day for five minutes to the Thing in front of me.

'Mad as a hatter, poor devil – or drunk. Max, try and get him to come home.'

Surely *that* was not Mrs. Wessington's voice! The two men had overheard me speaking to the empty air, and had returned to look after me. They were very kind and considerate, and from their words evidently gathered that I was extremely drunk. I thanked them confusedly and cantered away to my hotel, there changed, and arrived at the Mannerings' ten minutes late. I pleaded the darkness of the night as an excuse; was rebuked by Kitty for my unlover-like tardiness; and sat down.

The conversation had already become general; and under cover of it, I was addressing some tender small talk to my sweetheart, when I was aware that at the further end of the table a short red-whiskered man was describing, with much broidery, his encounter with a mad unknown that evening.

A few sentences convinced me that he was repeating the incident of half an hour ago. In the middle of the story he looked round for applause, as professional story-tellers do, caught my eye and straightway collapsed. There was a moment's awkward silence, and the red-whiskered man muttered something to the effect that he had 'forgotten the rest', thereby sacrificing a reputation as a good story-teller which he had built up for six seasons past. I blessed him from the bottom of my heart, and – went on with my fish.

In the fulness of time that dinner came to an end; and with genuine regret I tore myself away from Kitty – as certain as I was of my own existence that it would be waiting for me outside the door. The red-whiskered man, who had been introduced to me as Dr. Heatherlegh of Simla, volunteered to bear me company as far as our roads lay together. I accepted his offer with gratitude.

My instinct had not deceived me. It lay in readiness in the Mall, and, in what seemed devilish mockery of our ways, with a lighted head-lamp. The red-whiskered man went to the point at once, in a manner that showed he had been thinking over it all dinner time.

'I say, Pansay, what the deuce was the matter with you this evening on the Elysium road?' The suddenness of the question wrenched an answer from me before I was aware.

'That!' said I, pointing to It.

'*That* may be either *D. T.* or Eyes for aught I know. Now you don't liquor. I saw as much at dinner, so it can't be *D. T.* There's nothing whatever where you're pointing, though you're sweating and trembling with fright like a scared pony. Therefore, I conclude that it's Eyes. And I ought to understand all about them. Come along home with me. I'm on the Blessington lower road.'

To my intense delight, the 'rickshaw, instead of waiting for us, kept about twenty yards ahead – and this, too, whether we walked, trotted, or cantered. In the course of that long night ride I had told my companion almost as much as I have told you here.

'Well, you've spoiled one of the best tales I've ever laid tongue to,' said he, 'but I'll forgive you for the sake of what you've gone through. Now come home and do what I tell you; and when I've cured you, young man, let this be a lesson to you to steer clear of women and indigestible food till the day of your death.'

The 'rickshaw kept steady in front; and my red-whiskered friend seemed to derive great pleasure from my account of its exact whereabouts.

'Eyes, Pansay – all Eyes, Brain, and Stomach. And the greatest of these three is Stomach. You've too much conceited Brain, too little Stomach, and thoroughly unhealthy Eyes. Get your Stomach straight and the rest follows. And all that's French for a liver pill. I'll take sole medical charge of you from this hour! for you're too interesting a phenomenon to be passed over.'

By this time we were deep in the shadow of the Blessington lower road and the 'rickshaw came to a dead stop under a pine-clad, overhanging shale cliff. Instinctively I halted too, giving my reason. Heatherlegh rapped out an oath.

'Now, if you think I'm going to spend a cold night on the hillside for the sake of a Stomach-*cum*-Brain-*cum*-Eye illusion . . . Lord, ha' mercy! What's that?'

There was a muffled report, a blinding smother of dust just in front of us, a crack, the noise of rent boughs, and about ten yards of the cliff-side – pines, undergrowth, and all – slid down into the road below, completely blocking it up. The uprooted trees swayed and tottered for a moment like drunken giants in the gloom, and then fell prone among their fellows with a thunderous crash. Our two horses stood motionless and sweating with fear. As soon as the rattle of falling earth and stone had subsided, my companion muttered:– 'Man, if we'd gone forward we should have been ten feet deep in our graves by now. "There are more things in heaven and earth" . . . Come home, Pansay, and thank God. I want a peg badly.'

We retraced our way over the Church Ridge, and I arrived at Dr. Heatherlegh's house shortly after midnight.

His attempts toward my cure commenced almost immediately, and for a week I never left his side. Many a time in the course of that week did I bless the good fortune which had thrown me in contact with Simla's best and kindest doctor. Day by day my spirits grew lighter and more equable. Day by day, too, I became more and more inclined to fall in with Heatherlegh's 'spectral illusion' theory, implicating eyes, brain, and stomach. I wrote to Kitty, telling her that a slight sprain caused by a fall from my horse kept me indoors for a few days; and that I should be recovered before she had time to regret my absence.

Heatherlegh's treatment was simple to a degree. It consisted of liver pills, cold-water baths, and strong exercise, taken in the dusk or at early dawn – for, as he sagely observed:– 'A man with a sprained ankle doesn't walk a dozen miles a day, and your young woman might be wondering if she saw you.'

At the end of the week, after much examination of pupil and pulse, and strict injunctions as to diet and pedestrianism, Heatherlegh dismissed me as brusquely as he had taken charge of me. Here is his parting benediction:– 'Man, I certify to your mental cure, and that's as much as to say I've cured most of your bodily ailments. Now, get your traps out of this as soon as you can; and be off to make love to Miss Kitty.'

I was endeavoring to express my thanks for his kindness. He cut me short.

'Don't think I did this because I like you. I gather that you've behaved like a blackguard all through. But, all the same, you're a phenomenon, and as queer a phenomenon as you are a blackguard. No!' – checking me a second time – 'not a rupee, please. Go out and see if you can find the eyes-brain-and-stomach business again. I'll give you a lakh for each time you see it.'

Half an hour later I was in the Mannerings' drawing-room with Kitty – drunk with the intoxication of present happiness and the foreknowledge that I should never more be troubled with Its hideous presence. Strong in the sense of my new-found security, I proposed a ride at once; and, by preference, a canter round Jakko.

Never had I felt so well, so overladen with vitality and mere animal spirits, as I did on the afternoon of the 30th of April. Kitty was delighted at the change in my appearance, and complimented me on it in her delightfully frank and outspoken manner. We left the Mannerings' house together, laughing and talking, and cantered along the Chota Simla road as of old.

I was in haste to reach the Sanjowlie Reservoir and there make my assurance doubly sure. The horses did their best, but seemed all too slow to my impatient mind. Kitty was astonished at my boisterousness. 'Why, Jack!' she cried at last, 'you are behaving like a child. What are you doing?'

We were just below the Convent, and from sheer wantonness I was making my Waler plunge and curvet across the road as I tickled it with the loop of my riding-whip.

'Doing?' I answered; 'nothing, dear. That's just it. If you'd been doing nothing for a week except lie up, you'd be as riotous as I.

' "Singing and murmuring in your feastful mirth,
          Joying to feel yourself alive;
     Lord over Nature, Lord of the visible Earth.
     Lord of the senses five." '

My quotation was hardly out of my lips before we had rounded the corner above the Convent; and a few yards further on could see across to Sanjowlie. In the centre of the level road stood the black and white liveries, the yellow-panelled 'rickshaw, and Mrs. Keith-Wessington. I pulled up, looked, rubbed my eyes, and, I believe, must have said something. The next thing I knew was that I was lying face downward on the road, with Kitty kneeling above me in tears.

'Has it gone, child?' I gasped. Kitty only wept more bitterly.

'Has what gone, Jack dear? what does it all mean? There must be a mistake somewhere, Jack. A hideous mistake.' Her last words brought me to my feet – mad – raving for the time being.

'Yes, there *is* a mistake somewhere,' I repeated, 'a hideous mistake. Come and look at It.'

I have an indistinct idea that I dragged Kitty by the wrist along the road up to where It stood, and implored her for pity's sake to speak to It; to tell It that we were betrothed; that neither Death nor Hell could break the tie between us: and Kitty only knows how much more to the same effect. Now and again I appealed passionately to the Terror in the 'rickshaw to bear witness to all I had said, and to release me from a torture that was killing me.

As I talked I suppose I must have told Kitty of my old
relations with Mrs. Wessington, for I saw her listen
intently with white face and blazing eyes.

'Thank you, Mr. Pansay,' she said, 'that's *quite*
enough. *Syce ghora láo.*'

The syces, impassive as Orientals always are, had
come up with the recaptured horses; and as Kitty
sprang into her saddle I caught hold of the bridle,
entreating her to hear me out and forgive. My answer
was the cut of her riding-whip across my face from
mouth to eye, and a word or two of farewell that even
now I cannot write down. So I judged, and judged
rightly, that Kitty knew all; and I staggered back to the
side of the 'rickshaw. My face was cut and bleeding, and
the blow of the riding-whip had raised a livid blue
wheal on it. I had no self-respect. Just then, Heatherlegh, who must have been following Kitty and me at a
distance, cantered up.

'Doctor,' I said, pointing to my face, 'here's Miss
Mannering's signature to my order of dismissal and . . .
I'll thank you for that lakh as soon as convenient.'

Heatherlegh's face, even in my abject misery, moved
me to laughter.

'I'll stake my professional reputation' – he began.

'Don't be a fool,' I whispered. 'I've lost my life's
happiness and you'd better take me home.'

As I spoke the 'rickshaw was gone. Then I lost all
knowledge of what was passing. The crest of Jakko
seemed to heave and roll like the crest of a cloud and
fall in upon me.

Seven days later (on the 7th of May, that is to say) I
was aware that I was lying in Heatherlegh's room as weak
as a little child. Heatherlegh was watching me intently
from behind the papers on his writing-table. His first

words were not encouraging; but I was too far spent to
be much moved by them.

'Here's Miss Kitty has sent back your letters. You
corresponded a good deal, you young people. Here's a
packet that looks like a ring, and a cheerful sort of a note
from Mannering Papa, which I've taken the liberty of
reading and burning. The old gentleman's not pleased
with you.'

'And Kitty?' I asked dully.

'Rather more drawn than her father, from what she
says. By the same token you must have been letting out
any number of queer reminiscences just before I met
you. Says that a man who would have behaved to a
woman as you did to Mrs. Wessington ought to kill
himself out of sheer pity for his kind. She's a hot-headed
little virago, your mash. Will have it too that you were
suffering from *D. T.* when that row on the Jakko road
turned up. Says she'll die before she ever speaks to you
again.'

I groaned and turned over on the other side.

'Now you've got your choice, my friend. This
engagement has to be broken off; and the Mannerings
don't want to be too hard on you. Was it broken
through *D. T.* or epileptic fits? Sorry I can't offer you
a better exchange unless you'd prefer hereditary insanity.
Say the word and I'll tell 'em it's fits. All Simla knows
about that scene on the Ladies' Mile. Come! I'll give you
five minutes to think over it.'

During those five minutes I believe that I explored
thoroughly the lowest circles of the Inferno which it is
permitted man to tread on earth. And at the same time I
myself was watching myself faltering through the dark
labyrinths of doubt, misery, and utter despair. I wondered, as Heatherlegh in his chair might have wondered,

which dreadful alternative I should adopt. Presently I heard myself answering in a voice that I hardly recognized, –

'They're confoundedly particular about morality in these parts. Give 'em fits, Heatherlegh, and my love. Now let me sleep a bit longer.'

Then my two selves joined, and it was only I (half-crazed, devil-driven I) that tossed in my bed, tracing step by step the history of the past month.

'But I am in Simla,' I kept repeating to myself. 'I, Jack Pansay, am in Simla, and there are no ghosts here. It's unreasonable of that woman to pretend there are. Why couldn't Agnes have left me alone? I never did her any harm. It might just as well have been me as Agnes. Only I'd never have come back on purpose to kill *her*. Why can't I be left alone – left alone and happy?'

It was high noon when I first awoke; and the sun was low in the sky before I slept – slept as the tortured criminal sleeps on his rack, too worn to feel further pain.

Next day I could not leave my bed. Heatherlegh told me in the morning that he had received an answer from Mr. Mannering, and that, thanks to his (Heatherlegh's) friendly offices, the story of my affliction had travelled through the length and breadth of Simla, where I was on all sides much pitied.

'And that's rather more than you deserve,' he concluded pleasantly, 'though the Lord knows you've been going through a pretty severe mill. Never mind; we'll cure you yet, you perverse phenomenon.'

I declined firmly to be cured. 'You've been much too good to me already, old man,' said I; 'but I don't think I need trouble you further.'

In my heart I knew that nothing Heatherlegh could do would lighten the burden that had been laid upon me.

With that knowledge came also a sense of hopeless, impotent rebellion against the unreasonableness of it all. There were scores of men no better than I whose punishments had at least been reserved for another world; and I felt that it was bitterly, cruelly unfair that I alone should have been singled out for so hideous a fate. This mood would in time give place to another where it seemed that the 'rickshaw and I were the only realities in a world of shadows; that Kitty was a ghost; that Mannering, Heatherlegh, and all the other men and women I knew were all ghosts; and the great, gray hills themselves but vain shadows devised to torture me. From mood to mood I tossed backward and forward for seven weary days; my body growing daily stronger and stronger, until the bedroom looking-glass told me that I had returned to every-day life and was as other men once more. Curiously enough my face showed no signs of the struggle I had gone through. It was pale indeed, but as expressionless and commonplace as ever. I had expected some permanent alteration – visible evidence of the disease that was eating me away. I found nothing.

On the 15th of May I left Heatherlegh's house at eleven o'clock in the morning; and the instinct of the bachelor drove me to the Club. There I found that every man knew my story as told by Heatherlegh, and was, in clumsy fashion, abnormally kind and attentive. Nevertheless I recognized that for the rest of my natural life I should be among but not of my fellows; and I envied very bitterly indeed the laughing coolies on the Mall below. I lunched at the Club, and at four o'clock wandered aimlessly down the Mall in the vague hope of meeting Kitty. Close to the Band-stand the black and white liveries joined me; and I heard Mrs. Wessington's old appeal at my side. I had been expecting this ever since I came out; and was only surprised at her delay. The phantom 'rickshaw and I went side by side along the Chota Simla road in silence. Close to the bazaar, Kitty and a man on horseback overtook and passed us. For any sign she gave I might have been a dog in the road. She did not even pay me the compliment of quickening her pace; though the rainy afternoon had served for an excuse.

So Kitty and her companion, and I and my ghostly Light-o'-Love, crept round Jakko in couples. The road was streaming with water; the pines dripped like roof-pipes on the rocks below, and the air was full of fine, driving rain. Two or three times I found myself saying to myself almost aloud:– 'I'm Jack Pansay on leave at Simla – *at Simla*! Every-day, ordinary Simla. I mustn't forget that – I mustn't forget that.' Then I would try to recollect some of the gossip I had heard at the Club: the prices of So-and-So's horses – anything, in fact, that related to the workaday Anglo-Indian world I knew so well. I even repeated the multiplication-table rapidly to myself, to make quite sure that I was not taking leave of my senses. It gave me much comfort; and must have prevented my hearing Mrs. Wessington for a time.

Once more I wearily climbed the Convent slope and entered the level road. Here Kitty and the man started off at a canter, and I was left alone with Mrs. Wessington. 'Agnes,' said I, 'will you put back your hood and tell me what it all means?' The hood dropped noiselessly, and I was face to face with my dead and buried mistress. She was wearing the dress in which I had last seen her alive; carried the same tiny handkerchief in her right hand; and the same card-case in her left. (A woman eight months dead with a card-case!) I had to pin myself down to the multiplication-table, and to set both hands on the stone parapet of the road, to assure myself that that at least was real.

'Agnes,' I repeated, 'for pity's sake tell me what it all means.' Mrs. Wessington leaned forward, with that odd quick turn of the head I used to know so well, and spoke.

If my story had not already so madly overleaped the bounds of all human belief I should apologize to you now. As I know that no one – no, not even Kitty, for whom it is written as some sort of justification of my conduct – will believe me, I will go on. Mrs. Wessington spoke and I walked with her from the Sanjowlie road to the turning below the Commander-in-Chief's house, as I might walk by the side of any living woman's 'rickshaw, deep in conversation. The second and most tormenting of my moods of sickness had suddenly laid hold upon me, and, like the Prince in Tennyson's poem, 'I seemed to move amid a world of ghosts.' There had been a garden-party at the Commander-in-Chief's, and we two joined the crowd of homeward-bound folk. As I saw them then it seemed that *they* were the shadows – impalpable fantastic shadows – that divided for Mrs. Wessington's 'rickshaw to pass through. What we said during the course of that weird interview I cannot – indeed, I dare not – tell. Heatherlegh's comment would have been a short laugh and a remark that I had been 'mashing a brain-eye-and-stomach chimera'. It was a ghastly and yet in some indefinable way a marvellously dear experience. Could it be possible, I wondered, that I was in this life to woo a second time the woman I had killed by my own neglect and cruelty?

I met Kitty on the homeward road – a shadow among shadows.

If I were to describe all the incidents of the next
fortnight in their order, my story would never come to
an end; and your patience would be exhausted. Morning
after morning and evening after evening the ghostly
'rickshaw and I used to wander through Simla together.
Wherever I went there the four black and white liveries
followed me and bore me company to and from my
hotel. At the Theatre I found them amid the crowd of
yelling *jhampanies*; outside the Club veranda, after a long
evening of whist; at the Birthday Ball, waiting patiently
for my reappearance; and in broad daylight when I went
calling. Save that it cast no shadow, the 'rickshaw was in
every respect as real to look upon as one of wood and
iron. More than once, indeed, I have had to check
myself from warning some hard-riding friend against
cantering over it. More than once I have walked down
the Mall deep in conversation with Mrs. Wessington to
the unspeakable amazement of the passers-by.

Before I had been out and about a week I learned that
the 'fit' theory had been discarded in favor of insanity.
However, I made no change in my mode of life. I called,
rode, and dined out as freely as ever. I had a passion for
the society of my kind which I had never felt before; I
hungered to be among the realities of life; and at the same
time I felt vaguely unhappy when I had been separated
too long from my ghostly companion. It would be
almost impossible to describe my varying moods from
the 15th of May up to to-day.

The presence of the 'rickshaw filled me by turns with
horror, blind fear, a dim sort of pleasure, and utter
despair. I dared not leave Simla; and I knew that my
stay there was killing me. I knew, moreover, that it was
my destiny to die slowly and a little every day. My only
anxiety was to get the penance over as quietly as might

be. Alternately I hungered for a sight of Kitty and watched her outrageous flirtations with my successor – to speak more accurately, my successors – with amused interest. She was as much out of my life as I was out of hers. By day I wandered with Mrs. Wessington almost content. By night I implored Heaven to let me return to the world as I used to know it. Above all these varying moods lay the sensation of dull, numbing wonder that the Seen and the Unseen should mingle so strangely on this earth to hound one poor soul to its grave.

August 27. – Heatherlegh has been indefatigable in his attendance on me; and only yesterday told me that I ought to send in an application for sick leave. An application to escape the company of a phantom! A request that the Government would graciously permit me to get rid of five ghosts and an airy 'rickshaw by going to England! Heatherlegh's proposition moved me almost to hysterical laughter. I told him that I should await the end quietly at Simla; and I am sure that the end is not far off. Believe me that I dread its advent more than any word can say; and I torture myself nightly with a thousand speculations as to the manner of my death.

Shall I die in my bed decently and as an English gentleman should die; or, in one last walk on the Mall, will my soul be wrenched from me to take its place forever and ever by the side of that ghastly phantasm? Shall I return to my old lost allegiance in the next world, or shall I meet Agnes, loathing her and bound to her side through all eternity? Shall we two hover over the scene of our lives till the end of Time? As the day of my death draws nearer, the intense horror that all living flesh feels toward escaped spirits from beyond the grave grows more and more powerful. It is an awful thing to go down quick among the dead with scarcely one-half of your life completed. It is a thousand times more awful to wait as I do in your midst, for I know not what unimaginable terror. Pity me, at least on the score of my 'delusion', for I know you will never believe what I have written here. Yet as surely as ever a man was done to death by the Powers of Darkness, I am that man.

In justice, too, pity her. For as surely as ever woman was killed by man, I killed Mrs. Wessington. And the last portion of my punishment is even now upon me.

The Quincunx

Walter de la Mare

On opening the door and in no good humour at so late
and apparently timid a summons I fancied at first glance
that the figure standing at the foot of the four garden
steps was my old and precious friend Henry Beverley –
unexpectedly back in England again. At the moment
there was only obscured moonlight to see him by and he
stood rather hummocked up and partly in shadow. If it
hadn't been Henry one might have supposed *this* visitor
was the least bit apprehensive.

'Bless my heart!' I began – delight mingled with
astonishment – then paused. For at that moment a thin
straight shaft of moonlight had penetrated between the
chimney stacks and shone clear into the face of a far less
welcome visitor – Henry's brother, Walter.

I knew he was living rather dangerously near, but had
kept this knowledge to myself. And now in his miniature
car, which even by moonlight I noticed would have
been none the worse off for a dusting, he had not only
routed me out, but was also almost supplicating me to
spend the night with him – in a house which had, I heard
with surprise, been left to him by an eccentric aunt,
recently deceased, about two miles away.

Seldom can moonshine have flattered a more haggard
face. Had he no sedatives? Sedatives or not, how could I
refuse him? Besides, he was Henry's brother. So having
slowly climbed the stairs again, with a lingering glance of

regret at the book I had been reading, I extinguished my green glass-shaded lamp (the reflex effects of which may have given poor Walter an additional pallor), pushed myself into a great-coat, and jammed a hat on my head, and in a moment or so we were on our way, with a din resembling that of a van-load of empty biscuit-tins. I am something of a snob about cars, though I prefer them borrowed. It was monstrous to be shattering the silence of night with so fiendish a noise, all the blinds down and every house asleep. 'On such a night . . .' And as for poor Walter's gear-changing – heaven help the hardiest of Army lorries!

'Of course,' he repeated, 'it would be as easy as chalk to dismiss the whole affair as pure fancy. But that being so, how could it possibly have stood up to repeated rational experiment? Don't think I really care a hoot concerning the "ghostly" side of this business. Not in the least. I am out for the definite, I am dog-tired, and I am all but beaten.'

Beaten, I thought to myself not without some little satisfaction. But beaten by what, by whom?

'Beaten?' I shouted through the din. We were turning a corner.

'You see – for very good reasons I don't doubt – my late old aunt could not away with me. She found precious little indeed to please her in my complete side of the family – not even the saintly Henry. My own idea is that all along she had been in love with my father. And I, thank heaven, don't take after *him*. There is a limit to imbecile unpracticality, and,' he dragged at his hand-brake, having failed to notice earlier a cross-road immediately in front of us under a lamp-post.

'She never intended me to inherit so much as a copper bed-warmer, or the leg of a chair. Irony was not her strong point – otherwise I think she might have bequeathed me her wheezy old harmonium. I always had Salvation Army leanings. But Fate was too quick for her, and the *house* came to *me* – to me, the least beloved of us all. At first, merely out of curiosity, I decided to live in the place, but there's living and living, and there's deucedly little cash.'

'But she must have . . .' I began.

'Of course she must have,' he broke in. 'Even an old misbegotten aunt-by-marriage can't have lived on air. She *had* money; it was meant, I believe – she mistrusted lawyers – for my cousin Arthur and the rest. And' – he accelerated – 'I am as certain as instinct and common sense can make me that there are stocks, shares, documents, all sorts of riff-raff, and *possibly* private papers, hidden away somewhere in her own old house. Where she lived for donkeys' years. Where I am trying to exist now.' He shot me a rapid glance rather like an animal looking round.

'In short, I am treasure-hunting; and there's inter-ference. That's the situation, naked and a bit ashamed of it. But the really odd thing is – she knows it.'

'Knows what?'

'She knows I am after the loot,' he answered, 'and cannot rest in her grave. Wait till you have seen her face, my dear feller, then scoff, if you can. She was a secretive old cat and she hated bipeds. Soured, I suppose. And she never stirred out of her frowsy seclusion for nearly twenty years. And *now* – her poor Arthur left gasping – she is fully aware of what her old enemy is at. Of every move I make. It's a fight to – well, past "the death" between us. And *she* is winning.'

'But my dear Beverley . . .' I began.

'My dear Rubbish,' he said, squeezing my arm. 'I am as sane as you are – only a little jarred and piqued. Besides

I am not dragging you out at this time of night on evidence as vague as all that. I'll give you positive proof. *Perhaps* you shall have some pickings!'

We came at length to a standstill before his antiquated inheritance. An ugly awkward house, it abutted sheer on to the pavement. A lamp shone palely on its walls, its few beautifully-proportioned windows; and it seemed, if possible, a little quieter behind its two bay-trees – more resigned to night – than even its darkened neighbours were. We went in, and Beverley with a candle led the way down a long corridor.

'The front room,' he said, pointing back, 'is the dining-room. There's nothing there – simply the odour of fifty years of lavendered cocoon; fifty years of seed-cake and sherry. But even to sit on there alone, munching one's plebeian bread-and-cheese, is to become conscious – well, is to become conscious. In *here*, though, is the mystery.'

We stood together in the doorway, peering beneath our candle into a low-pitched, silent, strangely-attractive and old-fashioned parlour. Everything within it from its tarnished cornice to its little old parrot-green beaded footstool was the accumulated record of one mind, one curious, solitary human individuality. And it was as silent and unresponsive as a clam.

'What a fascinating old lady!' I said.

'Yes,' he answered in a low voice. 'There she is!'

I turned in some confusion, but only to survey the oval painted portrait of Miss Lemieux herself. She was little, narrow, black-mittened, straight-nosed, becurled; and she encountered my eyes so keenly, darkly, tenaciously, that I began to sympathize with both antagonists.

'Now this is the problem,' he said, making a long nose at it and turning his back on the picture. 'I searched the house last week from garret to cellar and intended to begin again. The doubloons, the diamonds, the documents are here somewhere, and as R.L.S. said in another connection, If she's *Hide*, then I'm *Seek*. On Sunday I came in here to have a think. I sat there, in that little chair, by the window staring vacantly in front of me, when presently in some indescribable fashion I became aware that I was being stared *at*.' He touched the picture hanging up on its nail behind him with the back of his head. 'So we sat, she and I, for about ten solid minutes, I should think. Then I tired of it. I turned the old Sphinx to the wall again, and went out. A little after nine I came back. There wasn't a whisper in the house. I had my supper, sat thinking again, and fell asleep. When I awoke, I was shivering cold.

'I got up immediately, went out, shut the dining-room door with my face towards this one, went up a few stairs, my hand on the banister, and then vaguely distinguished by the shadow that it was ajar. I was certain I had shut it. I came back to investigate. And saw – *her*.' He nodded towards the picture again. 'I had left her as I supposed in disgrace, face to the wall: she had, it seemed, righted herself. But this may have been a mistake. So I deliberately took the old lady down from her ancestral nail and hid her peculiarly intent physiognomy in that cushion:

> *Dare not wild heart, grow fonder!*
> *Lie there, my love, lie yonder!*

Then I locked windows, shutters and door and went to bed.

He paused and glanced at me out of the corner of his eye. 'I dare say it sounds absurd,' he said, 'but next morning when I came down I dawdled about for at least half an hour before I felt impelled to open this door. The chair was empty. She was "up"!'

'Any charwoman?' I ventured.

'On Tuesdays, Fridays and at the week-ends,' he said.

'You are *sure* of it?' He looked vaguely at me, tired and protesting. 'Oh, yes,' he said, 'last night's was my fifth experiment.'

'And you want me . . .?'

'Just to stay here and keep awake. I *can't*. That's all. Theorizing is charming – and easy. But the nights are short. You don't appear to have a vestige of nerves. Tell me who is playing this odd trick on me! Mind you, I *know* already. Somehow it's this old She who is responsible, who is manœuvring. But how?'

I exchanged a long look with him – with the cold blue gaze in the tired pallid face; then glanced back at the portrait. Into those small, feminine, dauntless, ink-black eyes.

He turned away with a vague shrug of his shoulders. 'Of course,' he said coldly, 'if you'd rather *not*.'

'Go to bed, Beverley,' I answered, 'I'll watch till morning . . . We are, you say, absolutely alone in this house?'

'Physically, yes; absolutely alone. Apart from *that* old cat there is not so much as a mouse stirring.'

'No rival heirs? No positive claimants?'

'None,' he said. 'Though, of course . . . It's only – my aunt.' We stood in silence.

'Well, good night, then; but honestly I am rather sceptical.'

He raised his eyebrows, faintly smiled – something between derision and relief, lifted the portrait from the wall, carried it across the room, leaned it against the armchair in the corner. 'There!' he muttered. 'Check! you old witch! . . . It's very good of you. I'm sick of it. It has relieved me immensely. Good night!' He went out quickly, leaving the door ajar. I heard him go up the stairs, and presently another door, above, slammed.

I thought at first how few candles stood between me and darkness. It was now too late to look for more. Not, of course, that I felt any real alarm. Only a kind of curiosity – that might perhaps leap into something a little different when off its guard! I sat down and began meditating on Beverley, his nerves, his pretences, his venomous hatred of . . . well, what? Of a dozen things. But beneath all this I was gazing in imagination straight into the pictured eyes of a little old lady, already months in her grave.

The hours passed slowly. I changed from chair to chair – 't.e.g.' gift-books, albums of fading photographs, old picture magazines. I pored over some marvellously fine needlework, and a few enchanting little water-colours. My candle languished; its successor was kindled. I was already become cold, dull, sleepy and depressed, when in the extreme silence I heard the rustling of silk. Screening my candle with my hand, I sat far back into my old yellow silk sofa. Slow, shuffling footsteps were softly drawing near. I fixed my eyes on the door. A pale light beyond it began stealing inwards, mingling with mine. Faint shadows zigzagged across the low ceiling. The door opened wider, stealthily, and a most extraordinary figure discovered itself, and paused on the threshold.

For an instant I hesitated, my heart thumping at my ribs; and then I recognized, beneath a fantastic disguise, no less tangible an interloper than Beverley himself. He was in his pyjamas; his feet were bare; but thrown over his shoulders was an immense old cashmere shawl that might have once graced Prince Albert's Exhibition in the Crystal Palace. And his head was swathed in what seemed to be some preposterous eighteenth-century night-gear. The other hand outstretched, he was carrying his candlestick a few inches from his face, so that I could see his every feature with exquisite distinctness beneath his voluminous head-dress.

It was Beverley right enough – I noticed even a very faint likeness to his brother, Henry, unperceived till then. His pale eyes were wide and glassily open. But behind this face, as from out of a mask – keen, wizened, immensely absorbed – peered his little old enemy's unmistakable visage. Miss Lemieux's! He was in a profound sleep, there could be no doubt of that. So closely burned the flame to his entranced face I feared he would presently be setting himself on fire. He moved past me slowly with an odd jerky constricted gait, something like that of a very old lady. He was muttering, too, in an aggrieved queer faraway voice. Stooping with a sigh, he picked up the picture; returned across the room; drew up and mounted the parrot-green footstool, and groped for the nail in the wall not six inches above his head. At length he succeeded in finding it; sighed again and turned meditatively; his voice rising a little shrill, as if in altercation. Once more he passed me by unheeded and came to a standstill; for a moment, peering through curtains a few inches withdrawn, into the starry garden. Whether the odd consciousness within him was aware of *me*, I cannot say. Those unspeculating, window-like eyes turned themselves full on me crouched there in the yellow sofa. The voice fell to a whisper; I think that he hastened a little. He went out and closed the door, and I'd swear my candle solemnly ducked when his was gone!

I huddled myself up again, pulled up a rug and woke again to find the candle-stub still alight in the dusk of dawn – battling faintly together to illuminate the little vivid painted face leaning from the wall. And that, on my soul – showing not a symptom of fatigue – in this delicate Spring daybreak, appeared more redoubtable than ever!

I sat for a time undecided what to be doing, what even to be thinking. And then, as if impelled by an inspiration, I got up, took down again the trophy from its nail, and with my pen-knife gently prized open the back of its gilded frame. Surely, it had occurred to me, it could not be mere vanity, mere caprice or rancour that could take such posthumous pains as this! Perhaps, ever dimly aware of it as he was in his waking moments, merely the pressing sub-conscious thought of the portrait had lured Beverley out of his sleep. Perhaps . . .

I levered up the thin dusty wood; there was nothing beneath. I drew it out from the frame. And then was revealed, lightly pasted on the back, a scrap of yellowed paper, scrawled with five crosses in the form of a quincunx. In one corner of this was a large, capital Italianate 'P'. And beneath a central cross was drawn a small square. Here was the veritable answer before my eyes. How very like old age to doubt its memory even on such a crucial matter as this. Or was it only doubt?

For whose guidance had this odd quincunx been intended? Not for Walter Beverley's – that was certain. Standing even where I was I could see between the curtains the orchard behind the house pale in the dawn with its fast-fading fruit-blossom. There, then, lay concealed the old lady's secret 'hoard'. We had but to exercise a little thought, a little dexterity and precaution; and Beverley had won.

And then suddenly, impetuously, rose up in my mind an obstinate distaste of meddling in the matter. Surely, if there is any such thing as desecration, *this* would be desecration.

I glanced at the old attentive face looking up at me, the face of one who had, it seemed, so easily betrayed her most intimate secret, and in some unaccountable fashion there now appeared to be something quite other than mere malice in its concentration – a hint even of the apprehension and entreaty of a heart too proud to let them break through the veil of the small black fearless eyes.

I determined to say nothing to Beverley; watch yet again. And – if I could find a chance – dig by myself, and make sure of the actual contents of Miss Lemieux's treasury before surrendering it to her greedy, insensitive heir. So once more the portrait was re-hung on its rusty nail.

He was prepared for my scepticism; but he did not believe, I think, that I had kept unceasing watch.

'I am sure,' he said repeatedly, 'absolutely sure that what I told you last night has recurred repeatedly. How can you disprove my positive personal evidence by this one failure – by a million negatives? It is you who are to blame – that tough, bigoted *common* sense of yours.'

I willingly accepted his verdict and offered to watch once more. He seemed content. And yet by his incessant restlessness and the curious questioning dismay that haunted his face I felt that his nocturnal guest was troubling and fretting him more than ever.

It was a charming old house, intensely still, intensely self-centred, as it were. One could imagine how unwelcome the summons of death would be in such a familiar home on earth as this. I wandered, and brooded, and searched in the garden: and found at length without much difficulty my 'quincunx'. The orchard was full of fruit trees, cherry, plum, apple: but the five towering pear trees, their rusty crusted bloom not yet all shed, might become at once unmistakably conspicuous to anyone in possession of the clue; though not till then. But how hopeless a contest had my friend set himself with no guidance, and one spade, against such an aunt, against such an orchard!

Evening began to narrow in the skies. My host and I sat together over a bottle of wine. Much as he seemed to cling to my company, I knew he longed for solitude. Twice he rose, as if urged by some sudden caprice to leave me, and twice he sat down again in even deeper constraint.

But soon after midnight I was left once more to my vigil. This time I forestalled his uneasy errand and replaced the portrait myself. I rested awhile; then, when it was still very early morning, I ventured out into the mists of the garden to find a spade. But I had foolishly forgotten on which side of the mid-most tree Miss Lemieux had set her tell-tale square. So back again I was compelled to go, and this time I took the flimsy, precious scrap of paper with me. Somewhere a waning moon was shedding light, for the mists of the garden were white as milk and the trees stood phantom-like above the drenched grasses.

I pinned the paper to the mid-most pear tree, measured out with my eye a rough narrow oblong a foot or two from the trunk and drove the rusty spade into the soil.

At that instant I heard a cautious minute sound behind me. I turned and once more confronted the pathetic bedizened figure of the night before. It was fumbling with the handle of the window, holding aloft a candle. The window opened at length and Beverley stood peering out into the garden. I fancied even a shrill voice called. And then without hesitation, with the same odd, shuffling gait Beverley stepped out on to the dew-damped gravel path and came groping towards me. He stood there, quietly watching me, not two paces distant; and so utterly still was the twilight that his candle-flame burned slim and unwavering in the mist, shedding its small, pale light on leaf-sprouting flowerless bough and dewdrop, and upon that strange set haunted face.

I could not gaze very long into the grey unseeing eyes. His lips moved. His fingers oddly bent twitched. And then he turned from me. The large pale eyes wandered to my spade, to the untrampled grasses, and finally, suddenly fixed their gaze on the tiny square of fading paper. He uttered a little cry, shrill and desperate, and stretched out his hand to snatch it. But I was too quick for him. I doubled it up, thrust it into my pocket and stepped back beneath the trees. Then, intensely anxious not to awaken the sleep-walker, I drew back with extreme caution, foot by foot, but soon perceived that, however gradual my retreat, he was no less patiently driving me into a little shrubbery where there would be no chance of eluding him, and we should stand confronting one another face to face.

I could not risk a struggle in such circumstances. A wave of heat spread over me; I tripped, and then ran as fast as I could back to the house, hastened into the room and threw myself down in my old yellow sleeping-place, closing my eyes as if I were lost to the world. Presently followed the same faint footfall near at hand. Then, hearing no sound at all, and supposing he had passed, I cautiously opened my eyes – only to gaze once more unfathomably deep into his, stooping in the light of his candle, searching my face insanely, entreatingly – I cannot describe with how profound a disquietude.

I did not stir, until, with a deep sigh, like that of a tired-out child, he turned from me and left the room.

I waited awhile, my thoughts like a disturbed nest of ants. What should I do? To whom was my duty obligatory? – to Beverley, feverishly hunting for wealth not his (even if it existed) by else than earthly right; or to this unquiet spirit – that I could not but believe had taken possession of him – struggling, only *I* knew how bravely, piteously and desperately, to keep secret – what? Not mere money or valuables or private papers or personal secrets which might lie hidden beneath the shadow of the pear tree. Surely never had eyes pleaded more patiently and intensely and less covetously for a stranger's chivalry, nor from a wilder ambush than these that had but just now gazed into mine. What was the secret; what lure was detaining on earth a shade so much in need of rest?

I took the paper from my pocket. Light was swiftly flowing into the awakening garden. A distant thrush broke faintly into song. Undecided – battling between curiosity and pity, between loyalty to my friend and loyalty to even *more* than a friend – to this friendless old woman's solitary perturbed spirit, I stood with vacant eyes upon the brightening orchard – my back turned on portrait and room.

A hand (no *man's* asleep, or awake) touched mine. I turned – debated no more. The poor jaded face was grey and drawn. He seemed himself to be inwardly wrestling – possessed against possessor. And still the old bygone eyes within his own, across how deep an abyss, argued, pleaded with mine. They seemed to snare me, to persuade me beyond denial. I held out the flimsy paper between finger and thumb.

Like the limb of an automaton, Beverley's arm slowly raised his guttering candle. The flame flowed soft and blue. I held the paper till its heat scorched my thumb. Something changed; something but just now there was suddenly gone. The old, drawn face melted, as it were, into another. And Beverley's voice broke out inarticulate and feverish. I sat him down, and let him slowly awaken. He stared incredulously to and fro, from the window to me, to the portrait, and at last his eye fell on his extraordinary attire.

'I say,' he said, 'what's this?'

'Seemingly,' I said, 'they are the weeds of the malevolent aunt who has been giving you troubled nights.'

'Me?' he said, not yet quite free from sleep.

'Yes,' I said.

He yawned. 'Then – I have been fooled?' he said. I nodded. I think that even tears came into his eyes. The May-morning choragium of the wild birds had begun, every singer seemingly a soloist in the enraptured medley of voices.

'Well, look here!' he said, nodding a stupid sleep-drowsed head at me, 'look here! What . . . you think of an aunt who hates a fellow as much as that, eh? What you think?'

'I don't know what to think,' I said.

The Apple Tree

Elizabeth Bowen

'Frightened!' exclaimed Lancelot. 'Of her? Oh, nonsense – surely? She's an absolute child.'

'But *that's* what I mean,' said Mrs. Bettersley, glancing queerly sideways at him over the collar of her fur coat. He still did not know what she meant, and did not think she knew either.

In a rather nerve-racking combination of wind and moonlight Simon Wing's week-end party picked its way back to his house, by twos and threes, up a cinder-path from the village. Simon, who entered with gusto into his new rôle of squire, had insisted that they should attend the Saturday concert in the village memorial hall, a raftered, charmless and icy building endowed by himself and only recently opened. Here, with numbing feet and creeping spines, they had occupied seven front seats, under a thin but constant spate of recitation, pianoforte duet and song, while upon them from all quarters draughts directed themselves like arrows. To restore circulation they had applauded vigorously, too often precipitating an encore. Simon, satisfied with his friends, with his evening, leant forward to beam down the row. He said this would please the village. Lancelot communicated to Mrs. Bettersley a suspicion; this was why Simon had asked them down.

'So I'm afraid,' she replied, 'and for church to-morrow.'

All the same, it had warmed them all to see Simon happy. Mounting the platform to propose a vote of thanks to the Vicar, the great ruddy man had positively expanded; glowed; a till now too palpable cloud rolled away from him. It was this recognition by his old friends of the old Simon – a recognition so instantaneous, poignant and cheerful that it was like a handshake, a first greeting – that now sent the party so cheerfully home in its twos and threes, their host ever boisterously ahead. At the tail, lagging, Lancelot and Mrs. Bettersley fell into a discussion of Simon (his marriage, his ménage, his whole aspect, marked by entire unrestraint; as though between these two also some shadow had dissipated. They were old, friendly enemies.

'But a child –' resumed Lancelot.

'Naturally I didn't mean to suggest that she was a werewolf!'

'You think she *is* what's the matter?'

'Obviously there's nothing funny about the house.'

Obviously there was nothing funny about the house. Under the eeric cold sky, pale but not bright with moonlight, among bare, wind-shaken trees, the house's bulk loomed, honourably substantial. Lit-up windows sustained the party with promise of indoor comfort: firelight on decanters, room after room heavy-curtained; Simon's feeling for home made concrete (at last, after wandering years) in deep leather chairs, padded fenders and sectional bookcases, 'domes of silence' on yielding carpets; an unaspiring, comfortable sobriety.

'She does seem to me only half there,' confessed Lancelot; 'not, of course, I mean, mentally, but –'

'She had that frightful time – don't you know? *Don't* you know?' Mrs. Bettersley brightened, approaching her lips to his ear in the half moonlight. 'She was at that school – don't you remember? After all *that*, the school broke up, you know. She was sent straight abroad – she'd have been twelve at the time I dare say; in a pretty state, I've no doubt, poor child! – to an aunt and uncle at Cannes. Her only relations; they lived out there in a villa, never came home – she stayed abroad with them. It was then Simon met her; then – all this.'

'School?' said Lancelot, stuttering with excitement. 'What – were they ill-treated?'

'Heavens, not that!' exclaimed Mrs. Bettersley. 'Worse –'

But just at this point – it was unbearable – they saw the party pull up and contract ahead. Simon was waiting to shepherd them through the gate, to lock the gate after them.

'I hope,' he said, beaming as they came up, 'you weren't too bored.'

They could not fail to respond.

'It's been a marvellous evening,' said Mrs. Bettersley; Lancelot adding, 'What wonderful talent you've got round here!'

'I don't think we're bad for a village,' said Simon modestly, clicking the gate to. 'The choral society are as keen as mustard. And I always think that young Dickinson ought to go on the stage. I'd pay to see him anywhere.'

'Oh, so would I,' agreed Lancelot cordially. 'It's too sad,' he added, 'your wife having missed all this.'

Simon's manner contracted. 'She went to the dress rehearsal,' he said quickly.

'Doesn't she act herself?'

'I can't get her to try . . . Well, here we are; here we are!' Simon shouted, stamping across the terrace.

Young Mrs. Wing had been excused the concert. She had a slight chill, she feared. If she ever did cast any light on village society it was to-night withheld. No doubt Simon was disappointed. His friends, filing after him through the french window into the library, all hoped that by now – it was half past ten – young Mrs. Simon might have taken her chill to bed.

But from the hearth her flat little voice said, 'Hullo!' There she still stood, looking towards the window, watching their entrance as she had watched their exit. Her long silver sheath of a dress made her almost grown up. So they all prepared with philosophy to be nice to young Mrs. Wing. They all felt this first week-end party, this incursion of old friends all knit up with each other, so knit up round Simon, might well be trying for young Mrs. Wing. In the nature, even possibly, of an ordeal. She was barely nineteen, and could not, to meet them, be expected to put up anything of 'a manner'. She had them, however, at a slight disadvantage, for Simon's marriage had been a shock for his friends. He had been known for years as a likely marrying man; so much so that his celibacy appeared an accident; but his choice of a wife – this mannerless, sexless child, the dim something between a mouse and an Undine, this wraith not considerable as a mother of sons, this cold little shadow across a hearth – had considerably surprised them. By her very passivity she attacked them when they were least prepared.

Mrs. Wing, at a glance from her husband, raised a silver lid from some sandwiches with a gesture of invitation. Mrs. Bettersley, whose appetite was frankly wolfish, took two, and slipping out inch by inch from her fur coat, lined up beside her little hostess in the firelight, solid and brilliant. The others divided armchairs in the circle of warmth.

'Did you have a nice concert?' said Mrs. Wing politely No one could answer. 'It went off well on the whole,' said Simon gently, as though breaking sorrowful news to her.

Lancelot could not sleep. The very comfort of bed, the too exquisite sympathy with his body of springs and mattress, became oppressive. Wind had subsided, moon-light sketched a window upon his floor. The house was quiet, too quiet; with jealousy and nostalgia he pictured them all sleeping. Mrs. Wing's cheek would scarcely warm a pillow. In despair Lancelot switched the light on; the amiable furniture stared. He read one page of *Our Mutual Friend* with distaste and decided to look down-stairs for a detective story. He slept in a corridor branching off from the head of the main staircase.

Downstairs the hall was dark, rank with cooling cigar-smoke. A clock struck three; Lancelot violently started. A little moon came in through the skylight; the library door was closed; stepping quietly, Lancelot made his way to it. He opened the door, saw red embers, then knew in a second the library was not empty. All the same, in there in the dark they were not moving or speaking.

Embarrassment – had he surprised an intrigue? and abrupt physical fear – were these burglars? – held Lancelot bound on the threshold. Certainly someone was not alone; in here, in spite of the dark, someone was watching someone. He did not know whether to speak. He felt committed by opening the door, and standing against the grey of the glass-roofed fall must be certainly visible.

Finally it was Simon's voice that said defensively: 'Hullo.' Lancelot knew he must go away immediately. He had only one wish – to conceal his identity. But

Simon apparently did not trust one; moving bulkily, he came down the long room to the door, bumping, as though in a quite unfamiliar room, against the furniture, his arm out ahead, as though pushing aside or trying to part a curtain. He seemed to have no sense of distance; Lancelot ducked, but a great hand touched his face. The hand was ice-cold.

'Oh, you?' said Simon. From his voice, his breath, he had been drinking heavily. He must still be holding a glass in his other hand – Lancelot heard whisky slopping about as the glass shook.

'It's all right,' said Lancelot; 'I was just going up. Sorry,' he added.

'You can't – come – in – here,' said Simon obstinately.

'No, I say; I was just going up.' Lancelot stopped; friendliness fought in him with an intense repulsion. Not that he minded – though this itself was odd; Simon hardly ever touched anything.

But the room was a trap, a cul-de-sac; Simon, his face less than a yard away, seemed to be speaking to him through bars. He was frightful in fear; a man with the humility of a beast; he gave off fear like some disagreeable animal smell, making Lancelot dislike and feel revolted by his own humanity, his own manhood, as though in too close proximity with a negro.

'Go away,' said Simon, pushing at him in the dark. Lancelot stepped back in alarm, a rug slipped under his foot, he staggered, grasping at the lintel of the door. His elbow knocked a switch; immediately the hall, with its four hanging lamps, sprang into brilliant illumination. One was staggered by this explosion of light; Lancelot put his hands over his eyes; when he took them away he could see Simon's face was clammy, mottled; here and there a bead of sweat trembled and ran down. He was standing sideways, his shoulder against the door; past him a path of light ran into the library.

Mrs. Simon stood just out of the light, looking fixedly up and pointing at something above her head. Round her Lancelot distinguished the big chairs, the table with the decanters, and, faintly, the glazed bookcases. Her eyes, looking up, reflected the light but did not flicker; she did not stir. With an exclamation, a violent movement, Simon shut the library door. They both stood outside its white glossy panels. By contrast with what stood inside, staring there in the dark, Simon was once more human; unconsciously, as much to gain as to impart reassurance, Lancelot put a hand on his arm.

Not looking at one another, they said nothing.

They were in no sense alone even here, for the slam of the door produced in a moment or two Mrs. Bettersley, who looked down at them from the gallery just overhead the zone of bright lights, her face sharpened and wolfish from vehement curiosity. Lancelot looked up; their eyes met.

'All right, only somebody sleep-walking,' he called up softly.

'All right,' she replied, withdrawing; but not, he guessed, to her room; rather to lean back in shadow against the wall of the gallery, impassive, watchful, arms folded over the breast of her dark silk kimono.

A moment later she still made no sign – he would have been glad of her presence. For the return to Simon of sensibility and intelligence, like circulation beginning again in a limb that had been tightly bound up, was too much for Simon. One side-glance that almost contained his horror, then – huge figure, crumpling, swaying, sagging – he fainted suddenly. Lancelot broke his fall a little and propped him, sitting, against the wall.

This left Lancelot much alone. He noted details: a dog-collar lying unstrapped, ash trodden into a rug, a girl's gloves – probably Mrs. Simon's – dropped crumpled into a big brass tray. Now drawn to the door – aware the whole time of his position's absurdity – he knelt, one ear to the keyhole. Silence. In there she must still stand in contemplation – horrified, horrifying – of something high up that from the not quite fixity of her gaze had seemed unfixed, pendant, perhaps swaying a little. Silence. Then – he pressed closer – a thud – thud – thud – three times, like apples falling.

This idea of apples entered his mind and remained, frightfully clear; an innocent pastoral image seen black through a dark transparency. This idea of fruit detaching itself and, from a leafy height, falling in the stale, shut-up room had the sharpness of an hallucination; he thought he was going mad.

'Come down,' he called up to the gallery.

Mrs. Bettersley, with that expectant half-smile, appeared immediately and came downstairs. She glanced at Simon's unconsciousness, for which she seemed to be grateful, then went to the library door. After a moment facing the panels, she tried the handle, cautiously turning it.

'*She's* in there,' said Lancelot.

'Coming?' she asked.

He replied 'No,' very frankly and simply.

'Oh, well,' she shrugged; 'I'm a woman,' and entered the library, pushing the door to behind her. He heard her moving among the furniture. 'Now come,' she said, 'come, my dear . . .' After a moment or two of complete silence and stillness: 'Oh, my God, no – I can't!' she exclaimed. She came out again, very white. She was rubbing her hands together as though she had hurt them. 'It's impossible,' she repeated. 'One can't get past . . . it's like an apple tree.'

She knelt by Simon and began fumbling with his collar. Her hands shook. Lancelot watched the access of womanly busyness.

The door opened again and young Mrs. Wing came out in her nightgown, hair hanging over her shoulders in two plaits, blinking under the strong light. Seeing them all she paused in natural confusion.

'I walk in my sleep,' she murmured, blushed and slipped past upstairs without a glance at her husband, still in confusion like any other young woman encountered by strangers in her nightgown, her appearance and disappearance the very picture of modest precipitancy.

Simon began to come to. Mrs. Bettersley also retreated. The fewest possible people ought, they felt, to be in on this.

Sunday morning was pale blue, mild and sunny. Mrs. Bettersley appeared punctually for breakfast, beaming, pink and impassible. Lancelot looked pale and puffy; Mrs. Simon did not appear. Simon came in like a tempered Boreas to greet the party, rubbing his hands. After breakfast they stepped out through the window to smoke on the terrace. Church, said Simon pressingly, would be at eleven.

Mrs. Bettersley revolted. She said she liked to write letters on Sunday morning. The rest, with a glance of regret at the shining November garden, went off like lambs. When they had gone she slipped upstairs and tapped on Mrs. Simon's door.

The young woman was lying comfortably enough, with a fire burning, a mild novel open face down on the

counterpane. This pretty bride's room, pink and white,
frilled and rosy, now full of church bells and winter
sunshine, had for Mrs. Bettersley, in all its appointments,
an air of anxious imitation and approximation to some
idea of the grown-up. Simon's bed was made and the
room in order.

'You don't mind?' said Mrs. Bettersley, having sat
down firmly.

Mrs. Simon said nervously she was so pleased.

'All right this morning?'

'Just a little chill, I think.'

'And no wonder! Do you often walk in your sleep?'

Mrs. Simon's small face tightened, hardened, went a
shade whiter among the pillows. 'I don't know,' she said.
Her manner became a positive invitation to
Mrs. Bettersley to go away. Flattening among the
bedclothes, she tried hard to obliterate herself.

Her visitor, who had not much time – for, the bells
stopped, they would be back again in an hour – was quite
merciless. 'How old were you,' she said, 'when *that*
happened?'

'Twelve – please don't –'

'You never told anyone?'

'No – please, Mrs. Bettersley – please, not now. I feel
so ill.'

'You're making Simon ill.'

'Do you think I don't know?' the child exclaimed. 'I
thought he'd save me. I didn't think he'd ever be
frightened. I didn't know any power could . . . Indeed, indeed, Mrs. Bettersley, I had no idea . . . I felt
so safe with him. I thought this would go away. Now
when it comes it is twice as horrible. Do you think it is
killing him?'

'I shouldn't wonder,' said Mrs. Bettersley.

'Oh, oh,' moaned Mrs. Wing, and with wrists crossed over her face shook all over, sobbing so that the bedhead rattled against the wall. 'He was so sorry for me,' she moaned; 'it was more than I could resist. He was so sorry for me. Wouldn't you feel Simon might save you?'

Mrs. Bettersley, moving to the edge of the bed, caught the girl's wrists and firmly, but not untenderly, forced them apart, disclosing the small convulsed face and fixed eyes. 'We've got three-quarters of an hour alone,' she said 'You've got to tell me. Make it come into words. When it's once out it won't hurt – like a tooth, you know. Talk about it like anything. Talk to Simon. You never have, have you? You never do?'

Mrs. Bettersley felt quite a brute, she told Lancelot later. She had, naturally, in taking this hard line, something to go on. Seven years ago, newspapers had been full of the Crampton Park School tragedy; a little girl's suicide. There had been some remarkable headlines, some details, profuse speculation. Influence from some direction having been brought to bear, the affair disappeared from the papers abruptly. Some suggestion of things having been 'hushed up' gave the affair, in talk, a fresh, cruel prominence; it became a topic. One hinted at all sorts of scandal. The school broke up, the staff disappeared, discredited; the fine house and grounds, in the West Country, were sold at a loss. One pupil, Myra Conway, felt the shock with surprising keenness. She nearly died of brain fever; collapsing the day after the suicide, she remained at death's door for weeks, alone with her nurses in the horrified house, Crampton Park. All the other children were hurried away. One heard afterwards that her health, her nerves had been ruined. The other children presumably rallied; one heard no more of them. Myra Conway became Myra Wing. So much they all knew, even Simon.

Myra Wing now lay on her side in bed, in her pink bedroom, eyes shut, cheek pressed to the pillow as though she were sleeping, but with her body rigid; gripping with both hands Mrs. Bettersley's arm. She spoke slowly, choosing her words with diffidence as though hampered by trying to speak an unfamiliar language.

'I went there when I was ten. I don't think it can ever have been a very good school. They called it a home school, I suppose, because most of us stayed for the holidays – we had no parents – and none of us were over fourteen. From being there so much we began to feel that this was the world. There was a very high wall round the garden. I don't think they were unkind to us, but everything seemed to go wrong. Doria and I were always in trouble. I suppose that was why we knew each other. There were about eighteen other girls, but none of them liked us. We used to feel we had some disease – so much so that we were sometimes ashamed to meet each other; sometimes we did not like to be together. I don't think we knew we were unhappy; we never spoke of that; we should have felt ashamed. We used to pretend we were all right; we got in a way to be quite proud of ourselves, of being different. I think, though, we made each other worse. In those days I was very ugly. Doria was bad; she was very queer-looking; her eyes goggled and she wore big round glasses. I suppose if we had had parents it would have been different. As it was, it was impossible to believe anyone could ever care for either of us. We did not even care for each other; we were just like two patients in hospital, shut away from the others because of having some frightful disease. But I suppose we depended on one another.

'The other children were mostly younger. The house was very large and dark-looking, but full of pictures to make it look homely. The grounds were very large, full of trees and laurels. When I was twelve, I felt if this was the world I could not bear it. When I was twelve I got measles; another girl of my age got the measles too, and we were sent to a cottage to get well. She was very pretty and clever; we made friends; she told me she did not mind me, but she could not bear Doria. When we both got well and went back to the others, I loved her so much I felt I could not bear to part from her. She had a home of her own; she was very happy and gay; to know her and hear about her life was like heaven. I took great trouble to please her; we went on being friends. The others began to like me; I ran away from Doria. Doria was left alone. She seemed to be all that was horrible in my life; from the moment we parted things began to go right with me. I laughed at her with the others.

'The only happy part of Doria's life and mine in the bad days were the games we played and the stories we told in a lonely part of the garden, a slope of lawn with one beautiful old apple tree. Sometimes we used to climb up in the branches. Nobody else ever came there, it was like something of our own; to be there made us feel happy and dignified.

'Doria was miserable when I left her. She never wept; she used to walk about by herself. It was as though everything I had got free of had fallen on her, too; she was left with my wretchedness. When I was with the others I used to see her, always alone, watching me. One afternoon she made me come with her to the apple tree; I was sorry for her and went; when we got there I could not bear it. I was so frightened of being lost again; I said terrible things to her. I wished she was dead. You see, there seemed to be no other world outside the school.

'She and I still slept in the same room, with two others. That night – there was some moon – I saw her get up. She tied the cord of her dressing-gown – it was very thick – round her waist tightly; she looked once at me, but I pretended to be asleep. She went out and did not come back. I lay – there was only a little moon – with a terrible feeling, like something tight round my throat. At last I went down to look for her. A glass door of the garden was open. I went out to look for her. She had hanged herself, you know, in the apple tree. When I first got there I saw nothing. I looked round and called her, and shook the branches, but only – it was September – two or three apples fell down. The leaves kept brushing against my face. Then I saw her. Her feet were just over my head. I parted the branches to look – there was just enough moon – the leaves brushed my face. I crept back into bed and waited. No one knew; no steps came. Next morning, of course, they did not tell us anything. They said she was ill. I pretended to know no better. I could not think of anything but the apple tree.

'While I was ill – I was very ill – I thought the leaves would choke me. Whenever I moved in bed an apple fell down. All the girls were taken away. When I got well, I found the house was empty. The first day I could, I crept out alone to look for the real apple tree. "It is only a tree," I thought; "if I could see it, I should be quite well." But the tree had been cut down. The place where it grew was filled with new turf. The nurse swore to me there had never been an apple tree there at all. She did not know – no one ever knew – I had been out that night and seen Doria.

'I expect you can guess the rest – you were there last night. You see, I am haunted. It does not matter where I am, or who I am with. Though I am married now, it is just the same. Every now and then – I don't know yet when or what brings it about – I wake to see Doria get up and tie the cord round her waist and go out. I have to go after her; there is always the apple tree. Its roots are in me. It takes all my strength, and now it's beginning to take Simon's.

'Those nights, no one can bear to be with me. Everyone who has been with me knows, but no one will speak of it. Only Simon tries to be there, those times – you saw, last night. It is impossible to be with me; I make rooms impossible. I am not like a house that can be burnt, you see, or pulled down. You know how it is – I heard you in there last night, trying to come to me –'

'I won't fail again: I've never been more ashamed,' said Mrs. Bettersley.

'If I stay up here the tree grows in the room; I feel it will choke Simon. If I go out, I find it darker than all the others against the sky . . . This morning I have been trying to make up my mind; I must go; I must leave Simon. I see quite well this is destroying him. Seeing him with you all makes me see how he used to be, how he might have been. You see, it's hard to go. He's my life. Between all this . . . we're so happy. But make me do this, Mrs. Bettersley!'

'I'll make you do one thing. Come away with me – perhaps for only a month. My dear, if I can't do this, after last night, *I'm* ruined,' exclaimed Mrs. Bettersley.

The passion of vanity has its own depths in the spirit, and is powerfully militant. Mrs. Bettersley, determined to vindicate herself, disappeared for some weeks with the haunted girl. Lancelot meanwhile kept Simon company.

From the ordeal their friend emerged about Christmas, possibly a little harder and brighter. If she had fought, there was not a hair displaced. She did not mention, even to Lancelot, by what arts, night and day, by what cynical vigilance she had succeeded in exorcizing the apple tree. The victory aged her but left her as disengaged as usual. Mrs. Wing was returned to her husband. As one would expect, less and less was seen of the couple. They disappeared into happiness: a sublime nonentity.

The Leaf-Sweeper

Muriel Spark

Behind the town hall there is a wooded parkland which, towards the end of November, begins to draw a thin blue cloud right into itself; and as a rule the park floats in this haze until mid-February. I pass every day, and see Johnnie Geddes in the heart of this mist, sweeping up the leaves. Now and again he stops, and jerking his long head erect, looks indignantly at the pile of leaves, as if it ought not to be there; then he sweeps on. This business of leaf-sweeping he learnt during the years he spent in the asylum: it was the job they always gave him to do: and when he was discharged the town council gave him the leaves to sweep. But the indignant movement of the head comes naturally to him, for this has been one of his habits since he was the most promising and buoyant and vociferous graduate of his year. He looks much older than he is, for it is not quite twenty years ago that Johnnie founded the Society for the Abolition of Christmas.

Johnnie was living with his aunt then. I was at school, and in the Christmas holidays Miss Geddes gave me her nephew's pamphlet, *How to Grow Rich at Christmas*. It sounded very likely, but it turned out that you grow rich at Christmas by doing away with Christmas, and so pondered Johnnie's pamphlet no further.

But it was only his first attempt. He had, within the next three years, founded his society of Abolitionists.

His new book, *Abolish Christmas or We Die*, was in great demand at the public library, and my turn for it came at last. Johnnie was really convincing, this time, and most people were completely won over until after they had closed the book. I got an old copy for sixpence the other day, and despite the lapse of time it still proves conclusively that Christmas is a national crime. Johnnie demonstrates that every human-unit in the kingdom faces inevitable starvation within a period inversely proportional to that in which one in every six industrial-productivity units, if you see what he means, stops producing toys to fill the stockings of the educational-intake units. He cites appalling statistics to show that 1.024 per cent of the time squandered each Christmas in reckless shopping and thoughtless churchgoing brings the nation closer to its doom by five years. A few readers protested, but Johnnie was able to demolish their muddled arguments, and meanwhile the Society for the Abolition of Christmas increased. But Johnnie was troubled. Not only did Christmas rage throughout the kingdom as usual that year, but he had private information that many of the Society's members had broken the Oath of Abstention.

He decided, then, to strike at the very roots of Christmas. Johnnie gave up his job on the Drainage Supply Board; he gave up all his prospects, and, financed by a few supporters, retreated for two years to study the roots of Christmas. Then, all jubilant, Johnnie produced his next and last book, in which he established, either that Christmas was an invention of the Early Fathers to propitiate the pagans, or it was invented by the pagans to placate the Early Fathers, I forget which. Against the advice of his friends, Johnnie entitled it *Christmas and Christianity*. It sold eighteen copies. Johnnie never really recovered from this: and it happened, about that time, that the girl he was engaged to, an ardent Abolitionist, sent him a pullover she had knitted, for Christmas; he sent it back, enclosing a copy of the Society's rules, and she sent back the ring. But in any case, during Johnnie's absence, the Society had been undermined by a moderate faction. These moderates finally became more moderate, and the whole thing broke up.

Soon after this, I left the district, and it was some years before I saw Johnnie again. One Sunday afternoon in summer, I was idling among the crowds who were gathered to hear the speakers at Hyde Park. One little crowd surrounded a man who bore a banner marked 'Crusade against Christmas'; his voice was frightening; it carried an unusually long way. This was Johnnie. A man in the crowd told me Johnnie was there every Sunday, very violent about Christmas, and that he would soon be taken up for insulting language. As I saw in the papers, he was soon taken up for insulting language. And a few months later I heard that poor Johnnie was in a mental home, because he had Christmas on the brain and couldn't stop shouting about it.

After that I forgot all about him until three years ago, in December, I went to live near the town where Johnnie had spent his youth. On the afternoon of Christmas Eve I was walking with a friend, noticing what had changed in my absence, and what hadn't. We passed a long, large house, once famous for its armoury, and I saw that the iron gates were wide open.

'They used to be kept shut,' I said.

'That's an asylum now,' said my friend; 'they let the mild cases work in the grounds, and leave the gates open to give them a feeling of freedom.'

'But,' said my friend, 'they lock everything inside. Door after door. The lift as well; they keep it locked.'

While my friend was chattering, I stood in the gateway and looked in. Just beyond the gate was a great bare elm-tree. There I saw a man in brown corduroys, sweeping up the leaves. Poor soul, he was shouting about Christmas.

'That's Johnnie Geddes.' I said. 'Has he been here all these years?'

'Yes,' said my friend as we walked on. 'I believe he gets worse at this time of year.'

'Does his aunt see him?'

'Yes. And she sees nobody else.'

We were, in fact, approaching the house where Miss Geddes lived. I suggested we call on her. I had known her well.

'No fear,' said my friend.

I decided to go in, all the same, and my friend walked on to the town.

Miss Geddes had changed, more than the landscape. She had been a solemn, calm woman, and now she moved about quickly, and gave short agitated smiles. She took me to her sitting-room, and as she opened the door she called to someone inside,

'Johnnie, see who's come to see us!'

A man, dressed in a dark suit, was standing on a chair, fixing holly behind a picture. He jumped down.

'Happy Christmas,' he said. 'A Happy and a Merry Christmas indeed. I do hope,' he said, 'you're going to stay for tea, as we've got a delightful Christmas cake, and at this season of goodwill I would be cheered indeed if you could see how charmingly it's decorated; it has "Happy Christmas" in red icing, and then there's a robin and . . .

'Johnnie,' said Miss Geddes, 'you're forgetting the carols.'

'The carols,' he said. He lifted a gramophone record from a pile and put it on. It was *The Holly and the Ivy*.

'It's *The Holly and the Ivy*,' said Miss Geddes. 'Can't we have something else? We had that all morning.'

'It is sublime,' he said, beaming from his chair, and holding up his hand for silence.

While Miss Geddes went to fetch the tea, and he sat absorbed in his carol, I watched him. He was so like Johnnie that if I hadn't seen poor Johnnie a few moments before, sweeping up the asylum leaves, I would have thought he really was Johnnie. Miss Geddes returned with the tray, and while he rose to put on another record, he said something that startled me.

'I saw you in the crowd that Sunday when I was speaking at Hyde Park.'

'What a memory you have!' said Miss Geddes.

'It must be ten years ago,' he said.

'My nephew has altered his opinion of Christmas,' she explained. 'He always comes home for Christmas now, and don't we have a jolly time, Johnnie?'

'Rather!' he said. 'Oh, let me cut the cake.'

He was very excited about the cake. With a flourish he dug a large knife into the cake. The knife slipped, and I saw it run deep into his finger. Miss Geddes did not move. He wrenched his cut finger away, and went on slicing the cake.

'Isn't it bleeding?' I said.

He held up his hand. I could see the deep cut, but there was no blood.

Deliberately, and perhaps desperately, I turned to Miss Geddes.

'That house up the road,' I said, 'I see it's a mental home now I passed it this afternoon.'

'Johnnie,' said Miss Geddes, as one who knows the game is up, 'go and fetch the mince-pies.'

He went, whistling a carol.

'You passed the asylum,' said Miss Geddes wearily.

'Yes,' I said.

'And you saw Johnnie sweeping up the leaves.'

'Yes.'

We could still hear the whistling of the carol.

'Who is *he*?' I said.

'That's Johnnie's ghost,' she said. 'He comes home every Christmas.'

'But,' she said, 'I don't like him. I can't bear him any longer, and I'm going away tomorrow. I don't want Johnnie's ghost, I want Johnnie in flesh and blood.'

I shuddered, thinking of the cut finger that could not bleed. And I left, before Johnnie's ghost returned with the mince-pies.

Next day, as I had arranged to join a family who lived in the town, I started walking over about noon. Because of the light mist, I didn't see at first who it was approaching. It was a man, waving his arm to me. It turned out to be Johnnie's ghost.

'Happy Christmas. What do you think,' said Johnnie's ghost, 'my aunt has gone to London. Fancy, on Christmas day, and I thought she was at church, and here I am without anyone to spend a jolly Christmas with, and, of course, I forgive her, as it's the season of goodwill, but I'm glad to see you, because now I can come with you, wherever it is you're going, and we can all have a Happy . . .'

'Go away,' I said, and walked on.

It sounds hard. But perhaps you don't know how repulsive and loathsome is the ghost of a living man. The ghosts of the dead may be all right, but the ghost of mad Johnnie gave me the creeps.

'Clear off,' I said.

He continued walking beside me. 'As it's the time of goodwill, I make allowances for your tone,' he said. 'But I'm coming.'

We had reached the asylum gates, and there, in the grounds, I saw Johnnie sweeping the leaves. I suppose it was his way of going on strike, working on Christmas day. He was making a noise about Christmas.

On a sudden impulse I said to Johnnie's ghost. 'You want company?'

'Certainly,' he replied. 'It's the season of . . .'

'Then you shall have it,' I said.

I stood in the gateway. 'Oh, Johnnie,' I called.

He looked up.

'I've brought your ghost to see you, Johnnie.'

'Well, well,' said Johnnie, advancing to meet his ghost, 'Just imagine it!'

'Happy Christmas,' said Johnnie's ghost.

'Oh, really?' said Johnnie.

I left them to it. And when I looked back, wondering if they would come to blows, I saw that Johnnie's ghost was sweeping the leaves as well. They seemed to be arguing at the same time. But it was still misty, and really, I can't say whether, when I looked a second time, there were two men or one man sweeping the leaves.

Johnnie began to improve in the New Year. At least, he stopped shouting about Christmas, and then he never mentioned it at all; in a few months, when he had almost stopped saying anything, they discharged him.

The town council gave him the leaves of the park to sweep. He seldom speaks, and recognises nobody. I see him every day at the late end of the year, working within the mist. Sometimes, if there is a sudden gust, he jerks his head up to watch a few leaves falling behind him, as if amazed that they are undeniably there, although, by rights, the falling of leaves should be stopped.

ALSO AVAILABLE AS BLOOMSBURY CLASSICS

Surfacing, Margaret Atwood
Wilderness Tips, Margaret Atwood
The Snow Queen and Other Fairy Tales, Hans Christian Andersen
At The Jerusalem, Paul Bailey
Old Soldiers, Paul Bailey
Flaubert's Parrot, Julian Barnes
Ten, A Bloomsbury Tenth Anniversary Anthology
The Piano, a Novel, Jane Campion and Kate Pullinger
The Passion of New Eve, Angela Carter
Emperor of the Air, Ethan Canin
Alice's Adventures in Wonderland, Lewis Carroll
A Christmas Carol, Charles Dickens
Poor Cow, Nell Dunn
The Lover, Marguerite Duras
The Birds of the Air, Alice Thomas Ellis
The Virgin Suicides, Jeffrey Eugenides
Utopia and Other Places, Richard Eyre
The Great Gatsby, F. Scott Fitzgerald
Bad Girls, Mary Flanagan
The Lagoon and Other Stories, Janet Frame
Mona Minim, Janet Frame
Owls Do Cry, Janet Frame
Across the Bridge, Mavis Gallant
Green Water, Green Sky, Mavis Gallant
Something Out There, Nadine Gordimer
Christmas Stories, Selected by Giles Gordon
Carol, Patricia Highsmith
The 158 Pound Marriage, John Irving
Setting Free the Bears, John Irving
Trying to Save Piggy Sneed, John Irving
Jimmy and the Desperate Woman, D. H. Lawrence
Einstein's Dreams, Alan Lightman
Bright Lights, Big City, Jay McInerney

Debatable Land, Candia McWilliam
Bliss and Other Stories, Katherine Mansfield
The Garden Party and Other Stories, Katherine Mansfield
So Far From God, Patrick Marnham
Lies of Silence, Brian Moore
The Lonely Passion of Judith Hearne, Brian Moore
The Pumpkin Eater, Penelope Mortimer
Lives of Girls and Women, Alice Munro
The Country Girls, Edna O'Brien
Coming Through Slaughter, Michael Ondaatje
The English Patient, Michael Ondaatje
In the Skin of a Lion, Michael Ondaatje
Running in the Family, Michael Ondaatje
Let Them Call it Jazz, Jean Rhys
Wide Sargasso Sea, Jean Rhys
Keepers of the House, Lisa St. Aubin de Téran
The Quantity Theory of Insanity, Will Self
The Pigeon, Patrick Süskind
The Heather Blazing, Colm Tóibin
Cocktails at Doney's and Other Stories, William Trevor
The Choir, Joanna Trollope
Angel, All Innocence, Fay Weldon
Oranges are not the only fruit, Jeanette Winterson
The Passion, Jeanette Winterson
Sexing the Cherry, Jeanette Winterson
In Pharaoh's Army, Tobias Wolff
This Boy's Life, Tobias Wolff
Orlando, Virginia Woolf
A Room of One's Own, Virginia Woolf